CHRISTINA'S CHALLENGE

She is not the sort of girl to turn and walk away from a man just because he's down . . . Not the sort of girl to pass up a little excitement because of a little danger . . . But she is just the sort of girl to hot up the cold war . . .

This time Christina Van Bell really goes under cover. Not-so-innocently involved with a mysterious young man who asks her to do him one more special favour, she finds herself more-or-less up to her pretty eyes in spies. Tracking down a very significant bottle of wine from New York to Paris to Rome, from back alley to front bedroom, Christina soon discovers that she is her own best secret weapon. For beneath those disguises and impassive expressions, a spy is still a man. And who knows better than Christina what to do with a man?

CHRISTINA'S CHALLENGE

Blakely St James

THE SHERIDAN
BOOK COMPANY

This edition published in 1994 by
The Sheridan Book Company

First published in Great Britain 1985
Random House, 20 Vauxhall Bridge Road, London SW1V 2SA
Arrow edition 1985

Printed and bound in Great Britain by
Cox & Wyman Ltd, Reading, Berkshire

ISBN 1–85501–523–4

CHAPTER ONE

"If I had been Bridget, I would have thrown that handsome stud of hers down on the floor and ripped those tight jeans right off him. Then I would have fucked him silly, and he would have forgotten all about the cause."

Clive Van Pelt, the play's producer, took a healthy sip of his scotch and eyed me suspiciously. He was trying to decide if I, the chief financial backer of this masterpiece, was serious. All around us the opening night party for the off-off-Broadway sensation, Sean Mulligan's *Famine and Fire*, was in full swing and we had to raise our voices to be heard over the tumult.

"This was a serious work," Clive finally said. "The hero was fighting for what he believed in. You can't just plop a sex scene down in the middle of a dialogue about the meaning of Irish independence."

"Causes are for men who can't get laid," I insisted. "A man who was sexually satisfied would not leave a hot cunt and a great pair of tits to go throw bombs at government buildings."

"You have a one-track mind," Clive teased. "But I must admit that if the woman was you, I wouldn't

1

get out of bed though the fate of the Republic depended on my throwing that grenade."

"You're trying to change the subject," I said.

"You have a great body."

"I know that. But I also have good commercial sense. If there had been a hot sex scene in the first act instead of all that boring, pretentious talk, you wouldn't have had half the critics stampeding out of the exits before the second scene was over."

"They didn't stampede," he said in a hurt tone. "I protest your use of the word stampede."

"You would have had a line at the box office tomorrow," I continued, "instead of the closing notice I presume you will have to post."

"I don't have to post it. I may let the play run a few more weeks. The audience was very enthusiastic."

I shot him a withering look. Thinking that an enthusiastic audience might sway the critics to temper their remarks, we had crammed the tiny theater to the rafters with friends and IRA sympathizers, all of whom applauded every line as if it had been written by Shakespeare himself. The seasoned journalists, however, had refused to be taken in by the theatrics of the gallery, which were in some ways more accomplished than those being performed on the stage.

"The play was not staged merely to make money," Clive continued, grasping at straws. "It was intended as a forum for serious ideas."

"That's all very well," I replied, "but as the punch line of that old joke about the man and the donkey goes, you have to get their attention first. If you had put some sex into that play you might have opened in a Broadway theater instead of closing in a SoHo loft."

"If you're so critical of the play, why the hell did you invest in it in the first place?" Clive demanded angrily. "As the principal backer you stand to lose more money than any of us."

"Oh, I don't care about the money," I said. "Sean is an old friend of mine, and I like to help my friends. I have more money than I can possibly spend, and if some of it can be used to make my friends happy, I like to oblige them. Besides, Sean's a really decent writer when he doesn't let his politics interfere with his art."

"Why, thank you, my dear," said a voice behind me. "I'll take that as a compliment." I turned and a lanky, red-bearded man in a brown turtleneck sweater, faded corduroy pants, and leather sandals embraced me passionately. I returned his kiss, slipping my arms around his waist and pressing myself against him.

"Don't worry, Sean," I said, hugging him. "Clive feels that the play is an intellectual, if not commercial success, and that's the important thing, isn't it? Who cares about the critics anyway?"

"Not me," Sean laughed. "Actually, the bad review will do more to help the cause than a successful run of the play. It's well-known that the play was boycotted in London, and the adverse publicity here will only be interpreted as further proof of the influence of British anti-Irish propaganda on the American press. The American Irish will send millions of dollars home in outraged protest at this prejudicial treatment of my genius."

"You're right," I agreed. "Failure is better than success. I'll make up any financial losses to Clive and the other backers and give the cast a month's pay."

"Hear, hear!" said Clive. "Let's drink to that!" He stopped a passing waiter and handed each of us a glass of champagne from the tray.

"To the cause," said Sean, raising his glass. "And to you, my dear."

"To Christina!" echoed Clive, downing his drink.

On that note we parted company. Clive had to attend to his duties as host, Sean wanted to get roaring drunk, and I decided to mingle with the usual oddball mix of people that attend opening night parties. Unlike his more successful contemporaries, who hold these parties in their East Side penthouses, Clive's rambling Riverside Drive apartment had belonged to his mother and was decidedly lacking in elegance. Untouched since her death, it was filled with Art Deco furniture, overstuffed velvet sofas with lace doilies, faded pink-flowered carpeting, and dusty rubber plants and potted palms. The food had been catered by the Second Avenue Deli, which, while not having the snob appeal of "21" or Lutèce, does have the best pastrami and chopped liver in New York. Clive had provided a good supply of cheap wine, beer, and domestic champagne, and some of the more thoughtful guests had brought various substances to be ingested through the nasal passages.

I exchanged small talk with several of Sean's writer friends, most of whom remained unpublished, the mistress of a Third World foreign ambassador, and the editor of an underground newspaper. There were several jet-setters in designer clothes and expensive jewelry, obviously slumming, and I carefully avoided their company. I detest people who flaunt their wealth or patronize those who have less money than they do. I do not feel it necessary to wear my diamonds and silk evening dress to an opening night in SoHo, and had chosen a pair of skin-tight jeans, knee-high black leather boots, and a plain black cashmere sweater.

I was starting on my third helping of stuffed derma when I noticed a small group of men and women sitting around a low coffee table, sharing a wicked-looking hash pipe. I walked over and they immediately made room for me between a comatose actress with bulging breasts and an extremely handsome young man with tousled blond hair and a gleaming smile. He offered me the communal pipe, and I sucked a healthy amount of the pungent smoke into my lungs.

"I recognize you from the play," I said, exhaling slowly. "You played the hero's brother, didn't you?"

"That's right," he said. "I was terrific, wasn't I?" Like many actors he made up for his lack of talent with a healthy dose of ego.

"Not bad," I said politely, but he accepted my faint praise as if it had been the most elaborate compliment. "It's too bad that the play will probably close tonight. You might have made a name for yourself."

"It doesn't matter," he said, taking another drag on the pipe. The hash was very potent, and his pupils were like pinpoints. "I already have a steady job. You probably recognize me from my television work, right? Most women do."

I shook my head. "I'm afraid I don't watch television," I said. "Are you on some show?"

"Only the hottest soap opera in the country," he announced proudly. "Have you ever heard of 'Road to Heartbreak'?" I said I hadn't. "I'm on that one. I play the handsome young Doctor Horn, and I've been balling every nurse in the hospital for several months. Two of them are carrying my babies, and I have an incurable illness that will either kill me or give me amnesia. The writers are still debating that point. If I don't get killed off, I'll wander away and be the subject of a widespread police search, which will end in my being framed for the wanton murder of the brother of one of the young nurses I have impregnated. So you see, I'm a pretty important guy on that show."

"It's nice to be devoted to one's art," I murmured.

"I like to do theater occasionally," he rushed on,

"but the soap is my major interest. I get letters from chicks all over the country. Fan mail, gifts, carnal offers, it's really amazing."

"You must make out like a bandit," I cooed.

"If I weren't gay, I'd be the happiest guy on earth," he sighed.

Deciding that I had had enough of talking about him, and knowing that he'd never be interested in talking about me, I smiled, patted his hand maternally, and murmuring some excuse about finding the little girls' room, I made a somewhat hasty exit.

It was growing late. Those who had come to see and be seen, to sample the food and the wine and to engage in verbal masturbation were gone. By common consent, those who remained wanted something more, and this, of course, made me the center of attention. Although someone as beautiful and as desirable as I am could easily become conceited, I have never been accused of this trait. I like to be admired, but I do not hold myself aloof. I rarely turn down an invitation to dinner, to a party, or to make love. As I let my eyes roam over the tempting display of potential partners, I began to wish I had a dozen cunts so that I could accommodate them all at the same time. As I turned to get a drink, I became aware of a tall black girl with gold beads threaded through her high, braided coiffure and a small diamond chip in her left nostril, who was staring at me intently. I have heard men refer to themselves as breast men or leg men or ass men, but to me all parts of the body are equally exciting. Sometimes it's the way a person moves that catches my eye, or the way they hold their heads. From her high-boned cheeks and full, sensuous lips to her shapely calves and trim ankles, this woman would have satisfied the most exacting of connoisseurs. She was wearing a loose-fitting dress of African design, the bright colors complementing the rich ebony of her skin. I felt an overwhelming desire to touch that skin, which glowed in the soft light of the room as if it had been polished, and I could tell by the expression in her eyes that I would not be rebuffed. I idly sipped my drink as I turned away for a moment to consider my approach. Should I be naive? seductive? direct? Women's lib has eliminated a lot of the pretense with which women traditionally shrouded their carnal desires, but still . . .

"My name is Ayisha," said a voice in my ear. It was her. "I've been watching you."

"Really?"

"There isn't a man or a woman in this room who can keep his or her eyes off you."

"I'm flattered."

"You shouldn't be." Ayisha smiled. "It's no more than your due."

"Then it's a mutual admiration society," I replied. "I was just wishing I could touch you. Your skin is beautiful."

"Black is beautiful," she quipped. "And the blacker the better." She laughed delightedly at her own remark and I laughed with her.

The lights had been dimmed. Many of the guests had wandered off to the bedrooms. Still others, in various stages of undress, drifted around the room, looking and touching and easing into the unrestrained atmosphere. We moved toward each other. I could smell the musk of her perfume and feel the warmth of her body through the thin material of her dress. Taking my hand, she led me to an empty bedroom. With mounting desire we hastily shed our clothes and lay down on the bed. Ayisha's dark eyes were like bright coals and my breath caught in my throat as I looked at the ample yet firm curves of her body set against the whiteness of the sheets.

I leaned closer, pressing my lips to hers. I felt her warm breath in my mouth and she entwined her arms around my neck, enveloping me in the heady fragrance that seemed a part of her. My lips parted as she deepened the kiss. I felt her tongue in my mouth, searching, stimulating me so that little electric currents raced along my spine. I melted against her, my hand reaching for her breasts. My own nipples were hard little points of pleasure as they rubbed against hers and she gave a soft moan as my hands began to caress the soft velvet of her skin. I moved down along her body, my lips tracing a hot, moist path over her breasts and her belly and the hollow where her thigh joined her hip. I buried my face in the lush blackness of her pubic hair, so different yet so similar to my own. She began to moan softly, tossing her head from side to side. Her body came alive under the expert ministrations of my hands and lips, and spreading her legs wide, she arched her hips upward as my lips found her nether lips and my tongue raked along the sensitive outer edge. I parted the folds of her pussy lips like a juicy plum, my tongue lapping eagerly at the moistness within. She put her hands against my head, urging me forward, her body trembling as I licked and sucked at the very center of her sex. She began to cry out, her body jerking spasmodically, and I gripped her buttocks in an effort to keep my tongue centered on her clit. I was breathing heavily now. Making love to a woman is, for me, a form of masturbation. In my mind's eye I saw our positions reversed and my own body began to respond to her passion. I was hot and hungry. My tongue and lips were eating her like a ripe fruit and she cried and whimpered with excitement.

Still gripping her ass cheeks, I slipped a finger into her anus. Her hips arched off the sheets and her buttock muscles tightened convulsively. The world seemed to hold its breath as she trembled on the brink of orgasm. Then, with a final scream her body stiffened and collapsed, her fragrant juices bathing my lips and tongue as her orgasm washed over her.

"You're pretty good for a white girl," Ayisha said, stretching languorously after it was over.

"*Pretty* good!"

"Well . . . actually you were great," she laughed, throwing her arms around me and pulling me down next to her on the bed. "You move good, you smell good and you taste good." She shifted position so that she held her weight poised above me. Then she slowly lowered herself so that her body covered mine. She brushed the damp hair off my brow, her fingers tracing the outlines of my face. She lightly kissed my forehead and my eyes and the tip of my nose as I ran my hands over the smooth contours of her back. Our lips met and held, her breasts crushing mine. She began to caress my body as she deepened the kiss, her tongue darting into my mouth. I sighed and relaxed as she touched my breasts and my belly. Her hands soothed and stimulated at the same time. They were comforting as well as erotic, different from the rougher lovemaking of a man.

Suddenly she changed her position so that her head faced my feet. I gave a low moan as her fingers massaged the hard bone at the top of my vagina. She slowly followed the outline of my cunt lips, down then up again until my hips began to undulate and I spread my legs. Her fingers slipped between my moistened lips, spreading them. She placed her mouth on my cunt, licking along the inside of my pussy. Her warm breath on my sex and the roughness of her tongue against my labia drove me to new heights of erotic tension. Her knees were on either side of my shoulders, the curve of her pussy almost touching my lips. I reached up and, putting my hands on her hips, eased her toward me. Her cunt was damp and the heady musk of her scent was an aphrodisiac. I placed my lips against her warm, fragrant lips and kissed her hungrily. I felt her body stiffen and her tongue drove deeper into my cunt. I probed her swollen cunt, opening her with my fingers and running my tongue inside to savor the sweet juice within. Our bodies moved together in a smooth, undulating motion as our mouths kissed, nibbled, and caressed each other's cunts. Our fingers teased and tantalized, our tongues reached toward hardened clits. Keeping our lovemaking deliberately slow, we prolonged the sensations past all bearing. I felt Ayisha come, a gentle, flowing climax, and as I lapped at the glistening juices pouring out of her cunt, my own tension broke and I was enveloped in slow undulations of pleasure.

Ayisha rolled over and, turning around, gathered me in her arms. We lay still for a long time, enjoying the special closeness that follows really great sex. We felt good about ourselves and about each other and had a mutual desire to share these feelings with others. Not bothering to dress, we left the room in search of further pleasures. We wandered through the dimly lit house, pausing to peek into the various rooms. I have always enjoyed the sight of people making love and even keep a pair of binoculars on the terrace of my New York penthouse so that I can spy on my neighbors.

One bedroom at the party held a group of people, most of whom were enjoying the sight of a voluptuous young woman performing fellatio on a number of men. She knelt in the center of the bed, totally naked and covered only by a veil of honey-colored hair that cascaded below her waist. Those who wanted her attentions stood around the sides of the bed, masturbating themselves to steellike erections as they waited their turn. She was eager and quick, and streams of pale, milky love juice flowed from the sides of her mouth and splashed onto her breasts.

"Now, that looks like fun," I whispered to Ayisha, who stood right in back of me.

"Not for me, thanks."

"Why not?"

"Too many calories. I have to watch my weight."

"Not if you were selective. Right now I'd like some action with that tall black man near the head of the bed. The one that's as dark as you."

"You're nothing if not consistent," Ayisha laughed. "That's Elton. He's my twin." He looked up at the sound of his name, and before I could recover from my surprise Ayisha beckoned him over and introduced us. A stockier, more powerful version of Ayisha, Elton had the same broad nose, flat high-boned cheeks, and coal-black eyes as his twin.

I could hardly contain my excitement as the three of us quickly found an empty room and stretched out on the bed. There is a special pleasure for me in a three-way love trio. Lying between Ayisha's feminine softness and Elton's masculine hardness, I felt like the creamy white filling in an Oreo sandwich cookie. I was aware both of their differences and their sameness, the subtle wooing of Ayisha and the insistent passion of her masculine twin.

Elton moved first. His lips found mine and his hand slowly began to caress the pale mounds of my breasts. I moaned softly as I slipped my arms around his neck, nibbling at his ear and the tender spot right beneath. I felt his hands move along my waist to the rounded curve of my buttocks. I felt Ayisha's hand lightly stroking my thigh, and my legs opened in response to her touch. As Ayisha continued to lovingly caress my inner thighs, Elton moved to my breasts. His firm lips kissed the sensitive flesh, his tongue licking the areolas and the nipples until they stiffened in response. The combined pleasure of masculine and feminine touch stirred the juices in my cunt. My body grew warm, quivering in anticipation as I spread my legs wider and Elton's huge body poised above mine.

"Fuck me," I moaned. "Please take me now."

His cock was long and hard as he forced my legs still wider apart with his knees. I felt a rush of cool air on the inside of my cunt and my stomach muscles tightened in erotic response. Ayisha's hands moved over his hips and between his legs. She fondled his balls and stroked the shaft of his cock, swelling his erection to its full size. My body flushed with desire as I watched Ayisha guide Elton's huge shaft toward my sopping cunt. I gasped as he entered me, stretching me with his size. Ayisha stroked her twin's back and buttocks as he began pumping me.

"You're great, baby," he crooned as I bent my knees and arched my hips off the sheets to allow him maximum penetration. He supported my buttocks with his hands as we ground together in our own special sexual rhythm. I caught a glimpse of Ayisha's face and could tell that she was enjoying the sight of her twin and her lover giving each other pleasure. She moved closer and, leaning down, began to suck and fondle my breasts. She moved her hand so that it encircled Elton's plunging cock. It slid through her fingers, leaving a sticky-sweet residue. She traced the outline of my lips and I grabbed at her hand, tasting my own love juice on her fingers.

Elton's thrusts became more demanding and I locked my legs around his waist, my hips rising and falling as Ayisha stimulated his cock and my pussy, bringing us both to a trembling peak of pleasure. As Elton's orgasm doused my steaming cunt, my own climax swept over me. I collapsed back against the pillows as Elton pulled his still-pulsing cock from my pussy and thrust it into Ayisha's eager mouth. She swallowed hungrily, then bent over and began to lick the last milky drops from my pussy.

At Ayisha's suggestion we changed positions so that Ayisha knelt on the floor with her mouth on the level of my cunt and Elton stood behind me, his swollen cock nudging my rear end. I spread my legs, and Elton parted the cheeks of my buttocks with his hands, easing the tip of his penis into my back passage. I gasped and stiffened, but he held me still, urging my legs wider apart until I relaxed and pushed back against him, placing my hands on Ayisha's head to steady myself. She immediately buried her face in my fragrant pussy and began tonguing me ecstatically. We began to move in a slow, undulating rhythm, Ayisha eating my cunt and her twin plunging deeper and deeper into my anus. My entire body trembled in the center of this sexy sandwich and I cried out, begging for release. The twins speeded up their motions to accommodate my need, and I sensed their own growing excitement as we moved together in a fevered, erotic congruence. Suddenly Elton's orgasm exploded in my asshole like a string of firecrackers that triggered my own climax. His warm cum filled my rectum and dripped down my legs as Ayisha gorged herself on my love juice and fingered herself to orgasm.

Totally exhausted at last, we lay together on the bed, trying to catch our breaths. Elton lay between Ayisha and me, his hands absently stroking our thighs and pussies in a loving, nonsensual way. We had experienced a perfect blend of giving and taking, satisfying both ourselves and each other. I felt a special intimacy with both of them, but as with all such rare moments, I knew it could not be prolonged. Giving them each a final fond embrace, I went in search of my clothes.

Most of the guests seemed to have gone, though the muffled sounds from the darkened rooms indicated that those who were left had paired off and were enjoying a quiet bit of erotic exercise. The smell of hash lingered in the air and the floors were littered with popper casings. I walked along the dimly lit hallway, trying to feel my way to the kitchen. I didn't want to disturb the romantic atmosphere by turning on a light, but I had smoked a great quantity of hash, expended a great deal of energy, and had a raging case of the munchies.

I tripped over what felt like someone's leg and heard a cry of pain from behind the sofa.

"Sorry," I whispered in the direction of the voice.

"S'okay," came a muffled reply. The voice sounded familiar.

"Is that you, Clive?"

"S'me," he mumbled.

"Did I wake you?" He sounded as if his face were buried in a pillow.

"Oh yes, baby, yesss, lick a little harder, honey," came a happy young female voice. I smiled as I realized that the conservative middle-aged producer had found something better to do than sleep, and quickly tiptoed away.

Like most of the prewar apartments on the upper West Side, Clive's kitchen was an immense expanse of painted white wooden cabinets, worn linoleum tile, and ancient wallpaper, showing teapots, rolling pins, and baking tins superimposed on a wavy red-and-white checkered background. Though he hadn't modernized the decor, Clive had equipped himself with just about every known gadget available for the up-and-coming gourmet cook, and while his devotion to his mother's memory was a subject of much humorous speculation, his culinary abilities were universally admired. An invitation to dine in his tacky Mediterranean dining room with its Austrian-crystal chandelier and red velvet drapes was considered a social coup, and the menu was talked about for months after the event.

I, on the other hand, couldn't cook my way out of a wet paper bag, or whatever it is one cooks one's way out of. When I enter a kitchen it's strictly to do battle with knife and fork, so I passed the stove, which I wouldn't know how to light anyway, and went straight to the refrigerator, hoping that it would contain something ready to eat.

I was rummaging through the shelves, opening jars and peering into little tinfoil-wrapped packages when I became aware that there was someone else in the room.

"Anything in there?" said a deep male voice behind me.

"Plenty of things," I replied, not turning around, "all of them requiring some form of preparation. Unfortunately, I'm not a cowboy so I'm not at home on the range. I need something I can just pop into my mouth."

"I can think of many things you could pop into your lovely mouth," the voice said. I winced at the obviousness of his remark. "Fruit, for instance, or cheese," he continued, and I laughed as I realized my companion wasn't a crude bore after all.

I stood up and turned around. The deep, sexy voice belonged to a heavyset young man with dark, almond-shaped eyes and even darker hair. He had a broad nose, prominent cheekbones, and a wide, thin-lipped mouth. A slight scar divided his left eyebrow, giving his face a slightly off-center appearance. He was wearing a plain black T-shirt and worn jeans. A silver cross flashed against his broad chest and a wide leather belt with metal studs was hitched around his trim waist. He wore a black leather wrist band and heavy motorcycle boots.

"Allow me," he said. His voice had a distinctly Eastern European accent.

I stepped away from the refrigerator. He looked over the contents, then proceeded to lay out some eggs, cheese, onions, green peppers, and mushrooms. He went to the spice rack and took half a dozen of the little jars off the shelves.

"Do you know what you're doing?" I asked suspiciously.

"Uh huh," he nodded, stepping over to the stove. "Can I help?"

"I think I can manage it," he grunted, pulling a bowl from a cabinet and breaking in half a dozen eggs. I watched enviously as he whipped, grated, sliced, chopped, stirred, and fried with complete confidence. If all the housekeepers and cooks in the world suddenly went on strike, I would certainly starve, but I could see that this interesting-looking young man would do all right. At least he would know how to make a cheese omelette for two, which was what he was doing right before my eyes.

While the omelette was cooking, he set the table and brewed some thick, dark coffee that looked as if it would melt the spoon if it was stirred.

"You're certainly a handy man to have around the house, Mr. . . ."

"Zelanko. Nicholas Zelanko." He handed me my plate and we sat down at the table.

"How do you do. I'm Christina van Bell. This smells delicious," I said, taking a forkful. "Do you cook for a living?"

"No. I write poetry. However, I used to help the cook in the army when I was not on duty. For extra food."

"I thought the army fed you well."

"I did not serve in your country. I have lived here for a few months only."

"You speak English very well."

"My government . . . my *former* government, excuse me, sent me to school on scholarship. Then army. I was translator. It was a hard life. I was hungry all the time. You could not understand this."

He was right. I had never so much as denied myself an Oreo cookie. "It sounds terrible," I agreed sympathetically. I looked up and caught him staring at me with a smoldering expression in his eyes that made my breath catch in my throat.

"Enough food?" he asked.

"Yes. Thank you . . ."

"Not for me. I'm still hungry." His eyes held mine, and I sensed that he wasn't talking about food. He leaned forward and touched my lips with his fingers. "You will come home with me," he said softly. It wasn't a question. It was a statement of fact.

"Why should I?" I snapped. "You're a cocky, arrogant bastard!"

"You want to," he said, smiling. "I can tell. You are frightened but you are curious too. You want to know what it will be like with me."

"Maybe," I said, looking into his hard eyes. "I don't know. Will you be cruel?"

"Do you want me to be cruel?" His hand slipped behind my head. He leaned closer and pressed his lips to mine in a harsh, searing kiss. Angry thoughts flooded my mind but my body responded with such intensity that I knew myself betrayed. "Come," he said shortly and I did not protest. Silently we found our jackets, and I followed him downstairs and into the cool night air.

CHAPTER TWO

As a wealthy and beautiful woman, I usually divide my time between the snow-peaked mountains of Switzerland, the sun-drenched beaches of the Riviera, and the most expensive and exclusive gaming clubs in the world. I am accustomed to being flattered, to giving orders and being in control. But tonight, the bizarre and kinky people at the party and my sexual encounter with the twins had whetted my appetite for something different. As I sat close behind Nicholas on his stripped-down Harley I had an uncontrollable urge to let myself go. My arms were around his waist and my cheek was pillowed against his broad back. The night wind whipped my hair as Nicholas steered the powerful bike downtown. I loved the feel of his body pressed against mine, the rich sweat-and-leather smell of his clothes. Images of *Easy Rider* and *The Wild One* flashed through my mind as we drove through the narrow, deserted streets at ninety miles an hour. The sexual tension simmered between us. I fantasized being conquered, dominated by this handsome, virile man, and my body flushed with sexual heat.

We pulled up in front of a decaying group of buildings on East 13th Street, barely missing the overflowing garbage cans at the curb. I slid off the bike,
shivering slightly in the damp air. I was out of my ele-
ment and began to regret my impulsiveness. I felt
awkward and a bit afraid. A starving cat brushed
against my leg, mewling pitifully.

"That's Tom," said Nicholas as if introducing us.
He reached inside his jacket pocket and withdrew a
crumpled paper napkin, which he handed to me.
"Cat's hungry," he said, avoiding my eyes. He was
obviously embarrassed, but the gesture touched me
and my apprehensions vanished. The napkin held
some bits of cheese and cold cuts, and I fed the scraps
to Tom while Nicholas removed the heavy chains
from his shoulder and used them to secure the motorcycle to a nearby fireplug.

He motioned for me to follow him, and we walked
up the front stairs and stepped through the brown
painted door into the hallway. The building was quite
old, but the interior showed that the owners, or at
least the superintendent and the tenants, cared
enough to keep it in an acceptable state of repair.
There were no graffiti on the faded yellow walls and
the linoleum had been scrubbed so often that the
original design had worn away. The hallway also
lacked the smells of decaying food and urine usually
associated with such places, and as I followed
Nicholas up the dark staircase, I noticed a holy
statue, in a niche on each landing. There were four
apartments on each floor. The walls were thin and
the apartments close together. As we passed the
closed doors, the sounds of raised voices, the late-
night movie, and a crying child were clearly audible.
Someone on the third floor was frying sausage and
onions, and the smell made me hungry all over again.

Nicholas had a small apartment on the fifth floor.

He unlocked the door and ushered me inside, turning on an old pewter floor lamp with an inverted white glass shade as he did so. The living room was simply furnished with a couch and several overstuffed chairs in mismatched floral prints, and there was an efficiency kitchen along one wall complete with an ancient white-and-gold flecked formica table and two red-plastic-upholstered kitchen chairs. Along the other walls were a battered black-and-white TV, a radio, and two bookcases crammed with volumes of political dogma. Magazines and newspapers in an Eastern European language lay on a makeshift coffee table in front of the couch.

Through an alcove space on the left I could see a neatly made double bed with plain white sheets and a gray wool blanket. A door to the right of the stove led to a small bathroom containing a toilet, a sink, and a prefabricated stall shower.

I ran a comb through my hair and then settled myself on the couch while Nicholas busied himself at the kitchen counter.

"Is Tom your cat?" I asked as he began to cut some black bread into neat little squares and arranged them on a plate.

"What's that?"

"The cat you were feeding out on the street. Is that your cat?"

"Tom? He's his own cat," Nicholas laughed. "I once considered taking him in but superintendent's wife wouldn't hear of it. She claims cat brings roaches because of food. I feed him whenever I see him, and in winter I sometimes sneak him into basement for the night. But he has been whole life on street and he survives. I guess we all survive."

He placed the plate containing the black bread on the coffee table, then set down another plate containing a brick of butter and what looked like caviar. There was a bottle of wine from a Rumanian vineyard I had never heard of. Rot-gut wine and California fish eggs, just my luck, I thought as I spread some butter on a square of the bread and topped it with a smear of the black eggs. My digestion will be ruined for a week. I took a careful bite.

"Is this beluga?" I asked in surprise, stuffing the rest of the canapé into my mouth and making myself another. If it wasn't, it was certainly an excellent imitation.

"Imported," said Nicholas, pouring out two glasses of wine.

"Where did you get it? Our relations with Russia and the Middle East have made it almost a black market item."

"I have my sources," he said. "I do not eat everyday, you understand. I save for special company. How do you like the wine?"

I sipped some of the pale yellow liquid. It had a light, fruity flavor, almost like champagne.

"This is terrific," I nodded enthusiastically. "Where did you buy it? I've never heard of the vineyard."

"Is private concern," Nicholas said. "Is not exported, but the owner is man from my village. He give me case when I come to America as gift."

He sat down next to me, refilled my glass, and poured one for himself. His face was in shadow but I could feel his eyes studying me intently. His knee pressed against my thigh and my heart began to beat faster. We ate and drank in silence, marking time, observing the conventions. I considered asking him to let me hear some of his poetry, another polite move, but decided against it. I hadn't come here to listen to bad verse or even good verse, for that matter. I was interested in his peter, not his meter. He seemed to sense my mood and, putting down his glass, he took mine from my hand and placed it on the table.

Without preliminaries he began to kiss me, his lips demanding rather than asking. His hands roughly fondled my body and he yanked my sweater out of my jeans to expose my bare breasts to his touch. My own passion was rising and my body tingled with excitement. His forceful lovemaking was turning me on, but as his hand fumbled for the snap on my jeans, I stiffened and pulled away. A look of surprise flickered in his eyes, then they narrowed angrily.

"Make me do it," I whispered. "Whatever happens, fuck me hard!"

Nick's eyes gleamed with excitement and I could tell that he was not averse to a little game playing. I also sensed that despite his extremely macho appearance, he would not really hurt me.

Grabbing my wrists, Nick held them behind my back with one hand, forcing my body against his chest as his lips closed over mine. His hand again reached for my breasts, his fingers searing the nipples as I struggled against him. I was wearing my hair tied back with a leather thong, and he suddenly spun me around and yanked the thong from my hair so that it spilled over my shoulders. He tied my wrists tightly behind my back and with a little push, released me.

I stood proudly before him, my naked breasts thrust forward by the position of my hands, my hair in wild profusion, framing my flushed face. My skin-tight jeans hugged my shapely ass and thighs, disappearing into knee-high, black leather boots. I wanted to be dominated by this forceful, sensual man, to be reduced to a mere cunt begging for his cock, but I am not submissive by nature. I did not flinch or hang my head but met his gaze squarely, daring him to go on.

Nick stepped closer and, holding me by one arm, roughly unsnapped the front of my jeans. He undid the zipper, then peeled the jeans over the rounded curve of my ass to my knees. I was not wearing underwear and as his eyes traveled over the flat hardness of my stomach to the golden triangle between my thighs, my pussy began to tingle and my buttock muscles tightened convulsively. I gasped as Nick thrust his fingers between the lips of my vagina, moving slowly in and out. I began to breathe heavily, my thighs trembling as Nick continued to tease my cunt, running his free hand over my buttocks and inserting a finger into my anus. He watched my reactions with an amused detachment, playing with me until my knees grew weak and the juices started to flow out of me.

"Cunt!" he said harshly. "You want it, don't you? You want my big hard cock reaming your ass. You want me to fuck your pussy till it's black and blue. Say it!"

I gasped, on the brink of orgasm, but shook my head, squirming away.

"Ohhh," Nick hissed. "Still the good little girl, eh? Miss Society, all cool and nice." He grabbed my hair and forced my face down on the bed, pulling my jeans inside out over my boots and flinging them aside.

He untied my hands and pulled my sweater over my head, leaving me naked except for my boots. He ran his hand along my back, letting it rest lightly for a moment on my upturned derriere. Though he hadn't threatened or hit me, I sensed the curbed power beneath his touch. I felt humiliated and vulnerable as he continued to stroke my quivering ass cheeks, running his hands along the inside of my thighs and touching the aching lips of my pussy. My heart was pounding and I literally shivered in anticipaton of his next move. My body began to grow warm. The gentle, methodical stroking held an implicit threat of punishment that increased the sexual tension until I thought I would explode. I felt like a violin string being stretched tighter and tighter. I gasped as his hand cracked across my naked behind

and my buttock muscles clenched in anticipation of
the next slap. He held back, forcing me to relax, then
delivered a blow that made me cry out with pain. He
continued to whack my defenseless behind until my
cheeks were burning, but each stroke fueled the fire
growing in my loins. My cries of pain turned to
moans of pleasure. I spread my legs, my hips rising
off the sheets as if to welcome each stinging slap.
Then, suddenly something inside me snapped and I
began to cry, my entire body shaken with great rack-
ing sobs. Nick immediately stopped spanking me. My
thighs were forced wide apart and I felt a large object
sliding into my aching pussy. The combination of the
intense pain of the spanking and the feeling of fullness in my cunt drove me to new erotic heights of
pleasure.

"Give it to me!" I screamed, my hips bucking with
his thrusts and my hands clawing at the sheets. "I
want all you've got! Give it to me good!"

"You've got it, baby," Nick crooned. "Not my
cock or my finger either. You've got my fist shoved
up your hole!"

The words had a cataclysmic effect. I could not
believe how open and wet I was. The experience was
such an emotional high that I climaxed with a shattering intensity that made the room spin.

I must have passed out. When I opened my eyes,
my boots had been removed and Nick was lying
naked beside me beneath the sheets. His skin felt cool
against my own as I snuggled against him. I felt the
welcome bulge of his cock along my thigh, and
though my ass still burned and my pussy ached from
our recent lovemaking, I wanted more than anything
to give him pleasure. Nick's hands were in my hair.
He kissed me passionately, his tongue probing my
mouth. Then he guided my head to his chest, matted
with thick dark hair. I ran my tongue over his
nipples, teasing them with my lips and teeth. I moved

downward into the warm cocoon of darkness under the sheet, my lips and tongue tracing a warm, moist trail over the muscled hardness of his rib cage and the taut skin of his stomach. The short springy hairs, now damp and fragrant with my saliva, brushed my breasts as I moved. I closed my eyes and breathed in the tangy male scent of his body as my lips touched the baby-soft skin of his cock. He gave a low groan as I cupped his balls, taking first one, then the other into my mouth. I kissed his pubic area and the hollow where his thigh joined his hip. I could see his cock in the half-darkness beneath the sheets, the wrinkled flesh now smooth and distended with passion. I wriggled farther down, nestling between his legs. I ran the tips of my nails lightly along his shaft, coaxing him to a steely erection. Then, placing my mouth over the helmetlike head of his cock, I eased my lips over his turgid pole, taking as much of him down my throat as I could. He cried out, his hips arching upward. His torso bucked spasmodically, and I dug my fingers into his ass cheeks, fighting to keep his thrusting cock in my mouth. Nick's hands were on my head and the entire bed vibrated as his hips bounced up and down. I sucked at him hungrily, humming deep in my throat so that my entire mouth vibrated as I worked. I sensed his whole body stiffen, then collapse as his control broke and waves of hot creamy cum spilled into my mouth. Like a starving woman, I swallowed his warm milk, relishing the rich texture and slightly salty taste. Then, totally exhausted, I pillowed my cheek on his now flaccid cock, my hand absently stroking his belly as I came slowly back to reality.

I felt his hands stroking my hair, and when I stirred, he quickly threw off the sheet and gathered me into his arms. I felt his lips on mine and as he deepened the kiss, I sighed softly, giving myself up to his embrace. He pushed me back against the pillows, his eyes burning with desire as he drank in the sight of my naked body, now soft and yielding, totally his.

"You're beautiful," he whispered. "I want to make love to you, not just your breasts or your ass or your cunt but to Christina. To all of you."

He began to kiss me, his lips moving over my face and neck, then concentrating on the rich fullness of my breasts. He kissed and licked each one in turn, the roughness of his tongue teasing the nipples until they stiffened and stood erect. Then he moved downward, his mouth leaving a hot, moist trail across my taut belly and the gentle swell of my inner thighs. I began to moan softly, my body writhing on the sheets. My love juices were flowing as my body came alive beneath his touch. I gave myself completely to the motions of his lips and tongue, squirming and whimpering with delight. When at last his mouth descended on my quivering quim, I was faint with excitement. His tongue was hard and slightly rough and he used it with an expertise that had me begging for more. I cried out again and again as my body responded to the steady rhythm of his tongue against my clit. He brought me to the brink of orgasm, then slowed his pace, producing sensations I had not thought possible.

When I could no longer hold back, I felt the welcome relief of his steely prick between my thighs, sliding into my aching hot slit.

"Oh God," I moaned. "That's so good!"

I wrapped my legs around his hips as he moved against me, slowly at first, then increasing the tempo, fucking me hard and fast. My desire reached a fever pitch as I urged him on with my hands and lips. I was like a cat in heat, craving nothing but the raw, bestial act. Like the bursting of a dam, his climax shattered inside me, triggering my own. He held me tightly against him, bruising me with his lips and hands as our bodies fused together with the heat of our orgasm. With a sigh of pleasure, Nick collapsed on top of me, and I drifted off to sleep with his prick still nestled between my thighs.

When I opened my eyes the next morning, daylight was streaming through the uncurtained windows, and the cheerful sound of a New York City garbage truck, motor grinding and puffing full tilt, drifted up from the street along with the choice comments of its crew.

"Back it up, come on, come on, y'got room," yelled one of the city's sanitation guardians as the truck lumbered to a crashing halt, knocking what sounded like sixteen full garbage cans into a clattering heap in front of the building. "That's it. Poifect!"

I groaned loudly and pushed my head under the pillow, trying unsuccessfully to block out the noise. They have a lot of nerve, collecting garbage at dawn, I thought angrily. I pried open my eyes and squinted at the battered alarm clock that sat ticking on a small nightstand next to the bed. It was past noon. I screwed my eyes shut and burrowed back under the covers. The alcove was very small and the head of the bed was right against the wall. I could hear someone walking around in the apartment on the other side. A window banged open.

"Pigs! Swine! I'll report this to the mayor!" a man shouted, then the window slammed shut. There was a momentary silence, then a blast of music so overpowering that it completely blocked out the noise from the street, came through the wall. As "The Damnation March" from *Faust* blasted forth, a nagging voice somewhere in the back of my mind reminded me that I had to be at the airport at five o'clock for a flight to France. I had a date for the opening of the Paris Opera the following day.

Reluctantly I swung my feet over the side of the bed. I took several deep breaths, wriggled my toes and, gathering up my clothes, padded naked into the living room. Nicholas was already dressed and clattering around the kitchen. I could smell fresh-brewed coffee and toast, and, grunting a greeting in the general direction of his back, I hurried into the bathroom.

I spent five minutes trying to figure out the mechanics of the shower before finally standing, eyes closed, under the needlelike spray, letting the warm water wash the last traces of the previous night's exertions from my body.

I stepped out of the shower, dried myself off and pulled on my sweater and jeans. I decided that shoes and combed hair were unnecessary for breakfast at the Zelanko house. I walked into the next room and sat down at the table. I am not a morning person and Nicholas was sensitive enough to realize that and refrained from making any cheerful comments. Besides, Nick didn't seem like much of a morning person himself. He put the food on the table, sat down opposite me and opened his newspaper.

I put three heaping teaspoons of sugar in my cup, poured half a cup of coffee, stirred, and filled the cup the rest of the way with milk. I buttered three pieces of toast and took a generous helping of scrambled eggs.

Nicholas was drinking his coffee black, and as I started on my second cup and fourth piece of toast he put down his paper and smiled across at me.

"It is rude of me to read," he said. "I beg your pardon."

"I don't mind," I replied. "I'm still half asleep."

"If you like we can go back to bed," he suggested. "We could make love, sleep a bit, make love again . . ."

"It sounds wonderful," I said, unromantically scraping the last of the eggs onto my plate, "but I'm afraid I can't. I have to catch a five o'clock plane to Paris."

"You're going to Paris? This evening?"

"Why not? Are the airports closed?"

"Aren't you cutting it rather close? It's almost two-thirty."

"My household staff knows I'm going. They'll pack my bags, confirm my reservations, get together my travel documents, and order a limousine. I'll just have to change clothes and go."

"Still, you must go home to change clothes," he said, looking at his watch and obviously calculating the time this would take. He seemed unusually interested in the details of my travel arrangements.

"It isn't my custom to eat and run, you understand, but I'm afraid this time I must."

"Well, I will forgive you . . . this time," he said, smiling. He opened his mouth as if to say something else, then changed his mind.

"Is there something on your mind?" I asked. I hoped it wasn't the usual morning-after plea for lifetime togetherness, fidelity, and marriage that I often get from my lovers. Though Nicholas had been an unusually interesting bed partner, it would take a lot more than a fancy set of moves between the sheets to make me even consider such a proposal. Domesticity should be confined to animals. Women, especially women such as myself, have better things to do.

"I was just wondering . . . No, it is too much an imposition."

"Ask me," I said, my curiosity piqued. "Maybe I'll say yes."

"Well, you're going to Paris, and it is coincidence I suppose, but I have something I wish to get to Paris. I've been holding off because I didn't want to send through mail . . ." He could see I didn't understand, and explained in detail. "It is bottle of Rumanian wine. You remember, I serve last night? You said that you like it."

"I did."

"I have been wanting to send bottle to friend who lives in Paris, but I do not trust mails. Wine is fragile, and very rare. You understand?"

"You want me to take the bottle to Paris with me, is that it?" I asked.

"It is terrible imposition, I know. Is just that my friend so loves this wine, it would be great thrill for him to get it . . ."

"I'll take the bottle," I said. I could see no real reason why I shouldn't. "I'll be in Paris for quite some time, and it will be no trouble to see that it's delivered to your friend."

"You are very generous. I cannot thank you enough."

"Consider it an even trade . . ." He started to demur. "For the breakfast," I continued, flashing him my most innocent smile.

He laughed out loud, then walked to his closet and took down a tall slender package, carefully wrapped in cardboard and brown paper. There was a label on the front with an address carefully typed on it. Obviously, Nick had wrapped it for mailing and had then had second thoughts.

"The address is on front," he said, handing me the package. It was heavy, about the weight one would expect a bottle of wine to be. "You will probably find him home in evening." I looked at the label and saw that it was addressed to an Andrei Denesovitch, who lived on a small street on the Left Bank of Paris between the Sorbonne and Notre-Dame. I nodded, indicating that I knew where to take the package.

I stood up, brushing toast crumbs off my sweater, and swallowed a last gulp of coffee. "I have to get going," I said. "Otherwise I'll miss my plane."

Nick slipped his arms around my waist and pulled me toward him. "I won't hold you," he murmured against my ear. "Is just to say good-bye."

I tilted my face upward and he crushed his lips to

mine in a searing embrace that almost made me change my mind about going.

"I'll call you when I return home," I whispered.

"Promise?"

I nodded, giving him a parting kiss, then slipped out the door. I walked quickly down the stairs and stepped outside. The sanitation truck had moved on, leaving half-emptied garbage cans scattered over the sidewalk and street, their spilled contents a sticky mess in the warm afternoon sun. The romanticism of the previous night was quickly dispelled as the sounds and smells of the lower East Side overpowered me. I looked about for a taxi. I wanted to escape, to leave the rotting vegetables and cacophonous noise for the cleanliness and order of my own upper East Side. I felt a pang of guilt at these manifest feelings of class-consciousness, and for a fleeting moment I wished that I could do something for all those who could not afford a cab ride uptown. I was about to start toward Second Avenue when a black cat, sniffing at a piece of fried chicken, caught my eye. It was Tom, the cat Nick had fed the previous evening. I frowned as I watched him pulling at the rotting piece of meat, the flies buzzing angrily around his head. Though Nick had insisted that Tom was fully capable of taking care of himself, I could see that the cat was painfully thin, with a matted, lackluster coat.

"Hello, old Tom. How are you today?" I whispered at the feline, who I noticed wasn't entirely black; he had white paws and chest and a white spot near his mouth. He looked up at me with enormous yellow eyes, and then began to rub himself back and forth against my leg. I reached down and scratched him behind the ears and he purred loudly, his entire body vibrating with the effort. I thought of Tom's life, of days spent rummaging through the garbage for scraps of food and of nights seeking shelter from the cold and rain. I thought of him dying of slow starvation or of possibly ending up under the wheels of one of the huge trucks that rumbled endlessly through the streets of this neighborhood. The more I thought about it, the more I knew that I couldn't let the cat stay on the street, no matter what Nick thought of his survival abilities. Nicholas' occasional feedings weren't adequate enough to insure the cat's future.

"How would you like to come home with me?" I asked. The cat sat down on my foot and vibrated happily. That made up my mind. I clumsily loaded the small creature into my arms along with my bottle of wine and set off for Second Avenue to find a taxi.

My luck was running strong that afternoon, for a cab was rumbling down the avenue just as I reached the corner, its ancient springs creaking and groaning loudly. It pulled up in front of me, and I managed to get the grimy door open and my package and Tom inside on the back seat. I slipped in, lifting the cat onto my lap, and slammed the door.

The driver waited for my instructions. I peered through the yellowing plastic shield that separated the driver from potential muggers, and saw that he was a thin middle-aged man with gray hair and large horn-rimmed spectacles. He wore an orange plaid shirt, which clashed nicely with his red polyester pants. I gave him my address, and he gunned the motor and steered the cab uptown.

"I have a passenger with me today," I said conversationally, holding the cat up so the driver could see him. "I've decided to give him a home."

"What's that?" he yelled back through the plastic panel. He seemed to be a little hard of hearing.

"Home," I yelled back. "I'm taking the cat home with me."

"Poem?"

"Home! I'm taking him home!"

"Sure, I'll take you home," the driver nodded.

"It's what I do for a living, you know. I'm a cabbie. I drive people where they want to go. It's no trouble. I like doing it."

"I mean the cat," I persisted. "You don't mind having the cat in the cab, do you?"

The driver glanced at me in his mirror and finally seemed to notice Tom. "Hey, you have a cat," he said. "Nice cat too. Don't let him pee on the seat, though."

"I'll watch him," I promised, stroking the cat's ears.

"I get a lot of strange animals in the cab," the driver continued. "Had a kangaroo in the cab once. Not alone. He had this guy with him who was taking him to some industrial show in midtown. It was the damnedest thing you ever saw, driving uptown with this kangaroo hanging out the window, looking at all the people. But the kangaroo wore a diaper, so it was okay with me. I don't mind animals, as long as they don't pee on the seats. That's where I draw the line. People, too. They can't pee on the seats either. House rule."

I started to wonder if he had heard the address I had given him.

"You got that address I gave you, didn't you?" I asked.

"Sure. I must say, though, I don't get many people from down here asking to go to a nice neighborhood like that. Most of the people going to that neighborhood look pretty ritzy. Nice evening gowns, expensive clothes . . ."

"I live up there."

"Pretty expensive place to live, isn't it?"

"I suppose so."

"Probably why you have to dress like that, with the crummy sweater and all. Spend all your money on rent, right?"

"This sweater is one hundred percent cashmere. It

was a very expensive sweater," I mumbled, knowing he wouldn't hear me.

"It's hard to find a nice safe place to live in this city," he continued as we turned west on 57th Street. "Rents are sky high. People pay an arm and a leg for an apartment that looks like a cell at Sing Sing with no heat or hot water and lousy landlords that never want to fix anything. And you'll get no help from the city, believe me. The goddamn mayor loves those landlords, gave 'em carte blanche. They run all over the little guy. Don't have a chance, the little guy, not with that bastard in City Hall." He paused in his lecture to navigate the cab through some difficult traffic, never reducing his speed below fifty as he did it. He screeched crazily around a truck and into oncoming traffic, narrowly pulling back into the lane just in time to avoid a large van heading our way.

"So," he said, "you got yourself a cat. Nice animal, cat, always wanted one myself."

"Why don't you get one?" I asked. "There are certainly plenty of them in the city. You could have your pick and get yourself a nice little companion."

"What's that?" he yelled.

"A companion!" I bellowed. "Get yourself a little companion!"

"I'd love to, but my wife won't let her live in the house with us. I'd be better off getting a cat. My wife doesn't like dogs."

"Would you like this cat?" I asked, holding the black cat up to the window. The cabbie looked at him through the rear-view mirror. "You could train him," I insisted. "They have seeing-eye dogs. Maybe the cat could tell you when the phone was ringing."

"Yep, that's a cat, wouldn't argue with you. Wouldn't mind having one like that."

"It's yours," I said as we arrived at my apartment house. He jammed down on the brakes, stopping in the middle of the street, and the traffic started to back up behind us, horns blaring and drivers cursing loudly. I pushed some money through the slot in the plastic shield and got out of the cab. I walked around to the driver's window and handed him the cat. Tom purred as the man stroked him.

"I'll call him Bastard, after the mayor," the driver promised. "We'll have a fine time together, won't we, fellow?" he whispered affectionately at the animal. "Do you like corn? I eat corn every night."

"Good luck," I said, waving as he gunned the engine and pulled away, I knew that the cat was in good hands. You can always trust a New York cabbie.

Up in my penthouse, I discovered that my staff, efficient as always, had packed my bags and arranged for a limousine, so all I had to do was change my clothes and leave my Paris address with my housekeeper. I made it to the airport with time to spare, and before the sun had set over the Big Apple, I was seated comfortably in the Concorde, a drink in each hand as we streaked over the Atlantic toward France.

CHAPTER THREE

I shivered as I drove the Maserati through the late night streets of Paris. I drew my black wool cape around me to keep out the early-autumn chill, then shifted the powerful car into first, depressing the accelerator to climb the steep hill of Rue de Rochechouart.

The miracle of supersonic flight and a stiff tail wind had enabled me to get to Paris from New York in a record three hours and six minutes. Due to the time difference, I had cleared customs at one-thirty A.M. Paris time, but to my body it was still eight-thirty P.M. the previous evening. I was wide awake and, despite having had dinner and several drinks on the plane, I was incredibly hungry.

My secretary had arranged for a car to be waiting for me at Orly airport. I used an exclusive executive service, which allowed the affluent customer to drive from the airport in something a little more elegant than a cardboard compact from the Renault cookie-cutter assembly lines. In this case it was a black Maserati with gray leather upholstery, the keys for which were provided by a sleepy company representative who was sitting all alone at his desk in the deserted airline terminal. He seemed very happy to see me.

"Now that you're here, I can close up and go home," he sighed, clicking off the little lamp on his desk.

"You mean you've been sitting here all night just to hand me the keys to the car?" I asked, feeling slightly guilty.

"I have, but don't let it bother your conscience," he said. "After all, it's part of the service you are paying through the nose for."

"Is there a porter on duty?" I asked, looking at the deserted terminal. "I have several bags to bring out to the car."

"There are no porters," the clerk said, shrugging his shoulders. "They are all on strike this week. They always strike at this time of year. Paris is beautiful in the fall and no one wants to be indoors lugging other people's suitcases and sweeping up piles of filth. Fall is a time for nature, for love, not sanitation."

"How romantic," I frowned. "That still leaves me with nine suitcases to get to my car."

"They will not all fit in the car, mademoiselle. Just two in the trunk and perhaps two on the back seat. I will have to send the rest to your residence by cab," the clerk said as he accompanied me to the car.

"Have them all sent then," I said, scribbling my address on a piece of paper. "Tell whoever answers the door to see to it they are unpacked." I handed him the paper and a large tip, and went out to the parking lot to locate my car. In minutes I had left the airport and was heading toward the center of Paris.

It was now after three A.M. as I drove through the streets of Paris. The Métro had stopped running and there were few taxis or private cars on the streets. I stopped and bought a bag of freshly baked beignets at an all night bakery. Covered with powdered sugar, they were still warm and smelled wonderful. I could hardly wait to get into the Maserati before devouring them.

Though I spend a great deal of time in Paris, I never tire of it. Even as I drove about at this late hour, it was blazing with a multicolored brilliance that makes the City of Lights one of the most beautiful in the world. The beignets had taken the edge off my appetite, and I drove contentedly through the streets and hills of Montmartre, circling the Basilique du Sacré-Coeur and heading down the Rue Caulaincourt, turning into Boulevard de Clichy to pass by the famous Moulin Rouge. The streets in the area were dark and deserted. Even the thrill-seekers and the low-lifes who preyed on them had crawled back to their beds by now.

I spent an hour driving around the city, down quiet tree-lined streets, past monuments and statues that were enchanting in their floodlit solitude, finally making my way to the famous Champs-Élysées, which led like the spoke of a bicycle wheel to the Arc de Triomphe. Circumnavigating the monument, I headed north to the seventeenth arrondissement and the home of Adaline Baudry.

I had met Adaline at the opening of an auction gallery in New York. We were instantly attracted to one another, and, discovering that we had an interest in antiques and several lovers in common, we soon became quite good friends. Based in Paris, Adaline was an antique dealer who catered to the wealthiest clientele, so her travels to acquire new and unusual treasures took her all over the world. We often met on the Continent, and once, during a weekend party on the yacht of a Greek shipping magnate, we had spent several happy hours in each other's arms, though this had not become a regular thing.

Adaline was presently in Rome, but when she had heard through the social grapevine that I would be in Paris, she had called me in New York the previous week and offered me the use of her townhouse. "You will be so much more comfortable than at the Bristol," she insisted, "and you will have much more privacy. I have a full-time housekeeper and a part-time cook. You will be well taken care of." Of course I accepted. I had been to Adaline's home many times and, though the house was small by American standards, it was quite comfortable. I speak French fluently and do not need the services of an English-speaking hotel staff, and I was intrigued with the idea of living like a native Parisian while in Paris. After graciously accepting her offer, I had packed enough clothing for an indefinite stay.

Adaline's townhouse was a narrow, two-story, gray stone structure. It was attached on both sides, as are most of the city's houses, and located on a quiet street on the outer fringes of Paris. As I pulled the car into the private parking space in front of the house, I noticed that a light was burning in one of the downstairs windows. I realized that I did not have a key and immediately regretted gadding about the city while Adaline's housekeeper stayed up all night to wait for me.

My ring was answered by a spare middle-aged woman in a worn blue flannel robe and fuzzy blue slippers. Her graying hair hung in a single braid down her back and she stifled a yawn as she let me into the house. I remembered that her name was Madame Poret.

"I was beginning to think you had been in an accident," she said in French, closing the door behind me. "It's good to see you again, Miss van Bell."

"I'm sorry that you had to stay up so late to wait for me," I said apologetically. "The city is so beautiful at night that I was driving around and completely lost track of the time. I forgot that I didn't have a key until I saw the light in the window."

"It was not a problem," she assured me. "I was

watching television and fell asleep on the sofa. Your luggage arrived several hours ago. I have prepared your room and a light snack in case you are hungry. I know how terrible airplane food can be.''

I thanked her and insisted that she take herself off to bed. "I can manage perfectly well on my own," I said. "I'll probably sleep late tomorrow, since my body is still operating on New York time, but I must be up in time to get to the opera tomorrow night."

"I'll be sure to wake you in plenty of time," she promised, slipping away.

The way in which someone arranges and uses his or her living space tells a great deal about that person. Adaline's house was an extension of her interests and her work, the rooms a jumble of mismatched furnishings and objets d'art that changed frequently as she became bored with, or sold off, the items. The rooms were cluttered and disorganized. Bookshelves and desks and tabletops were littered with photos, personal mementos, and gifts from friends all over the world and, looking around, I had the feeling that Adaline was just in the next room instead of thousands of miles away.

I went into the kitchen and took the tray containing my snack out of the refrigerator. I sat at the small round kitchen table, eating cold Chicken Cordon Bleu and reading that day's copy of *Le Monde* to catch up on current events in France. I wanted to be well informed in case I met some high-level government official at the opera and he wanted my opinion on the French stance in the Middle East or somewhere else.

The sky was just beginning to lighten above the roofs of the nearby houses when jet lag caught up with me. I went upstairs to find my room all prepared; my clothes put away, my robe and slippers laid out, and the bed covers turned down for the night. Madame Poret had placed Nicholas' wine bottle, still in its neat brown wrapping, on a small round table near the window. I made a mental note to see that it was delivered the next day. I took a quick shower and slipped between the pink-checked, Belgian cotton-flannel sheets, pulling the pale pink comforter over my head. Within seconds I was dead to the world.

That evening found me at my second theatrical opening of the week. There was a considerable difference, of course, between the opening of a small political play in a SoHo loft and the seasonal opening of the Paris Opera. In contrast to the whitewashed walls and bare wood floors of the loft, the Paris Opera House was a glittering palace of crystal, gold, and velvet. The grand staircase was crowded with opening night celebrants, all dressed to the nines in furs, gowns, and jewels, and I smiled as I thought of how the jeans and sweater I had worn to *Famine and Fire* would look in this setting. Though I had enjoyed the opening of Sean's play and my night with Nicholas, I knew in my heart that I had not fit in. *This* was my world, and although I do not usually flaunt my wealth, on this occasion I had given in to the demands of my social position. My gown was of electric blue taffeta with a long, full skirt and a fitted sequined bodice that left my neck, shoulders, and arms bare. I wore diamond earrings and a necklace and bracelet of diamonds and sapphires, and my hair was swept off my neck and held in place with diamond combs.

My escort for the evening was Marshall Franchot, a wealthy Parisian who had made his fortune in the perfume business. His scents were well known in Europe, at least among the small clientele who could afford his outrageously expensive products. Marshall's age was as much a secret as his formulas, though most people placed him in his midfifties. He was a tall slender man with the type of body that looks best in evening attire. He had a long bony face with a prominent nose and firm, straight lips. His light brown eyes had a directness and an intensity that reminded one of a hawk, and they gave his face a rather stern expression. Though he wasn't a swinger, he had the charm of manner and appreciation of the finer things in life that made him an enviable escort, and I was quite fond of him.

He had picked me up in his chauffeured limousine, a silver Rolls-Royce Corniche with custom coach work and gray leather upholstery, and we had driven to the Opera in grand style, sipping champagne in the spacious back seat and watching the Paris crowds bustling along the Rue Saint Honoré and the Avenue de l'Opéra.

"You are certainly drawing your share of attention this evening, Christina," Marshall commented as he slipped a cigarette from his gold cigarette case and lit it. It was the first-act intermission, and we were mingling with the opening night crowd. Marshall was a principal benefactor of the Opera and was somewhat of a celebrity in opera circles, but I was not exactly unknown to Parisian society myself and encountered many familiar faces on the steps of the grand staircase.

I snatched a glass of champagne from a passing tray and sipped it while Marshall acknowledged the greetings of passing friends.

"Are you enjoying tonight's performance?" he asked me.

"Yes, though I was surprised to see they were performing *Mefistofele* for the opening night," I said. "Boito isn't exactly a popular favorite, though I've always liked the opera myself."

"It's the Faustian aspect of the story that appeals to you," Marshall commented. "Like most hedonists, you are intrigued with the idea of making a pact with the devil."

"I'd like to do more than make a pact with this one," I said wickedly. "I'd like to . . ."

". . . go backstage! Of course," said Marshall hastily as a very old man with thin white hair and a drooping mustache shuffled up to us. "This is Count Bronsky, Christina."

"How do you do," said the Count, taking my hand and looking at me with sad, myopic eyes. "Do you like the opera, my dear?"

"Very much," I said. "I'm looking forward to the ballet in the second act. I hope they haven't left it out of this version."

"It would be sacrilege," said the Count gravely. "The Paris Opera has always had dance in the second act. Not good dance, mind you, but dance all the same. Are you a dancer?" I shook my head. "You could be, you know. You're very pretty. Franchot is a lucky man." He patted my hand and shuffled away.

"He's right," said Marshall. "You have grace and charm and I'm a very lucky man." He leaned down and kissed me softly on the cheek.

"When I was a little girl, I attended ballet classes," I confided. "My aunt felt it would give me poise. We studied the Dance of the Witches from this opera in my senior year at the school."

"That's a rather esoteric dance to teach little girls, isn't it? Whatever happened to *Swan Lake*?"

"It was a very bohemian school," I laughed. "Do you know, I can still remember some of the movements." I began to hum the music, waving my arms and twirling around.

"I would love to have seen you," Marshall smiled. "Perhaps you will perform it for me sometime . . ."

"How about tonight?"

"Tonight? You mean after the party? I'm rather old-fashioned, Christina, and I don't generally enjoy theatrics in the bedroom."

"Not in the bedroom, dummy! On the stage. I could go out there and dance with the company."

"Really, Christina, you have the most incredible nerve sometimes."

"Where's your sense of fun?" I chided him. "You said you wanted to see me dance. I can't sing opera, but this is not the Royal Ballet and I'm up to anything those cows in the corps can do. You're a patron of this place, aren't you?"

"Well, yes . . . but . . ."

"Then we can go backstage and check out a costume. There's plenty of time. Their entrance isn't until the second scene."

"You'll probably get me thrown off the board of directors," Marshall muttered darkly. "There are rules about this sort of thing, you know . . . unions . . . insurance . . ."

"Don't look so grim. I'll stick to the back of the group. Who's going to notice one extra witch?"

"There *are* a lot of witches," he agreed reluctantly. "Well, why not, if you really want to. Come along, Isadora, we'll get you a costume."

The orchestra was tuning up as we quickly went backstage. The place was a beehive of frenetic activity as singers, dancers, and production crew prepared for the second act. Singers were humming snatches of the score while the dancers stretched and bent to keep their muscles warm. Huge panels of scenery were being lowered into place, and men with clipboards and headsets barked orders to the lighting crew.

Marshall led me to a small room and spoke briefly to the wardrobe mistress. She nodded and disappeared, returning moments later with a costume and a pair of ballet shoes, which she handed to me.

"I told her you were a last minute replacement," Marshall said. "I'll find you an empty dressing room to change in, then you're on your own."

"Where will you be?"

"Back in our seats. If anyone misses you, I'll say you went to the toilet. There's always a long line at the ladies' room and you wouldn't be the first woman to miss the second act. If you do anything to botch up this performance, however, I will deny knowing you."

"Coward," I said.

"That's true," he sighed. "I don't know why you put up with me."

"You always smell nice," I said. "I find that irresistible."

The costume consisted of stripes of black and brown silk that flowed over my arms and hung to midcalf. This open construction allowed the dancer to move freely, but unfortunately the flesh-colored body stocking worn underneath had been made for an anorexic, flat-chested ballerina and there was no time to hunt up another. By the time I was dressed, the first scene had ended and the dancers were taking their places. The lights had been dimmed and everyone was concentrating on the cues. No one said anything when I joined the dancers' ranks.

Whether it's the Paris Opera House or Lucy Bennett's School of Dance, the tension and excitement of opening night is the same. My face was flushed and my heart was thudding against my chest as I hurriedly did a few stretches to warm up my muscles.

The second scene of Act Two is set in the heights of the Harz Mountains on an eerie, desolate crag. There was a blood-red moon and wisps of fog, produced by a dry ice machine in the wings, drifted across the stage. Faust and Mefistofele were singing an opening duet from their position on the crag, and as they finished, the dancers in the wings began to drone "Rampiamo rampiamo che il tempo" and started to move onto the stage. I hastily took up the tune and began the deliberately sensuous movements that signaled the witches' welcome of the sabbath. While

Mefistofele seated himself on his throne, attended by some of the witches, the rest, myself included, danced around, muttering incantations. Unlike the rest of the corps, I did not dance six hours a day, seven days a week, and as the tempo of the dance increased, I found it difficult to chant and dance at the same time. To save my breath, I stopped chanting and concentrated on the steps. I was grateful for the dim lighting and the dry ice machine which camouflaged any mistakes I made.

Mefistofele was handed a glass globe by one of the witches, the orb representing the world being handed to his satanic eminence. He sings the aria "Ecco il mondo" in which he comments on the degraded condition of mankind and the world he inhabits. This catalogue of infamy so delights Mefistofele that with a thundering laugh, he hurls the globe to the ground. This is the signal for the corps to begin a frenzied orgiastic dance, and, caught up in the music and the strange erotic mood, I launched myself about the stage with enthusiastic, if not entirely professional, abandon. My costume fluttered around me, revealing tantalizing flashes of naked breast and thigh, and from the corner of my eye I could see that the immense singer who played Mefistofele was watching my erotic gyrations with a look of naked desire that made my body tingle. I fantasized that I was indeed a witch, performing for the living incarnation of evil on earth. My eyes were on my master, my mind and body totally his. His voice echoed in my ears and his gaze burned my flesh as the scene reached its climax. As I passed in front of his throne, he half rose from his seat and stretched out a hand as if to touch me, but I was caught up in the forward motion of the dance and the moment was lost. With a final cry of "Sabòe har Sabbath," the witches danced offstage as the curtain crashed down to sonorous applause.

Marshall had made his way backstage, and I collapsed into his arms, breathless and giddy with triumph.

"Bravo, my little ballerina," Marshall cried, hugging me tightly. "A marvelous performance! You were the best witch of the group."

"I didn't think I would last," I gasped. "I'm not used to the strain. But it was so exhilarating, I was carried away. I felt great out there . . . Only now I feel like I've been beaten."

"Poor Christina," Marshall murmured sympathetically. "Why don't you go to the dressing room and rest for a while? You can join me after the next act. There's plenty of time. The opening night party doesn't begin until eleven P.M."

"Good idea," I said. "I could use a bit of a rest."

I staggered back to the dressing room on rubbery legs. There was a bottle of scotch on the dressing table and I gratefully poured myself a drink. The liquor burned my throat but my limbs stopped trembling and my breathing slowed. A feeling of languidness stole over me. There was a faded gold brocade chaise longue behind a chipped wooden screen. Putting down my empty glass, I dropped my aching, sweat-filmed body onto its soft surface and closed my eyes. I was beginning to drift off to sleep when I heard the door open softly.

"Well, well," said a deep, booming voice. "What have we here?"

I opened my eyes and found myself staring up at Mefistofele, standing beside the chaise longue with his legs wide apart and his hands on his hips. He was broad-chested and powerfully built, with flashing black eyes and a thick full beard. I could see his cock and balls straining the thin material of his tights, and as his eyes devoured my supine form, my heart began to thud against my chest and my flesh tingled in anticipation of his touch.

"Speak of the devil," I whispered.

"You seem to have forgotten part of your costume," he said, moving the stripes of silk aside and baring my breasts to his hot gaze. "You're not wearing a body stocking."

"I couldn't find one that fit," I murmured as his hands cupped the rich fullness of my breast. "They're made for flat-chested ballerinas."

"You're certainly not that," the Devil agreed, leaning over and taking one of my firm orbs into his mouth. I sighed with pleasure as his lips bruised the tender flesh. The sheer size and power of his hands and body was heightened by the costume and make-up which he still wore. I felt small and vulnerable, helpless before this masterful incarnation of evil. He crushed my breasts together with his hands, licking the crevice between them. Then he began to move downward, his lips and tongue licking and tasting every inch of salt-sweet flesh. My body began to tremble and I thrashed about on the chaise longue as my passion rose to the boiling point. When he descended on my pussy, it was like a jolt of electricity. He knelt at the foot of the chaise longue, pulling me toward him and gripping my buttocks in his huge hands. His beard brushed the sensitive flesh of my inner thighs as his hot tongue probed the lips of my cunt. I hooked my legs over his broad shoulders and wriggled forward, angling my hips upward to provide him a maximum of entry space. My hands were on his head, urging him on, and I literally ground my sopping cunt against his face like a cat in heat. He lifted my buttocks off the couch in his huge hands, flailing his tongue in my steaming slit. His lips closed over my cunt, his tongue tip darting at the swollen knob of my clit. I squirmed and moaned, totally out of control as my fingers scrabbled for a handhold in the thick velvet of his doublet. His tongue drove deeper and deeper into the hidden folds of my rose-sweet cunt until I flowered open, exploding in a shuddering series of orgasms.

I lay on the couch, still dazed from the force of my orgasm. The massive singer sat down next to me and I lazily tickled his ear with my fingertip as he unzipped the rich velvet doublet and eased it over his shoulders. His body was broad, almost unwieldy, and covered with a thick pelt of dark hair. I turned on my side and traced the line of his back as he bent over to pull off his boots. There was nothing hurried or furtive about his movements. He was completely sure of himself, and of me. He stood to remove his tights and my hand strayed to his ass. My finger lightly stroked the crack between his cheeks, and his buttock muscles tightened involuntarily. He was not indifferent to my touch and, wanting to give him pleasure, I slipped off the couch and knelt on the floor in front of him.

He put his hands on my head to steady himself as I began to massage his swelling member. I let my tongue slide over every inch of engorged flesh, from the purple-veined base to the helmetlike head. I licked his balls too, taking first one and then the other into the hot, moist cavity of my mouth. He began to groan loudly, his thighs quivering as I took as much of his huge prick into my mouth as I could, relishing the taste and feel of it. I buried my face in his pubic hair, breathing in the pungent smell of his maleness. My nails raked his naked flesh as he crushed me to him. I relaxed my throat muscles as his thrusting hips drove his cock deeper and deeper into my throat.

When I came up for air his shaft had grown to its full hardness, and as I saw it my stomach muscles tightened and my body flushed with sudden heat. I could have brought him to orgasm in my mouth but I wanted something more. I wanted that huge phallus between my thighs, buried to the hilt in my sopping cunt. As I hesitated, he sensed my need. Urging me back onto the soft, thick carpeting, he spread my thighs and with one swift movement, thrust his steel rod into the well-lubricated passage of my cunt. His cock filled me completely, stretching the tender flesh of my pussy so that for a moment I could hardly move. He moved slowly at first, allowing me to adjust to his size. I wound my arms around his neck, digging my heels into the carpeting and arching my pelvis upward as my body began to respond to his demands. The pain and tiredness in my limbs was wiped out as I clung to him with a fierce hunger born of my own growing desire. I looked into his burning eyes, my lips finding his. I couldn't think or cry out. I could only feel as he pounded his cock into me with such force that I heard a ringing in my ears and the room began to spin. I moved with him, matching his rhythm with a surge of strength I hadn't known I possessed. Our bodies soared toward orgasm, reduced to a single sweating, grinding mass of bestial flesh. I felt him stiffen, then with an animallike cry of pure joy, he let go. I braced myself as the force of his orgasm burst against the flaming walls of my cunt. His cock ground against my clit, splitting me in half as my own orgasm exploded in rippling waves of pleasure.

We lay on the carpeting with our limbs entwined, our senses slowly returning to normal. Mefistofele brushed the damp hair from my face, tracing the outline of my lips with his finger.

A sharp rap on the door intruded on our intimacy. "Let's get a move on," a voice called from outside. "We have an opera to perform here!"

"Coming, coming," the Devil called back. He helped me to my feet, then hastily gathered up the scattered pieces of his costume. He fixed his makeup, racing the clock as the bell rang, signaling the cast to take their places for the third act.

We had not exchanged names but somehow I preferred to keep it that way. My dance with the corps and our subsequent lovemaking had been like a dream. But the sabbath had ended and it was time to return to reality. I reached up and, drawing his head down, kissed him tenderly on the lips.

"Good-bye, my little witch," he said thickly. "I will not forget you." He crushed me to him one last time, then turned and hurried from the room.

There was a small bathroom in the dressing room. I stood in the shower for a long time, letting the hot steamy water relax my tired muscles and wash away the last traces of sweat and grime. I put on my gown, combed my hair and re-applied my makeup. The little witch had been transformed. Christina van Bell was ready to join the Prince and go to the ball.

I returned to my seat just in time to catch the final curtain calls and applauded enthusiastically with the rest.

"Something must have happened," Marshall commented as the crowd began to leave the theater. "The third act was quite late in starting."

I started to smile but instead gave a discreet cough. Marshall gave me a sharp look. "You had something to do with that," he said accusingly. "I might have known. What was going on back there?"

"I made a pact with the Devil," I laughed. "Didn't you notice that his voice was lower in the last act?"

"I only notice that you're the most beautiful woman here tonight," he replied diplomatically. "May I escort you to the gala, Christina?"

"Only if you promise to dance with me," I said, hugging him fondly.

CHAPTER FOUR

I was dreaming that the house was being demolished. Men and women, children and old people had seized on any kind of tool they could find—hammers, fireplace pokers, axes, chisels—and were tearing up the pavement in front of the house, breaking the windows and chipping away at the mortar between the bricks to loosen them. The din was incredible but I refused to respond. I would not open my eyes though the house were pulled down around my ears. There was another noise now, more persistent and annoying than the sharp, confused clamor of metal against stone. I hovered at the fringes of wakefulness, then reluctantly opened one eye. The sky was a clear, bright blue with white puffs of cloud, and a shaft of bright yellow sun streamed through the unshuttered window of my room. In the street below my window, a group of raucous teenagers were singing a discordant, murderously inaccurate French version of "Nineteenth Nervous Breakdown." The appropriateness of the title was not lost on me. I ran a mental check of my physical systems and realized without surprise that I was in very bad shape after my night at the opera. My head was pounding, my eyes burned, my stomach ached, and my limbs felt like lead weights. It was not an auspicious beginning to the day.

The little band of singers moved off down the street, obviously deciding to spread their complete lack of rhythm throughout the neighborhood. I turned over, put a pillow over my head, and attempted to go back to sleep.

I was almost unconscious when the door banged open and Madame Poret paraded in. "Good morning, Miss van Bell," she said cheerfully. She put something down on the table, then opened the window, letting a blast of cold fresh air into the room. "It's such a beautiful afternoon. I was sure that you wouldn't want to stay in bed all day and miss it."

"Who says?" I groaned from under the pillow. "What time is it anyway?"

"Almost two o'clock," she said. "I know you came in late last night . . ."

"It was five A.M.," I interjected, still under the pillow.

". . . but eight hours of sleep is enough for anyone," she continued. "If you don't get up now, you will not be able to sleep tonight."

"If I wanted advice," I muttered into the sheet, "I'd ask for it. You get my drift?"

I don't think my sarcasm translated well in French because the remark sailed over her head like a helium balloon. I screwed my eyes shut but she made no attempt to leave. I heard the click of china and silverware, then the odors of fresh-brewed coffee and warm sweet bread wafted across the room. I began to feel hungry.

"Sit up," Madame Poret instructed, pulling the

pillow off my head. "I've brought you a hot breakfast. It will make you feel better."

I surrendered to the conspiracy of the French to keep me from sleeping and did as I was told. Madame Poret placed a breakfast tray over my legs and set about straightening the room. I poured half a cup of coffee and added hot milk and three teaspoons of sugar. There was fresh fruit salad, a plate of seafood crepes with a white cream sauce, and a piece of walnut coffee cake, still warm and glazed with cinnamon. Madame Poret had been right. The food was delicious and did much to improve both my physical ills and my general outlook on life.

"My compliments to the cook," I said as I poured a second cup of coffee. "I think I'll get dressed and stroll around the city for a while. There is always something new to see in Paris."

"You can go to the site of the old Les Halles market," said Madame Poret. "They have completely rebuilt the area and there are many new shops and galleries, including the De Gaulle Museum. It is a modern art museum with a most unusual design."

"Museums are full of dead things," I grumbled. "I had something a little more energetic in mind. Perhaps I'll walk along the Seine and ogle the Frenchmen."

"It's you who will be ogled," Madame Poret replied. "But I don't think you will mind, eh?"

It was my turn to pretend that I didn't understand the sarcasm. I moved my breakfast tray and slipped out of bed, stretching languorously. I was wearing apple-green silk pajamas but the room was chilly and I looked about for a robe. My eyes fell on the tall package, wrapped in brown paper, still sitting on the table where Madame Poret had left it.

"Shit!" I said.

"Pardon?" said Madame Poret.

"Merde!" I translated, slipping back into French. "I just remembered that I promised to play delivery girl for that package."

"Would you like me to have it sent?"

"Yes . . . No, never mind. I'll take it myself. I had nothing definite planned for the afternoon and this will give me a destination."

"Will you be home for dinner?"

"I don't know but I will probably be late in any case. Why don't you have the cook leave a cold meal in the refrigerator and take the rest of the day off. I promise not to forget my key."

"Thank you, Miss van Bell, I will," she replied, picking up my breakfast tray and opening the door with her foot. "I think I will go to the De Gaulle Museum."

"Have a good time," I said as the door closed behind her.

There is something about Paris that makes me more aware of my clothes. It is a style-conscious city and even the shopgirls dress with a sophistication and élan not seen in London or even New York. I chose my outfit with care, a muted pink and gray tweed cashmere suit with a short jacket and a pencil-thin skirt, slit up the front to midthigh. A soft silk blouse in the same delicate shade of pink as the suit, a gray leather shoulder bag, and a pair of high-heeled shoes to enhance the graceful line of my legs completed the ensemble. I felt confident of my appearance and ready to tackle what was left of the day.

Clutching my brown paper parcel, I walked with a leisurely stride along the sunny streets, enjoying the sights and sounds of northern Paris and the looks of open admiration from passersby. Before I knew it, I had reached Place Pereire, where I had no trouble flagging down a taxi.

The cab, like most of the ones in Paris, was a compact affair with a rakish middle-aged driver. He had a thin black mustache, which I suspected was dyed, and was wearing a garish array of mismatched polyester clothes. Despite the savoir-faire of most Parisians, some things, like cabbie fashion, are universal.

I gave the driver an address on the Left Bank. He flipped on the meter and lurched into traffic without any apparent concern as to whether or not the oncoming cars would yield. Maintaining an average speed of seventy-five miles per hour, he weaved through the heavy traffic on Avenue Niel and headed for the traffic circle around the Arc de Triomphe. He entered this traffic circle at the same breakneck speed, forcing crowds of pedestrians to scamper from his path in panic.

"You're an American, aren't you?" he asked in French, turning fully around to look at me. The fact that his eyes weren't on the road did not seem to suggest to him that, just perhaps, he should reduce his speed.

"Shouldn't you be watching the road?" I asked nervously, ignoring his remark.

"What for?" he demanded. "I know what's in front of me. Too many cars, too many tourists, busloads of snotty Britishers and nuns and teachers from Iowa, horny Parisian couples rubbing their hands up and down each other's asses." He turned forward for a moment and corrected the starboard drift of the cab, bringing it back into its proper traffic lane as it careened around the circle. He seemed indifferent to the fact that he had already gone around twice. "I'm a lifelong resident of this city," he continued, "and I've driven a cab for twenty years. I know what's out there." He jerked his thumb at the windscreen, and

the car swerved dangerously. A group of stolid-look-
ing people cursed at us in German as we missed them
by inches. "But how often do I get to see a beautiful
woman like you, even if you are an American?"

"There's nothing wrong with being an American,"
I said defensively. "And I'd feel better if you'd
watch the road. Call it a silly, mad desire on my part
to live past the next two minutes."

He obediently turned around in his seat. "You are
the kind of woman I have sought my whole life," he
said, wrenching the wheel and turning us into the
Champs-Élysées, never slackening his pace. "How
would you like to come home to meet my mother?"

"It isn't high on my list of priorities," I said.

"She'd love you. Your French is good. She'd probably never guess you're an American. She hates all
Americans. She says that they insulted de Gaulle. She
says that Eisenhower kept de Gaulle from smashing
the Nazi machine during World War II in an attempt
to keep all the glory for the United States."

"That's not the way I heard it," I said.

"She's a bit shell-shocked from the war and she
holds a grudge. You can't really blame her."

"The war has been over for more than thirty years.
That's more than just holding a grudge," I pointed
out.

"We'll have to be careful when you meet," he
said, pulling into Rue de Rivoli. "I'll tell her you're a
Canadian. From Quebec, eh? It will help explain that
terrible North American accent of yours."

"I didn't know I had a North American accent.
I've always been told that my French was perfect," I
said, miffed by his remark.

"It's very good, but I can hear the difference. It
comes with being French. You get to know the
language intimately."

Supercilious bastard, I thought. I decided to put

an end to his game. "Won't your wife object to
your bringing me home?" I asked innocently. He
wrenched around in his seat and eyed me suspiciously.

"How did you know about her?" he demanded.

"You're wearing a ring," I said, pointing to his
left hand.

"She's very sick. Spends all her time in bed," he
said hurriedly.

"I'll bet."

"Also she's out of town a lot. She's a sales-
woman."

"Does your mother like her?"

"She's crazy about her. You'd think she'd stick up
for her only son, but not her. Always takes my wife's
side in a fight. She says I'm not good enough for
her."

"She's probably right," I agreed as the cab pulled
up at the Quai de la Tournelle, situated on the Left
Bank of the Seine and overlooking the great Notre-
Dame Cathedral, just on the other side of Pont au
Double.

The sun was beginning to set as I stepped out of the
cab, the red glow softening the gray stone walls of the
cathedral and lighting the dark waters of the Seine.
The evening air was cool, and a quiet had settled over
the city as work stopped and strolling couples returned home for their evening meals.

The concierge of the small but elegant stone building directed me to apartment 3B, and I took the
creaky, ancient lift to the third floor. According to
the label, the grateful recipient of my package was
an Andrei Denesovitch. Probably a fat old man with
gout, I thought sourly as I stepped out of the lift and
peered at the faded numbers on the doors. I'll just
hand him the package and leave.

My knock was answered promptly by a handsome

man in his midthirties with thick, straight brown hair and deep-set dark brown eyes. He had prominent cheekbones, a wide, straight mouth, and a charming smile. I was instantly attracted to him, and I could tell that the feeling was mutual.

"This is a pleasant surprise," he said in accented French.

"Pleasanter than you thought, Mr. Denesovitch," I said, waving the package. "I've brought you a surprise from America. May I come in?"

"Only a fool would say no, Miss . . ."

"Van Bell. Christina van Bell."

". . . Miss van Bell." He relieved me of the package and stepped aside to let me enter the apartment.

The living room was spare and clean, the furniture functional, modern, and expensive. There were some framed posters of French gallery exhibits on the walls and a small ornamental onyx clock on a mirrored glass coffee table in front of the couch. We sat down and I quickly explained to Andrei, as he insisted on being called, how I had met Nicholas at a party in New York and had agreed to bring the bottle of wine with me to Paris, leaving out the more intimate details of our evening together.

"So, you are just a Good Samaritan," said Andrei, unwrapping the package and placing the bottle of wine on the table in front of us. "That's good, very good," he repeated. He seemed inordinately pleased about this point.

"I had some of that wine in Nicholas' apartment," I said. "It was exceptionally good."

"You must share some with me now," he insisted. "It is made by a man from our village. Did Nicholas tell you we were childhood friends?"

"No, only that you knew each other. But then, we just met the other night."

Andrei nodded thoughtfully, then uncorking the

bottle he poured out two glasses of the wine and offered me a toast. "To old friends and new," he said, his eyes burning into mine. My hand trembled slightly, and I took a hasty gulp of my drink.

Andrei sipped his slowly, closing his eyes and savoring the wine on his tongue. "A fine wine, like a fine woman, must be approached in the right way," Andrei said softly, moving closer to me on the couch so that his shoulder brushed my arm and his knee pressed against my thigh. "They must both be taken slowly to be fully enjoyed."

"I believe that you can't tell a really fine wine without drinking it first," I said. "Sometimes a fancy bottle can hold a very inferior product." I put down my glass and leaned back against the cushions of the couch. Slowly and carefully, I raised my skirt over my knees to reveal the shapely curve of my thighs. He took the hint and slipped to the floor in front of me, running his hand along either leg and then picking up each foot and taking off my shoes. He slipped his hands beneath my skirt to slip off my garters, letting his fingers brush against my pussy through the thin material of my bikini briefs. He began to remove my stockings with the same lavish care, his lips and tongue caressing the smooth naked flesh of my thighs as they were uncovered inch by inch. My body began to grow warm and a tingling sensation spread outward from the center of my sex. I began to breathe more heavily and my pussy juices started to flow as his hands moved to the waistband of my silken briefs. I barely felt him take them off. I spread my legs as he bunched my skirt up around my waist and I felt the cool, buttery leather of the couch against my naked behind.

"You have a beautiful cunt," he murmured, running his fingers lightly along the outer curve of the lips. "It is like a precious chalice and the juices of your pussy are like the nectar of the gods." He gently separated the lips of my vagina with his fingers. I felt a rush of cool air that made me gasp, then his tongue tentatively licked the sensitive tissue within. I wriggled in pleasure and my stomach muscles tightened. I hooked my legs around his neck, letting my knees fall open. I closed my eyes and thrust my hips upward to provide the maximum of entry space for his probing tongue.

Suddenly I felt the remnants of the wine being poured into my upturned cunt. The sensation was not unpleasant and was followed immediately by Andrei's thirsty tongue probing the depths of my cunt. He gripped my buttocks, almost splitting me in half as his tongue drove deeper and deeper into my lush pink well, lapping up the wine-drenched juices of my pussy. My upper body thrashed about, and I clawed at the cushions of the couch as Andrei's gifted tongue raised me to fevered heights of pleasure. I climaxed explosively, my body trembling from my exertions as Andrei gently lowered my buttocks to the couch and eased my legs off his shoulders.

"I thought only the French were that good with their tongues," I gasped as Andrei gently pushed the damp hair from my forehead and helped me sit up.

"I have been in Paris several years," he smiled, "and have learned some of the customs of my adopted country."

"What else did you learn?" I asked, snuggling next to him and beginning to open the buttons on his shirt.

He did not answer. Slipping his arms beneath me, he crushed me against him, his lips closing over mine in a kiss that took my breath away. Standing up, he carried me into the bedroom, kicking the door shut behind us with his foot. He set me on my feet. His hot, restless eyes bored into mine, promising and commanding at the same time. I slipped off my jacket and skirt and unbuttoned my blouse. I unhooked my cream lace bra, cupping my breasts in my hands and offering them boldly to him as I stood naked before him. I heard the sharp intake of his breath, and his eyes clouded with desire as he gazed at my voluptuous body from my creamy white shoulders to my trembling thighs. He undid his belt and stepped out of his pants, his eyes never leaving me as he undressed. He was not overly tall and had a broad, heavy-set body. He came toward me and crushed me against his chest, his lips fiercely demanding. I ran my hands along the bulging muscles of his upper arms and back, and my body thrilled to the feel of his hard, hot cock pressing against my thigh. His hands moved down my back, cupping the twin cheeks of my ass, and I pressed myself against him, grinding my cunt against his groin. Our elaborate session of foreplay had left me particularly horny, and I was wet and open, aching for the feel of his cock between my thighs.

He turned me around and had me bend over the bed, then he placed a cushion under my hips so that my ass was higher than my head. He massaged my breasts and then ran one hand down along my belly while the other descended my back to the taut skin of my buttocks. He inserted a finger into the puckered hole of my anus so that I cried out and my body jerked spasmodically. He moved between my spread legs, forcing them farther apart, then plunged abruptly into my sopping pussy, skewering me against the pillow. I tightened my vaginal muscles around his cock as he moved with a steady rhythm. His hands continued to stroke my body as his cock cored my cunt from this rear-entry position and little tongues of fire lapped at my flesh. I love getting it this way, like a cat in heat, all sweaty and hot and begging for it. I tossed my head wildly, arching my body and pushing my hips back to meet his thrusts. My fingers plucked helplessly at the covers of the bed as he kept fucking me. Then suddenly, with a final yell, he emptied his load into me, triggering a volcanic series of orgasms. As his love milk poured into my spasming cunt, I squeezed the diminishing length of his cock to extract the last precious drops, then crawled exhausted into the bed and wrapped myself in the covers.

By the time I recovered my equilibrium, Andrei had showered and dressed. I trailed off to the bathroom to do the same, and I was standing naked before the bathroom mirror, combing my hair, when I heard a loud pounding coming from the direction of the front door. I hastily wrapped a towel around myself and peered into the bedroom. Andrei was standing near the bed as if frozen.

"Are you expecting someone?" I asked. He shook his head but a worried frown creased his face. The pounding commenced again.

"Andrei Denesovitch, this is the police," called a deep voice from the other side of the door. "We know you're in there! Open the door!"

"Cochon!" Andrei muttered under his breath. He began to scramble around the room, gathering piles of papers and stuffing them beneath the mattress of the bed. Fear is catching, and though I hadn't done anything wrong, I began to suspect that I might have difficulty explaining this to the police. Dropping my towel, I quickly gathered up my clothes and began pulling on my stockings with trembling hands.

"What do they want?" I asked, watching him tidy up the bed. He bit his lip, then snatched up a bag of white powder and flushed it down the toilet.

"It could be anything," he said. "I am active in many political causes. Save the whales, world peace . . ."

"I don't think the police are interested in whales," I said as the pounding began again, "but if it's all the same to you, I'd rather not hang around to find out." There was a rush of footsteps in the hall, followed by a loud thud as something smashed against the door.

"You're right," said Andrei. "We'll use the fire escape in the other room."

We hurried to the living room. Signs of our recent activities were still evident—the pillows of the couch scattered on the floor and the empty wine bottle and glasses on the table. With a loud cry, Andrei seized the bottle and stood looking around the room.

"I don't think we have time for a drink," I began, but I didn't get a chance to finish my thought. With a splintering sound, the lock on the door gave way and the body of a uniformed policeman stumbled headlong through the shattered portal. He was quickly followed by four more policemen, all holding large, lethal-looking guns.

"Hold it right there!" the first policeman said as Andrei, still holding the bottle, began to back toward the window. Andrei hesitated, then suddenly turned, but the policeman quickly tackled him, throwing him to the floor and pressing a gun against his head. He cocked the hammer and calmly removed the bottle from Andrei's grasp.

One of the other policemen grabbed my arm and began to push me toward the door.

"Let me go, you big ox," I said in French. "I'm an American citizen!"

"You're under arrest, Miss America," he said imperturbably, neatly sidestepping the vicious kick I aimed at his shins.

Two of the policemen hauled Andrei to his feet and, handcuffing him securely, dragged him from the room. The rest of us followed, using the stairs rather than the lift. We stepped outside the building, and, followed by the curious stares of the neighbors, we were forced into a waiting police van. The door slammed shut, and with sirens wailing, we drove off down the street.

CHAPTER FIVE

Inspector Claude Flambeau had a back that was almost as broad as the window in his office at the Palais de Justice. It was turned toward me now, and the Inspector, puffing on his pipe, hands clasped behind his back, stood regarding the blurred lights of passing cars on the Quai Mégisserie below. He was totally ignoring me and I was not used to being ignored.

"You fucking cossack!" I shouted in French. "You have a lot of nerve, dragging me down here and detaining me illegally. I'm an American citizen. I demand to call my attorney. I demand bail and habeas corpus and mal dicket mal docket. I demand to see the American Ambassador!"

The massive shoulders of the middle-aged inspector shrugged expressively, and he turned slowly to look at me through heavy-lidded eyes. The blue smoke from his pipe drifted through his thick black mustache, obscuring his features in the dim light of the room.

"I suspect he is having his dinner at this hour, Miss van Bell," he said calmly, tapping his pipe against the heel of his hand. "You should be having yours as well, and so should I, but we have business to finish here first.''

"What have you done to Andrei?" I continued. "I haven't seen him since you pulled me in here."

"He is being questioned, Miss van Bell. I assure you that we already have ample evidence to hold him, and you too, for that matter, unless you come to your senses and answer some questions."

"What will you do if I refuse? Use a rubber hose? Give me the third degree? I warn you, if you don't let me go this instant, I'll have your job!"

The Inspector walked slowly to his desk and lowered his bulk heavily into his chair. He turned to look at a handsome young man who had been sitting silently in a corner of the room, his chair tilted at a dangerous angle against the wall and his feet braced against the radiator. He was chain-smoking and a small tin ashtray on the floor was overflowing with butts. Stubbing out his cigarette, the young man got to his feet and came toward me.

He was just below six feet in height with platinum blond hair and clear blue eyes. His skin was very fair with no hint of a tan, and his features were almost classic in their handsomeness. He wore a pair of gray slacks, a light blue shirt with the sleeves rolled up, and a navy tie.

"Miss van Bell, you don't seem to understand what's going on here," he said, flashing me a warm smile. He spoke carefully, as if searching for the right words. French was not his native language.

"Well, you've all been a generous font of information, haven't you?" I snapped. "So far you've done nothing but bully and threaten me, an American citizen I might remind you, and a helpless woman to boot."

The young man grinned broadly. "An American citizen maybe, but helpless, never. I've never seen a less helpless woman in my life. Or a more beautiful one," he added, giving me a look that made my breath catch in my throat.

"You're an American!" I said accusingly, suddenly recognizing the accent. "What are you doing eavesdropping in a French police station?"

"I wasn't eavesdropping," he said, switching to English. "I'm here at Inspector Flambeau's express invitation. On official business." He reached into the pocket of his trousers and pulled out a small black leather case. Flipping it open he showed me an identification card stating that Mr. David Patrick Sean Connelly was an agent of the Central Intelligence Agency.

"How'd a good-looking guy like you end up a Fed?" I said sarcastically. "Why aren't you modeling designer underwear?"

"I have scars on my knees from playing football in college," he said, shrugging.

"Football, huh? West Point?"

"Notre Dame."

"I bet you were in the Army too."

"Green Berets." He smiled.

"I might have known," I said, sinking into a chair.

Mr. Connelly took this as a sign of acquiescence. "Now then, Miss van Bell," he said, sitting on the edge of the Inspector's large desk and lighting another cigarette, "let me explain the situation. We're in France and not the United States, and we have to play by French rules. They don't have to give you a lawyer or anything else, and they can hold you here until you cooperate. So what about it? Just answer a few questions, and if you have nothing to hide and this is all just an innocent mistake, as you have claimed, you'll be out of here in no time and Inspector Flambeau can get home to his dinner."

I looked at Inspector Flambeau, puffing imperturbably at his pipe, his hands laced across his portly middle like a Buddha in a baggy tweed suit.

"Mr. Connelly tells me that if I answer your questions, you will let me go," I said, switching back to French. "And I am keeping you from your dinner."

"That is true, mademoiselle. And a very good dinner it is too."

"I don't like this," I said, "but obviously I've no choice. I'm asking for *Gideon's Trumpet* and you're giving me *Les Miserables*. Ask your questions, Inspector. It seems I must cooperate or sit here and rot."

Inspector Flambeau asked me to tell him how I came to be in the apartment of Andrei Denesovitch, and I told him the whole chronology in a simple, straightforward manner. I explained how I had met Nicholas Zelanko and under what circumstances, leaving out the more intimate details of our evening together. I explained how, when I had mentioned that I was coming to Paris, Nicholas had asked me to deliver the wine bottle to Andrei.

The Inspector sat with his eyes half closed and his head sunk on his chest. He did not seem to be paying much attention, but I noticed that Mr. Connelly was listening intently and taking notes in a small notebook.

"Then your meeting with Mr. Zelanko was entirely by chance?" the Inspector asked when I had finished.

"Completely," I assured him. "He seemed like a nice fellow, and he was so anxious for his countryman to have that damned bottle of wine. I didn't see any reason to refuse his request."

The Inspector grunted and looked over at Mr. Connelly. He nodded his head, and the two men rose and excused themselves for a few moments. They retired to a corner of the room, and though I couldn't hear what they were saying, I could see that the American agent was doing most of the talking. When they had completed their discussion, Inspector Flambeau came over to me and held out his hand.

"Miss van Bell, thank you for your assistance," he said simply. "I do not think we will have further need of you in this matter." He placed his pipe lovingly in the ashtray on his desk, buttoned his jacket, and took a hat and scarf from a coatrack near the window. "Now, if you will both excuse me, Madame Flambeau has a roast in the oven and I've had a long day. Good night." He slipped out the door, leaving me alone with David Connelly.

"Now, was that so difficult?" he asked, rolling down his shirt-sleeves and buttoning the cuffs. "Just a few simple questions and you can go home and forget that you ever saw this place."

"Is that all this was to you? A few simple questions? These proceedings were totally out of order. What if I had had the wrong answers instead of the right ones? I could have ended up in a cell with an iron cot and a hole in the floor."

"You've seen too many movies," David grinned.

"The moment I get back to my house," I continued, "I'm going to call the American Ambassador. He'll protest to the head of your department."

"Who will deny knowing me," David sighed. "Listen, Christina, it's getting late. I'm out of cigarettes and neither of us has eaten. Why don't you let me take you to dinner?"

"Dinner? With you?"

"I don't see anyone else here," he said, looking around. "Come on. Consider it an apology for the rough treatment you received. I'll even let you in on a few government secrets. You must be curious as to what's been going on here."

I considered his proposal. To agree would be tantamount to accepting his apology. I could hardly go out to dinner with the man and then file a formal complaint against him the next day. On the other hand, I had never met a real spy before, and I was curious as to what was behind the afternoon's events. I was also hungry.

"Okay, James Bond, let's have some chow," I agreed suddenly.

"Terrific," he said enthusiastically. "I know just the place too." He slipped on a Harris Tweed sports jacket, and we took the lift downstairs. I was expecting some type of government car and, sure enough, David led me to a blue Peugeot 404 sedan that was indistinguishable from the dozen or so other cars in the lot. Driving into Saint-Germain, we went to Rue Jacob, a narrow, twisting street near the medical school, where he led me to a small restaurant called Le Petit Escargot.

The regulars at the bar all seemed to know David and greeted him heartily. David smiled and responded in his careful French, but the Parisians, usually contemptuous of anyone who misused their language, did not seem to mind in his case. I noticed that they called him "Monsieur Crockett."

"Who do these people think you are?" I whispered as David handed me a glass of wine.

"An American reporter for a paper in Iowa," he shrugged. "I don't think any of them knows where Iowa is, but that just makes it seem all the more important to them."

"Do you eat here often?"

"As often as I can. It's comfortable, the food is good, and the owner speaks some English, so I don't have to struggle with a fancy menu and an arrogant waiter."

We were approached by a tall thin man with curly black hair and a neatly trimmed goatee. He gave us a broad, friendly smile and clapped David on the back.

"Monsieur Crockett, how good to see you again," he said. "It has been too long a time. And you are in luck because I have your favorite meal on the menu this evening."

"Christina van Bell, Maurice Christin," David said, introducing us. "Maurice is the owner of this esteemed establishment."

"David tells me you have some of the best food on the Left Bank," I said to Maurice.

"We do," Maurice said, beaming. "But he would not know it. He is uncultured. An oaf. A nitwit." He said this last word in English, glaring at David. "That he cannot conjugate beyond the grade school level I can forgive, but his eating habits are an insult to French culinary art."

"Come now," David said. "My taste isn't as bad as all that."

"You're right," said Maurice, giving me an approving look. "You have brought this incomparable beauty into my humble restaurant. Come, I will give you a table in the private dining room upstairs."

As Maurice escorted us to the stairs, all of the regulars seated at the bar got up and hurried behind a small curtained doorway just behind us.

"Is that a mass exodus to the toilet?" I asked.

"Uh . . . not exactly," David stammered, flushing slightly. "It's something of a tradition in this place. They go under the stairs and look up your skirt as you walk upstairs. I hope you're wearing clean underwear."

"I'm not wearing underwear," I said as we mounted the stairs. "In my hurry to get dressed when the police were breaking down Andrei's door, I forgot to put my panties on." I didn't give a hoot in hell if the local barflies looked up my dress, but I enjoyed the look of consternation on David's face. Christina one, flatfoot nothing, I thought happily as Maurice led us to a side table and handed me a menu.

"Aren't you getting a menu too?" I asked David.

"No, Maurice knows what I'm having."

"It is always the same thing," Maurice sighed. "I have tried to broaden his tastes but without success."

"And what is this fabled meal that you always order?" I asked David.

"Boeuf sans Oeuf," David replied. "That's a hamburger without the fried egg. For some inexplicable reason, the French have a tradition of putting a fried egg on top of their hamburgers. Also pommes frites. That's french fries, though for some reason they don't have catsup. I asked for it once and Maurice banned me from the place for a week."

"How can you come to the cuisine capital of the world and order cattleburgers and fries?" I said. "I don't blame Maurice for wanting to kick you out."

"Bravo mademoiselle," said Maurice approvingly. "And what will you have this evening?"

I looked over the menu. "I'll have the special of the day," I said, "and a bottle of your best Bordeaux."

"Langue de Boeuf Braisée au Madère," Maurice smiled. "You are perfection, mademoiselle. It is a pleasure to have you eat in my establishment. Perhaps you will have a positive influence on this barbarian." He bowed very low and backed away.

David glared across the table at me, and I flashed him my most innocent smile.

"Aren't you the waiter's pet," he snapped. "What did you order that made such a big impression on him?"

"Tongue braised in Madeira sauce."

"Tongue?"

"Beef tongue, you idiot. From a cow."

David turned a little pale. "That's revolting," he said. "I could never eat anything that came out of a cow's mouth."

"You eat eggs, and they come from a worse place than a cow's mouth," I pointed out.

"Never mind! I was raised in Texas and I know what part of a cow's edible and what's not."

At this point Maurice returned with our food.

David served the wine and I noticed that, though he wasn't a partisan of French cooking, he didn't object to a glass of fine wine. Several glasses, in fact. The tongue was delicious, served over a bed of noodles and surrounded with braised carrots and onions. There was hot French bread and a tossed green salad with an excellent vinaigrette dressing.

"When do I hear the state secrets?" I asked between mouthfuls.

"When you're too drunk to remember them," David teased. "This wine is perfect. Have a glass."

"I've had three already."

"Four, but who's counting. Don't worry. I'll carry you home if necessary."

"I think I'd like that," I murmured, giving him a wicked look.

He looked at me thoughtfully for a moment, then settled back in his chair and lit a cigarette. "Have you ever heard of Dr. Zlave Krupp?" he asked. I shook my head. "Dr. Krupp works for one of our friends in the Eastern bloc," he continued. "He's not too well known, even to the world scientific community, because the communists keep him under a tight security wrap. He's one of their best scientists, a genius in his particular field."

"And what's his field?" I asked. I was beginning to wonder what all this had to do with wine bottles.

"Biological warfare. I can't be too specific, but suffice it to say that Dr. Krupp developed a formula that, if implemented, could be dangerous to our national security."

"He developed some sort of weapon, is that it?"

"It was just at the theoretical stage when we learned of it. No working model had been constructed. One of our agents working under cover in the area managed to appropriate the formula. It was a brilliant piece of work."

"Three cheers for our side!" I teased, dividing the

last of the wine between us.

"It's the name of the game in my line of work," he grinned. "First our agent broke the formula down into six components and placed each component on a microdot. Then his problem was how to get the microdots to our agents in Western Europe without arousing suspicion. So he took the six microdots and stuck them onto the labels of six bottles of wine that had been earmarked for shipment to France. By putting the dots on the same place on each label, they could easily be retrieved by someone who knew where to look for them."

"Did those bottles have any connection to the one I delivered to Andrei?" I asked.

"They did," said David, "but let me explain that point when I get to it. Everything went okay until the bottles got to the airport. Then some stupid, larcenous, son-of-a-bitch airport employee decided to help himself to the wine. The six bottles were in a crate of twenty-four, the only twenty-four bottles with that label. They were the product of a private vintner who only produced the wine for friends. We didn't realize that the bottles had been stolen until they failed to show up here a week later, and by that time the airport employee had sold off the wine. Lots of collectors of rare wine would like to get their hands on one of only twenty-four bottles of an excellent privately produced wine, and the bottles were easily fenced to dealers via the black market."

"So the formula is lost."

"Not yet. I'll admit that retrieving it seems a Herculean task, but we've handled tougher jobs than this. We've assigned all our available staff to searching out the whereabouts of those bottles, and we've managed to get a line on some of them."

"How can you tell which bottles have the microdots?"

"Those that do look like there is a printing imperfection on the label, a small smudge near one of the letters of the name. Unfortunately, we don't know in advance whether a bottle will have a micro-dot or not. We have to follow up every lead and this wastes a great deal of valuable time."

"It seems to me that if you're just persistent you should eventually be able to reassemble the formula," I said. "Why the hurry?"

"Unfortunately, the communists have found out about our security gaffe," David said ruefully. "They have their own agents tracking down the same bottles. It's become an international free-for-all, and I'm afraid that in the process someone might get hurt."

"I thought risking your life was part of playing macho spy," I said.

"I didn't mean our agents," David laughed, "or the commies either, for that matter. Most of the bottles we've located so far have been in the hands of private citizens. We can't just barge into their houses and demand to see their wine bottles. Many aren't even American citizens. We have to find some way to check out the wine bottles without the owners know-ing it and without tipping off the communists, who are much more heavy-handed in their methods. In one case, they burglarized the home of a bottle owner and knocked over a lamp during their escape, causing a three-alarm fire in which the owner was burned to death. The bottle was one of the blanks."

"How many bottles have you accounted for so far?" I asked.

"Six. But only the bottle that you delivered to An-drei had a microdot. We were lucky; the communists almost had that one."

"That leaves eighteen bottles and five microdots to go," I said. "I certainly don't envy you your task."

"It's all in a day's work," David replied. His tone was light, but his eyes looked troubled. He was not as nonchalant as he was trying to appear. He stubbed out his cigarette and smiled across at me. "That's enough about secret weapons and national security," he said. "How about some dessert?"

"Have you found a place that serves American apple pie and ice cream?" I teased.

"The French don't make anything that can in all honesty be called apple pie," he sighed. "They make something called an apple tart, but it's full of brandy and covered with warm apricot jam and soft whipped cream."

"Sounds great," I said. "Let's go!"

We left the restaurant, accompanied by the hearty farewells of Monsieur Christin and the regulars at the bar and turned left onto Rue Jacob. We made our way down to the quais, where we found several small cafés which specialized in French pastries and café au lait. We ate and talked and I found myself increasingly attracted to this intelligent, good-looking man with his old-fashioned courtesy and shy sense of humor. If he was any good in bed, he would be irresistible.

"Would you like a nightcap?" I asked as we prepared to leave.

"I don't usually drink those sickeningly sweet brandies," he replied. He patted his pockets with a look of concern. "But I could use a cigarette and I'm out."

"We'll get some on the way," I suggested.

"Where are we going?"

"To my place," I replied. "If you're nice to me, I may let you cop a cheap feel in the car."

"There's nothing cheap about you," David said, smiling, as he helped me to my feet. The touch of his hands sent little tremors along my spine.

It was late when we arrived at Adaline's house and I let us in. I had explained to David that the house belonged to a friend, and I could see that he was giving the place more than a cursory look as I scrawled a note for Madame Poret and left it in her box in the kitchen. Though he made an effort to appear indifferent to what went on around him, I had learned that this was just a pretense. David was a man with a keen eye, a good memory, and a strong set of principles. He was not a man who would be easily deceived, and I knew that though I hadn't actually stated my desire, he had a good idea why I had invited him home.

Adaline's bedroom was a large, comfortable room. It was decorated in her usual eclectic style with everything from Chinese Chippendale to French Bombay, but all in varying shades of pink. There were pink velvet drapes on the windows and a pink flowered Chinese rug on the floor. There were two pink-brocade Victorian love seats and a pink-glass Art Deco coffee table grouped in front of the gas fireplace, which was the room's only source of heat. David lit the fire and settled onto one of the couches with a scotch on the rocks and a cigarette, while I went to the bathroom to freshen up.

I took a long hot shower and slipped into a floor-length white satin robe, embroidered down the front and along the hemline and sleeves with a border of flowers and birds, all hand-stitched in gold thread. It was a replica of the one made for the Duc de Lorraine's mistress in the twelfth century. Adaline had bought it from the old Frenchwoman who had made it and gave it to me on my last birthday. Now looking at my image in the mirror, I knew that I had never looked lovelier. My fair hair spilling over my shoulders had been turned to pale gold by the whiteness of the satin, and my eyes shone like green fire against the delicate ivory of my skin. As I entered the bedroom, I heard the sharp intake of David's breath. I could feel his eyes watching me as I slowly walked to the small rolling bar near the window and poured myself a brandy. I turned and met his gaze squarely, and his fair skin flushed so that I seemed to feel the heat of him even across the room. No starving man had ever looked with such longing at a crust of bread, but I remained motionless, sipping my drink. If David wanted me, he would have to make the first move.

He came toward me and lightly stroked my hair. He picked up some of my hair so that it caught the light, then let it fall through his fingers in a shower of gold. He brushed some strands from my face, then kissed my temple and my eyelids and the tip of my nose. I sighed softly and lifted my face to his. My lips were slightly parted, and as my eyes met the fierce, hungry look in his, I felt my knees grow weak with desire. He kissed me, gently at first, then with growing passion. His lips promised, then redeemed that promise, his tongue snaking around mine. He lifted me effortlessly in his arms and carried me to the bed, laying me down as if I were made of glass. Slowly he unfastened my robe. His hand went to my breasts and he caressed the soft, white mounds. He took first one, then the other into his mouth, teasing the nipples to erect points of pleasure. I was breathing more heavily now, my body warm and tingling with excitement. He shifted his attentions to my stomach, his lips and tongue sending waves of electric current to the center of my sex.

Deliberately ignoring the aching triangle between my thighs, he touched and explored every curve and crevice of my body as if committing it to memory. He was an expert in the art of foreplay, his tongue and lips and hands creating sensations I had not thought possible. I groaned loudly and spread my legs. He was stretched out between my thighs, and I separated my pussy lips with my fingers so that the hard pink knob of my clit was clearly visible. He took the hint and gently ran first his finger, then his tongue along the inner edge of each lip. A spasm of pure pleasure shot through me at his touch and my stomach muscles tightened convulsively. He continued to tease my pussy with his tongue, moving deeper and deeper inside my steaming slit. He gripped my buttocks, pulling me toward him, his tongue making little stabbing motions at my clit as I bent my knees and spread my legs even wider apart. My entire body was on fire. I tossed my head and thrashed about, almost out of control as his tongue continued its unrelenting assault on my exposed sex.

I felt my body race toward orgasm and I struggled to hold back, to prolong the sensations as long as possible. His entire face was buried in my sopping cunt and he suddenly reached beneath me and pushed his forefinger into my anus. That pushed me over the edge and with a final cry I let myself go. I closed my eyes and tightened my sphincter muscles around his finger as my orgasm rippled through me.

When I opened my eyes he was stretched out beside me. There were no lights in the room but through the open window I could see a canopy of stars above the dark shapes of the houses. Their cold brilliance silvered David's hair, and his eyes were like clear blue water. As I stretched and sighed, he smiled down at me and my heart turned over as I looked at him.

"My God, Christina," he said at last, "you take a man's breath away. I feel like a young boy—all blushes and trembling hands."

"You don't make love like one," I teased.

"You're like a queen, all gold and white."

"It's the robe," I said thoughtfully. "And it's you. You make me feel like someone special."

"You *are* special. You're beautiful . . . intelligent . . . articulate . . . sensitive . . ." He punctuated these compliments with kisses, and I threw my arms around his neck and returned them with equal fervor.

He was still fully dressed and impatiently I reached

up, tugging at his tie and fumbling with the buttons on his shirt. He smiled and grabbed my hands. He kissed each one, then rolled away from me and got off the bed. He began to undress in a more leisurely manner, placing his clothes in a neat pile on a chair that stood near the bed. I enjoy seeing a man undress and I now lay watching him with half-closed eyes. His body was silhouetted in the semidarkness, but I could see that he had broad shoulders, a trim waist, and well-defined calves and thighs. A feeling of pleasurable anticipation stole over me. I slipped out of my satin robe and flung it aside, then moved over on the bed to make room for him.

He lay down next to me, pulling the blankets over our nakedness. I smiled at his modesty, but when one of the senses is blocked, it brings the others into sharper focus. Though I couldn't see him, I was acutely aware of the feel of David's body against my own, the scent of his cologne and the sound of his breathing as he leaned over me. He kissed me long and deeply and I could taste my sex on his lips. He ran his tongue over my lips, then kissed me again, moving over on top of me. The hardness of his chest crushed my breasts and I could feel his cock lengthening against my leg. I clasped my arms tightly around his neck and pulled him to me, sucking his tongue into my mouth. I could feel every muscle in his body tightening in response and the beating of his heart against my chest. I ground my hips against the steely stiffness of his cock. Our tongues were like an electric arc, sending lightning charges through our bodies as they touched. We were both so hot and horny we could have climaxed right then, but David pulled his mouth from mine. He loosened the grip of my hands from around his neck, indicating he wished to slow the pace of our lovemaking.

He began to shower kisses on my face, on my fore-head and cheeks and eyes and lips, like a hot, moist rain, until my face glowed with pleasure and my breath came in short sobbing gasps. He kissed his way along my neck and over my shoulders and chest. His tongue lapped at my breasts and my stomach like a flame. My skin began to burn and hot waves of excitement washed over me. He kissed and caressed my body until every inch of flesh was begging for his lips and tongue. I was crying and whimpering, begging for release as my senses soared to new erotic heights.

Throwing off the blanket, he shifted his position so that he was crouched over my body, his hands gently stroking my inner thighs and his face buried in the lush golden forest of my pubic hair. I spread my legs, arching my hips to meet his mouth. I felt his fingers on my pussy lips, pulling them apart, then a rush of cool air against the inside of my cunt. His tongue rasped along the sensitive inner edge of each lip. I cried out, clenching my buttock muscles and thrusting my hips higher as his tongue reached deeper inside. He leaned closer until his entire mouth was around my cunt, his tongue licking the sticky-sweet juice. His cock and balls were tantalizingly close to my face, his penis swollen with excitement. I stretched out my tongue and licked a milky drop of pre-cum from the tip, then, overcome with desire, I took him hungrily into my mouth. I felt him stiffen for just an instant, then he moved back against me, his prick sliding deeper into my throat. I felt it grow in my mouth as I tongued the smooth, hard shaft. My hands played with the soft, downy skin of his balls, lightly stroking the line between his ass cheeks, tickling the puckered hole of his anus. I bent my knees and curled my pelvis upward as he licked his way down to my anus. I shivered with pleasure and, separating his ass cheeks, I thrust my tongue into the tiny orifice between. The rhythm of our lovemaking was a perfect blend of giving and receiving as we lapped at each other's genitals. We trembled and moaned, touching, tasting, and inhaling the fragrance of each other's sex. I wanted to come and I wanted to hold back, to prolong the special feelings between us. Reaching between his legs, I held his long hard cock in my warm hand, and suddenly the desire for this symbol of his manhood overwhelmed me. I pushed him off my body and wriggled around under him.

"Now—take me now!" I begged.

He hesitated for just a second, and I pulled him down on top of me, his chest crushing my breasts and my mouth fused to his.

"Oh God . . . yes!" I cried as I felt his steellike shaft push between the lips of my pussy, deeper and deeper until he was buried to the hilt inside of me and I could feel his balls brush against my ass. He began to move slowly, pulling his cock out almost to the tip, then plunging into me again with a swift, sure movement. I shuddered and climaxed but he did not stay his thrusts. He continued to fuck me till I screamed and writhed, grinding myself against him and squeezing his cock with the inner muscles of my cunt. I climaxed again, then again, and still I wanted more. I wanted it to go on forever, the feeling of his cock pounding into me, his body moving against my own.

Suddenly he stiffened, his cock buried deep inside me. He gave a harsh cry and his orgasm shattered against the walls of my cunt. I wrapped my legs around his hips, my hands clawing at his back as his cum spurted into me, and I came again myself with a flood of passion that was frightening in its intensity.

Totally spent, I nestled against him as he stroked my trembling limbs and pulled the covers over us both. He bent over and kissed me gently on the cheek, then rocked me in his arms, humming softly as I drifted off to sleep.

CHAPTER SIX

Contrary to popular belief, getting up at the crack of dawn, eating bran and granola, popping vitamins, and jogging around the neighborhood in sweat pants and Adidas sneakers do not promote good health. These activities promote the excessive use of liniment for sore muscles and elastic bandages for torn ligaments, and encourage boring, pedantic conversation at the breakfast table. I remembered falling asleep in David's arms and was now perturbed to see that although it was only twelve-thirty P.M., his side of the bed was empty. He had probably decided to exercise vertically instead of horizontally, which was not my idea of the proper way to spend a Saturday morning, but one's upbringing always shows.

I got out of bed and walked to the window. I looked out over the rain-washed streets, watching the antics of the pedestrians as they tried to avoid the puddles of water and struggled to keep their umbrellas from blowing inside out. It generally rains two hundred and fifty days of the year in the City of Lights, and though I had enjoyed the unseasonably pleasant weather during the past few days, it was comforting to have things back to normal.

I heard footsteps in the hallway. Thinking it might be David come to his senses and returning to bed, I opened the door, but it was only Madame Poret.

"Good morning, Miss van Bell," she said.

"Good morning," I mumbled, my first attempt at making my voice work a partial failure. "Did Mr. Connelly go downstairs?"

"He came downstairs about an hour ago," she replied. "He seemed very agitated and was swearing in English under his breath. He spent about twenty minutes going through every drawer in the house."

"Did you ask him what he was doing?"

"I tried, but his French is deplorable. I could not make out what he wanted."

"Where is he now?"

The housekeeper shrugged expressively. "He went out, mademoiselle."

"Never mind," I said. "If he comes back before I make it downstairs, have the cook make him some breakfast. I'll eat after I've showered."

I returned to the bedroom and decided to take a quick shower in the small pink Art Deco bathroom rather than a more leisurely bath upstairs. David's behavior troubled me. Though there could be any number of rational explanations for what he had done, the fact that he was a CIA agent made me suspicious. The memory of my detention at the Palais de Justice the previous evening was still fresh in my mind, and I hadn't forgotten David's part in that ordeal. Perhaps he still suspected me of being involved in the plot to steal the microdots and was searching the house for evidence. His ardor last night had seemed genuine enough, but perhaps my fabulous body was not the only reason for his taking me home. These and other similar questions kept running through my mind, and by the time I had stepped out of the shower, I had worked myself into a state of indignation.

I slipped into a peach satin-and-lace teddy and wrapped myself in a long-sleeved, floor-length peach velour robe. I dislike slippers and never wear them. I put up with shoes as a necessary accoutrement of civilized attire, but I refuse to allow society's dress codes to intrude on my private space.

When I arrived downstairs, David was seated at the dining room table, talking to Madame Poret, who was glaring at him with Gallic hostility. He got to his feet as I entered, and I was struck again by this almost courtly gesture that seemed so at odds with the rest of him.

"Christina, you're a sight for sore eyes," he said. "How do you manage to look so beautiful without a trace of makeup?" The look in his eyes and the warm tone of his voice mollified my anger. Devious or not, he was a damned attractive man.

"Have you had breakfast?" I asked, taking my seat.

"I would like to," he said, "but this confounded woman is pretending that she doesn't understand my French."

"He is murdering the language," muttered the housekeeper darkly. "He makes sounds, but it is not French. It is gibberish!"

"Madame Poret is from Provence," I explained to David. "She's having difficulty understanding your accent. What are you trying to say?"

"I want to order breakfast, but I don't know the French word for cornflakes."

"Are you mad? You can have any sort of exquisite French delight for breakfast, prepared by a cook who is a graduate of the Cordon Bleu School and you want cornflakes?"

"I refuse to have that cat food they eat over here for breakfast just to be polite," David growled defensively. "There's nothing wrong with cornflakes. I just want some plain wholesome food with a name I can pronounce.''

"I'll see what I can do," I said. I explained to Madame Poret that Mr. Connelly was terminally ill and that he needed special food to make it through his last few days. "You may personally find scrambled eggs, a hard roll with butter, and hash brown potatoes revolting,'' I said to her, "but poor Mr. Connelly must choke it down or his last days will be forfeit.''

"Your friend is not ill," said Madame Poret, giving David a hard look. "He is a dolt, an idiot . . .''

"Un badaud," said David helpfully, recognizing what the housekeeper was saying.

"Oui!" she replied.

"Just do your best," I said in French.

"It will be an act of charity," the housekeeper sighed, walking back to the kitchen. "I will be remembered in heaven.''

"She's getting you some nice American food," I assured him. "Just like the seventy-nine-cent special you probably eat every morning at the local greasy spoon.''

David nodded appreciatively and took a deep drag on his cigarette. "I wish you had been here earlier," he said. "I was desperate for a cigarette, but she didn't seem to understand me when I asked if there were any in the house. I damn near turned the place upside down looking for one.''

"Madame Poret said that you were looking for something. Was that it? You were looking for cigarettes?''

"There isn't a scrap of tobacco in the house. Hash, cocaine, but no tobacco. I finally gave up and went down the street to a tobacco shop. What did you think I was doing? Searching the house for state secrets?''

"Of course not," I mumbled defensively, but I could tell that he didn't believe me.

Madame Poret came in carrying the breakfast tray as far away from her body as was possible. "If he asks for salt, the cook says he will give notice," she said to me as she set a plate of scrambled eggs down in front of David.

"I will not ask for catsup either," David promised in French, "though it's the best thing for scrambled eggs," he added in English, taking a forkful.

"He sends his compliments to the cook," I translated diplomatically. "He has never tasted better scrambled eggs."

"Of course not," Madame Poret said. "The Americans are even worse cooks than the English."

"At least American food is served hot," I said. "The English seem to eat everything at room temperature."

"That is true," the housekeeper conceded. "I am glad I am not English *or* American." She poured out the coffee and left, obviously pleased at having had the last word.

"What are you eating?" David asked conversationally, crunching into his buttered roll.

"Pain de Poisson," I said. "I wonder if I can steal Adaline's cook?"

"You mean fish? A fish pie?"

"Not exactly."

"You're having fish for *breakfast*? Where did you grow up? In a Dickens novel? That's the kind of thing they served Oliver Twist in the orphanage."

"You have the culinary tastes of a barbarian," I sighed. "I suggest that we discuss something less controversial, like politics or religion. The rift between us in the cuisine department seems too wide to breach."

David nodded amiably and stubbed out his cigarette. "I'll talk about anything you want," he said. "I just want to hear your voice. I'm going to miss that," he added softly, looking at me in a way that made my blood pound through my veins.

"Where are you headed when you leave here?" I asked, keeping my voice deliberately cool. I was more attracted to David Connelly than I cared to admit and didn't relish the thought of his walking out of my life.

"I have to contact one of our agents in Rome. He uses the name Marc Baxter."

"Is David Connelly your real name?" I asked, suddenly wanting some tangible proof of his existence.

"It is. But I don't use it here. Most people know me as Bob Crockett, the newspaperman from Iowa. Except for the people at my hotel, who think I'm Walter Brown, the European representative for a New York electronics firm. It helps explain why so many people come and go from my room. I just tell them we're having business meetings."

"What will Mr. Baxter do in Rome?"

"We've located the whereabouts of another one of those wine bottles. We have to get to it before the other side does."

"Who's the unlucky recipient of the wine?" I asked. David lit another cigarette, his blue eyes narrowed thoughtfully.

"His name is Marcello Cordova. He owns a five-star restaurant in Rome called Ristorante Cordova. Have you heard of it?"

"Of course," I nodded. "It's one of the finest restaurants in Rome. I've eaten there many times. The food is excellent but the restaurant is known mainly for its wine. There's an extensive cellar, which Mr. Cordova oversees personally, but I'm told that the best stuff is kept for his private consumption."

"You seem to know a great deal about him," said David, watching me carefully through a haze of blue smoke.

"Society gossip mostly," I said unselfconsciously. "Though we've never met, we travel in the same social circles. Besides, I had been thinking of doing an article on Mr. Cordova's wine collection for my magazine."

"Are you a reporter?"

"I own *World* magazine. We do feature stories on many famous people."

"That's quite a coincidence," he mused. "You could do that story, Christina, and gain access to Cordova's wine cellar at the same time."

"Now, hold on a minute," I said, raising my hand defensively. "I'm not going to risk my neck on some sort of harebrained caper. This isn't my fight. I mean, I'm as patriotic as the next person but this is out of my depth."

"Do you think I'd let you do this if there were even the slightest risk?" said David. "Mr. Cordova is an innocent man. He doesn't know that he has anything in his cellar but a rare bottle of wine. All you have to do is get him to show you the bottle, see if there's a microdot, and if there is, sneak it off the bottle and get it back to me."

"It wasn't Mr. Cordova I was worried about," I said. "What if your communist friends show up?"

"They won't if we move quickly," David replied. "Don't you see, that's the beauty of this scheme. *World* magazine is a perfect cover. If we use one of our own agents, we're likely to attract attention. But you're just the sort of person one expects to see at a fancy restaurant like that. No one will suspect a thing."

"Forget it," I said firmly. "I'm not about to spend my vacation acting out a scene from a Mack Sennett movie."

"You're right," said David cheerfully. "Forget and forgive. That's the best way."

"I do forgive you, David," I said sweetly. "That arrest was just an innocent mistake."

"Oh, I don't mean that," he replied. "I mean the fact that Nicholas and Andrei made a fool out of you."

"Who made a fool out of who?" I snapped.

"Whom," he corrected, a glint of amusement in his eyes. "Look, you carried that wine bottle through Paris customs without knowing what you were involved in. Now, I know you don't go around waving an American flag, but I'm sure you wouldn't have willingly worked against the interests of your own country."

"What do you take me for?"

"An innocent bystander, of course. Well, not exactly a bystander. If we hadn't already been onto their operation, that microdot would have been in communist hands right now."

"And I would have been instrumental in putting it there, is that what you're saying?"

"It's not your fault," he hastened to assure me. "Those men are professionals. They use people like you all the time. It's part of the game. It could have been anyone."

"But it wasn't anyone," I said. "It was me." I had been played for a fool by two Slavic slobs who had taken advantage of my generous, warm-hearted nature and my natural inclination to help my fellow man. I had been fucked, all right. In more ways than one.

"Forget and forgive," David reminded me, then ducked as the sugar bowl sailed over his head.

"Those bastards!" I yelled.

"Don't get angry," David said softly. I shot him a hard look.

"What do I get?"

"Get even."

"How?"

"Help me get to that wine bottle. Tit for tat. We get a step ahead of the commies and you get to go on with your life with a clear conscience."

"I have a clear conscience," I muttered. "What if Cordova won't grant me an interview? Nobody else has ever gotten one."

"Call and talk to him personally," David suggested. "I guarantee he won't be able to refuse. No man could refuse you anything. By the way, how's your Italian?"

"It's better than your French," I said. "Will you come with me?"

"I can't. It would arouse too much suspicion. But Baxter will look out for you. He's a good man."

"You really think this will work, huh?"

"I know it will. I'm betting my job on it. The Agency frowns on private citizens getting mixed up in our business and I wouldn't risk it if it weren't fool-proof. You just be sweet, charming, and sexy—yourself, in fact—and you'll be out of there in two days. Three at the most."

I looked at his open, boyish face and the thought occurred to me that the entire conversation had been a ruse. David had tricked me just as much as Zelanko had. Sweet, charming, and sexy, that's how he had referred to me and, considering the past twenty-four hours, I could not really blame him if he saw me in that way—a dizzy blonde bombshell, easily flattered and manipulated. But there is more to Christina van Bell than a beautiful face and a fabulous figure, and it was suddenly important to prove to David that I was as well-endowed mentally as I was physically.

He was relaxed now, the square line of his jaw softer, the blue eyes less steely. I smiled at him and he smiled back. I found myself wanting him again, the feel of his hands against my flesh, his lips against mine, and I could tell from the expression on his face that he was thinking the same thing.

He put down his coffee cup and ground the butt of his cigarette into the ashtray. He stood up, negotiated the perimeter of the breakfast table and knelt in front of me. He took my hands and held them for a moment, turning them upward and pressing his lips against the vulnerable flesh of the palms. A delicious shiver of excitement went through me.

He picked me up and carried me upstairs to the bedroom, placing me gently on the bed. The sheets were rumpled and still slightly damp, redolent of the ripe odors of our previous lovemaking. He lay down beside me and kissed me softly, lingeringly. He loosened the front of my robe to reveal the soft swell of my bosom, veiled in its peach-colored satin and lace teddy. He slipped the straps from my shoulders, imprisoning my arms, as he bared those luscious mounds to his hungry gaze. My heart was beating painfully. I found myself drawn again to his compelling strength, which came from more than mere physical size. His lips found mine, forcing them apart. His tongue thrust its way into my mouth, searching, demanding. I gave a soft moan, struggling against the confines of my clothes. He laughed at my attempt to escape and, sliding one arm around my waist, he lifted me against him, removing my robe and flinging it aside. I slipped my arms from the restraining straps of the teddy, letting it fall around my waist. I wound my arms around his neck, pressing myself against him. I felt the roughness of his jacket against my naked, burning flesh and the hard, cold buckle of his belt through the satin material of the teddy.

I fumbled with his belt and the fastening of his pants, reaching down to release the pole of his manhood from the tight confines of his Jockey shorts. He lay back and I sprawled on top of him. Placing one hand on each shoulder, I raised myself up, brushing the nipples of my breasts against his lips. His tongue flicked each one as I moved, teasing him, then he suddenly brought his hand down sharply on my up-turned derriere and I lost my balance and collapsed on top of him. My legs were spread, straddling his thighs, and I ground my pussy against his bulging prick as his hand rubbed my satin-covered ass. He slid his hand beneath the loose folds of fabric at my waist, his fingers tracing the crack between my cheeks. My buttock muscles tightened convulsively, then relaxed as his middle finger pushed insistently at the entrance to my back passage. My body flushed with desire. I reached back to pull the teddy over my hips, then spread my ass cheeks to allow his finger maximum penetration. My hips began to move harder and faster against his groin as he finger-fucked my ass. Our mouths were still pressed to-gether and his other hand fondled my breast.

I could feel my body racing toward orgasm, but I wanted something more. I wanted the feel of his naked flesh against my own, of his hard hot cock against my clit.

"Not yet," I gasped, tearing at his jacket with my hands. "Not this way!"

He understood and slowed his pace. He fumbled with his clothes while I slipped my sweat-filmed teddy over my trembling thighs and flung it aside. David's breathing was heavy. I could tell that he was as excited as I was as his eyes devoured my totally unclad form. He had stood up to undress, and as he stared down at me, his stiffened cock stood out be-tween his muscular thighs. A pearl of moisture tipped the helmetlike head, and my mouth watered as I looked at it. I slid off the bed and, kneeling on the thick-carpeted floor, I stretched out my tongue with deliberate slowness. I ran its entire length over the purplish-pink tip of David's cock in a way that made him gasp for breath and put his hands on my head to steady himself. I continued my ministrations at the same tantalizing pace. We were both so primed from our earlier foreplay that any quick move would catapult us into orgasm. I wanted to come but the exquisite pleasure of holding back, of prolonging the sensations past all bearing was a mind-blowing experience.

Finally I could deny myself no longer. I moved closer and, grasping his buttocks with my hands, eased my lips over the smooth hardness of his erect shaft. He gave a long, low moan of pleasure and I felt his buttock muscles quiver in my hands.

I cupped his balls, opening my mouth wide and tilting my head back to take the entire length of him deep into my throat. The smell of his sex, the feel of his slick rod in my mouth, and the soft down of his balls against my lips drove me to a frenzy. He was moving now, fucking my mouth with long, powerful thrusts. My hand strayed to my cunt, the lips puffy and damp. My fingers eased into my love canal, seeking the hard red knob of my clit. I moved my hips up and down in congruence with the rhythm of David's cock in my mouth.

He came without warning, shooting his hot load, filling my mouth and silvering my lips with his creamy gift. My own pussy was steaming, and with a final thrust of my finger I brought myself to a dizzying climax.

I was still on the floor. David's hand brushed the long strands of damp hair from my face and his lips brushed my forehead in a tender, chaste kiss.

"That was terrific," he murmured as he lifted me to my feet.

"It was just a tease," I replied. "A bit of foreplay to get you ready."

"Really? What do you do for an encore?"

I didn't reply. I slipped my arms around his neck,

pressing my pelvis against his as my tongue pushed its way between his lips. I felt his penis hardening against my bare thigh and I reached down to stroke it lovingly. My mind filled with images of what it would feel like inside me. I yearned for him, wanted him in the most primary, fundamental way. The way Eve wanted Adam, the way a woman wants a man. He lifted me in his arms and laid me gently on the bed. I spread my legs, and like a sword being returned to its sheath, his steellike shaft penetrated my pussy in one sure clean thrust.

I gave a low groan and tightened my vaginal muscles to hold the welcome hardness of his prick. He spread his own legs, forcing mine still farther apart. He pulled out almost all the way, then drove back in, making me gasp at the impact of his swollen member against the farthest reaches of my cunt. The force of his thrusts drove me upward along the sheets and I arched toward him, my fingers searching for a handhold on the broad muscles of his back. I continued to work the inner muscles of my cunt, combining the tight, wet resistance of a virginal passage with the experienced moves of a first-class hooker.

I wrapped my legs around his thighs, moving with the pounding rhythm of his thrusts. I pulled him closer, wanting every part of me touching every part of him. My nails raked his back and my teeth sought out the hollows in his collarbone as his manhood fired my lust. I was like a wild animal, grinding and bucking in a frenzy of raw carnal passion. Still working my vaginal muscles, I stuck a finger in my mouth, wetting it liberally with my tongue. Then I slid my hands down the long curve of his spine to the line between his buttocks. I spread his ass cheeks and plunged my finger into the puckered hole of his anus. I heard him gasp and he stiffened, his penis skewering my clit. I kept my finger still and he bucked his hips up, begging for more. Slowly and deliberately, I worked my finger in his back passage, alternating with the rhythm of his pistonlike strokes.

Our groans and whimpers were clearly audible and the bed moved and vibrated with our passion. Suddenly his anus tightened around my finger and with a final animal cry he let himself go. The hot jets of cum exploded into the far reaches of my cunt, triggering my own wild, sweet orgasm. I held on to his pulsing tool to savor the final shuddering spasm as he collapsed on top of me, then I slowly withdrew my finger from the tightness of his asshole and unwrapped my legs from around his thighs.

I must have drifted off to sleep, for when I opened my eyes the rain had stopped and wisps of white cloud streaked a lead-colored sky. David was still beside me, his bare thigh warm against my hip. He was smoking a cigarette, and the ashtray, balanced precariously on the blanket, was overflowing with butts. Though time was of the utmost importance, he had let me sleep and I liked that. I wriggled against him and he hastily stubbed out his cigarette and moved the ashtray to a safer place. Then he leaned over and kissed me.

"If I'm going to get to Rome," I said, "you'd better not kiss me again. It's getting late and I have to pack."

"The mind is willing, but the flesh is weak," groaned David, kissing me again. "Will you call Mr. Cordova?"

"When I get there," I said. "It will be harder for him to turn down my request for an interview when I tell him that I've come to Rome exclusively in the hope of seeing him."

"Good thinking," David said. "While you're packing, I'll make your hotel and plane reservations and get word to Baxter to expect you."

"Make them first class and book the room at the Excelsior," I said, pulling him on top of me. "How will I find Mr. Baxter?"

"He'll find you. He'll use a code word so you'll know it's him."

"What's the code word."

"Let's see," David said, his lips against my ear. "Tomorrow is Thursday, so . . . ah, yes, the code word is cunnilingus."

"Liar!" I laughed, pushing him roughly away. "Your agency would never allow the use of a word like that."

"I like to pull their beards a bit," he whispered hoarsely. "Why don't you try it and see what happens?"

An hour later I trailed off to shower and dress while David went to what he called a "safe" phone outside the house to make preparations for my debut as an undercover agent. By the time he had returned, I was ready to leave.

"We still have a few hours till your flight leaves," David said. "How about some dinner, then a crash course on locating and securing microdots?"

"Only if you let me select the restaurant," I said. "Don't worry, I'll translate everything on the menu for you, but I have a craving for Ris de Veau and few places prepare them like Les Trois Gourmands."

"Don't even tell me what that is," said David as he picked up my suitcases. "Just order me a hamburger."

"I know," I said. "Sans oeuf."

As it turned out, the restaurant was not far from David's hotel, which was located near Gare du Nord in the tenth arrondissement. For security reasons we used David's government car, which he handled with the skill of one long used to the peculiarities of Paris traffic.

"Your driving is better than your French," I teased him as we sped along the crowded avenues after dinner. "You drive like a true Parisian."

"The secret to successful driving in Paris," David replied, "is to completely ignore anything you were ever taught in Driver's Ed at your old high school. You cannot drive defensively in Paris because you will never get anywhere. The Parisians do not yield and they will risk their lives for the cheap thrill of cutting into traffic at ninety miles an hour while passing a red signal. You must be aggressive, thoughtless, and rude, or they'll eat you alive."

"Don't the police hand out tickets?" I asked.

"Hundreds, maybe thousands, per motorist. The Parisians stick them in their bureaus or kitchen drawers and ignore them. Parisians ignore everything. For example, there has been a law in Paris for years that car headlights must be turned on after dark. Do the Parisians drive with their headlights on?"

"Never," I laughed. "They're afraid of wearing out their batteries."

"That's right. They drive in the dark, the police hand out tickets, the drivers ignore the tickets, everyone knows his place, and everyone's happy."

The staff at David's hotel all greeted him as Mr. Smith.

"I thought you told me they all think you're Walter Brown here," I hissed.

"No. That's my mistake. Walter Brown was in the London hotel my last assignment. In this hotel I'm Paul Smith, an international businessman specializing in computers. I have to start keeping an index card file or something. One of these days I'm gonna get my head blown off, and the Agency won't know what name to stick on the tombstone."

"Does the desk clerk think I'm a business associate?" I asked.

"Either that or a terribly high-priced whore," David teased.

"Same thing," I shrugged as he opened the door of his room and stepped back to let me enter.

The room, like the car, was lacking in any detail that might make it stick in a person's mind. It was also lacking in comfort and elegance, but I kept these opinions to myself.

David closed the curtains and turned on the small light over the wood-grained formica coffee table. He took a bottle of scotch from the bottom of his closet and a fresh pack of Camels from the top drawer of his night table. He lit a cigarette and inhaled appreciatively. "There's nothing like an American cigarette," he sighed. "I'll smoke anything in a pinch, but this is sheer heaven." He put the bottle and two water glasses on the table and poured me a drink. "We have an hour till your flight leaves," he said, glancing at his watch. "I don't want to frighten you with warnings about enemy agents and national security, but I want you to make contact with Mr. Cordova as soon as possible. If you stay in Rome too long asking about wine, someone will put two and two together and the results might be very unpleasant."

"I'll get an interview for tomorrow afternoon," I promised.

"You're going to have to do more than get him to *talk* about his collection," David said. "You're going to have to get him to show you his private cellar and the particular bottle of wine we're interested in. Have you given any thought as to how you're going to do that?"

"David darling," I said, giving him a look that made him blush. "I have never had any trouble getting any man to produce anything I have asked for. Trust me. I will get the bottle of wine."

"That's about the way I figured it," said David wryly. "Here, take a close look at the label on this bottle. It's the one you delivered to Andrei. As you can see, it's a drawing depicting an angel sitting on a pile of grapes in the sun, with the name of the wine, ZECE, over his head. On a label containing the microdot, there is what looks like a small smudging of the ink where the last letter—the E—is out of register. Have you got that?"

"I'm with you so far," I said. There were certainly a lot of technicalities involved in spying these days. Mata Hari had a far easier time of it.

"You see this lipstick?" he asked, producing a small metal tube.

"That's a cheap lipstick," I said, wrinkling my nose.

"Don't worry, you won't have to wear it. The contents have been replaced by a small magnifying lens." He twisted the top of the tube to show me how to produce the lens and then had me duplicate his movements. "Use the lens to help locate the microdot," he continued. "Then lift it off with this little stick. It has an adhesive substance that will remove the dot without damaging it." He demonstrated how the stick was secreted inside a phony mascara tube. "Once you've secured the microdot, you press the button on this wristwatch and the front will spring open. Just deposit the microdot inside. You can use the magnifier to double-check. Remember, Cordova isn't at all suspicious, so if he catches you in the middle of all this, just pretend it's part of your makeup routine. The whole thing should take less than a minute if you keep your wits about you and stay calm. Now, do you have everything straight? Because unless something goes very wrong and we have to pull you out, once you're in Rome you'll be on your own."

"Don't worry, chief," I said, snapping a salute. "I'll be back with the goods in thirty-six hours or my name isn't Countess Kleitche von Dulow."

"It isn't." David frowned.

"You have a million names," I said, shrugging. "I thought I'd start a collection of my own."

CHAPTER SEVEN

Sam Brentwood leaned impatiently on the horn of his 1932 dark blue Rolls Silver Shadow and assaulted a bored traffic warden with a barrage of Italian insults that the officer blithely ignored. He sighed heavily and leaned back against the gray leather seat with an air of defeat. All around us a stagnant sea of fume-spewing, horn-blaring automobiles basked motionless in the midmorning Roman sunshine. I slipped off the jacket of my beige silk suit and opened the top buttons of my blouse. The day was already warm and the antique car did not have air conditioning.

"How long has the traffic been like this?" I asked.

"Since Forty-two B.C.," Sam growled. "Augustus Caesar was delayed on his way home from Gaul because of a six chariot pile-up outside the Colosseum. I think he's still stuck somewhere out there. Rome is a giant traffic jam surrounded by two-thousand-year-old buildings." He looked at me irritably. "My doctor ordered me to give up driving my car during daylight hours," he said. "The tension is bad for my blood pressure."

"Poor Sam," I said, lightly stroking his cheek with

103

my finger. "What were you doing at the airport, then? You were the last person I expected to see."

"I wanted to make sure that some paintings I'm shipping to a gallery in Brussels got on the right plane," he replied. "Those jokes about Italian inefficiency are soundly based on fact. I was angry about having to fight traffic in the heat of the day but it's turned out for the best."

"You're still fighting traffic," I pointed out.

"Yes, but I got to see you again," he said, smiling suddenly. He was a short, stocky man with thinning hair and a good deal of extra padding around his middle, but when he smiled his face lit up in a way that made my knees feel weak. Sam was an expatriate American who had become disenchanted with the rat race on Wall Street. On his fortieth birthday, he had quit his job, sold his house, taken his bankroll, and headed for Europe to paint. After several years his art had earned him more money than he had ever made on the stock market and many of the health problems that had developed during his years in New York had vanished. I owned several of his paintings and had spent three weeks one summer in his seaside villa, alternating between mind-blowing sex and food orgies and a serious study of acrylics. My artistic efforts had been less than successful, but Sam and I had formed a lasting friendship based on a mutual enjoyment of oral sex that endured to this day.

"Are you sure you won't stay in my apartment instead of going to a hotel?" Sam asked as the car inched forward. "I have plenty of room."

"I would love to," I sighed, "but I'll only be here for one night and I have work to do. I have an interview with Marcello Cordova this afternoon. Have you heard of him?"

"The restaurant owner." Sam nodded. "Times must be tough at that magazine of yours when they have to send the owner out to do the work. What's the matter, Christina, are your cub reporters on strike?"

"I'm as capable as any reporter," I said, "and this is the kind of article that requires a cultured point of view. How can some idiot reporter hope to bring the panache, the style, the knowledge of fine wine I have to an article?"

"And since Superman was unavailable, you decided to do it yourself," Sam laughed.

"Very funny," I snapped. "Cordova has refused interviews from every major magazine in the world, but when I called and asked, he agreed to see me. Obviously he has heard of me."

"Not exactly," muttered Sam, blushing furiously.

"What do you mean?"

"Do you remember those nude sketches I did of you?"

"How could I forget? I never held such tortuous positions for so long in my life."

"I did a series of five oil paintings using the best of those sketches and called them *Christina's World*."

"The name of my magazine," I murmured, suddenly understanding Cordova's desire to meet me. "Which one did Cordova buy?"

"The one of you bent over a chair, looking back over your shoulder. You've got a great ass, Christina. I had intended to keep that painting for myself, but he drove such a hard bargain, I couldn't refuse."

"I should demand a part of the profit," I laughed, "but this interview with Cordova is payment enough. It means a great deal to me, and I can see now that you were instrumental in my getting it."

"I couldn't have painted what wasn't there," he sighed, his hand caressing the rounded curve of my bottom.

"You're a fine artist," I said sincerely. "And a talented lover," I added, moving closer and nibbling gently at the lobe of his ear.

"You were an inspiration, Christina. Oh, I've had my share of models: tall, short, blonde, dark, but there has never been anyone like you. In bed or out. I'd like to sketch you again. I'd like to make love to you again too," he said wistfully as we pulled up in front of the Excelsior Hotel on Via Vittorio Veneto.

"Why don't I call you when I'm through with my assignment?" I said. "I could postpone my return to France for a few hours."

"I won't leave my apartment till I hear from you," Sam said as he signaled for a bellhop to take my suitcases into the hotel. "It will be like old times." His kiss held a promise, and I knew I would not fail to redeem that promise.

Knowing my dislike of small dark spaces, David had reserved a suite of rooms that overlooked the street. The hotel was located just north of the Piazza Barberini, and from the huge picture window I could see people strolling leisurely through the plaza. It was afternoon siesta time, when most businesses and stores close for three hours to allow the Romans to have a quiet meal, a contemplative walk through the park, or a hot session of lovemaking before resuming the business of the day. It is this civilized attitude that has undoubtedly accounted for the longevity of the Italian culture.

Like most restaurants in the city, Ristorante Cordova would not be open for business until after seven in the evening, as Romans tend to have their evening meal quite late. I had arranged to meet Mr. Cordova just before six so that we could converse uninterrupted before the demands of his business cut into our time.

I had several hours before I needed to dress so I ordered a meal from room service and trailed off to take a bath while I waited for it to be delivered. I felt nervous about my upcoming interview, for, despite my boast to David, a lot of things could go wrong.

I took out my gold cigarette case and lit up a joint, forcing myself to relax. I opened my notebook and checked the list of instructions David had given me on the way to the airport. Being a good novice spy, I had asked if I should memorize the list and swallow the paper, but David had assured me that it wouldn't be necessary. I reviewed the equipment I would have to use if I found the microdot, making sure that I could operate each piece quickly and efficiently.

It was obvious that Mr. Cordova's desire to meet me had more to do with my *ass*ets than my position as owner of a world-famous magazine, though I wasn't averse to a sexual encounter if it would get him to show me his precious wine collection and help me locate the microdot. I selected a form-fitting red wool dress with long sleeves and a scooped neckline that plunged to a deep V in back, exposing the upper part of my buttocks. If my natural charm and good looks were not enough to captivate Mr. Cordova, this outfit would surely cast the deciding vote.

Satisfied that I was ready for my first foray into the murky world of international intrigue, I wrapped myself in a thin, gray-plaid mohair shawl and took the lift downstairs. The Excelsior Hotel was in the same neighborhood as Ristorante Cordova and, having an hour to go until my appointment, I decided to forgo a taxi and walk to the restaurant.

I strolled along the winding Via Vittorio Veneto. The afternoon sun was low in the sky, turning my hair to a halo of gold around my face, and my fair skin and brightly colored clothing attracted stares of open admiration from men and women alike. Some of the men were more demonstrative in their attentions and my bottom was pinched a number of times, but I took it all in the good-natured way it was intended. You always know where you stand with the Italians. Their reactions, both positive and negative, are always refreshingly direct.

I turned right into Via Pinciana, walking along the giant park that comprises the Villa Borghese with its fountains, glades, statues, and museums until I reached Via Giovanni Sgambati. This is a small street a few feet from the famous Casino Borghese, which houses Canova's nude of Pauline Borghese, Napoleon's sister, reclining realistically on her couch. It was on this choice bit of real estate that Ristorante Cordova was located.

It was a modest two-story building with a spacious dining area downstairs and private dining rooms on the second floor. Signore Cordova's famous wine cellar was under the pavement, reportedly extending for some distance beyond the restaurant.

I went through the front door and found myself in a large dining room done in a simple, straightforward style. The wooden floor had been polished to a soft shine and the brass chandeliers gleamed brightly, their lights reflecting in the mirror-covered walls. A handsome young waiter in a black uniform and a long white apron was busily setting the tables with snowy-white cloths and silverware in anticipation of that evening's trade.

"Excuse me, signorina," he stammered in Italian. "The door should not have been open. We will not be serving for at least an hour."

"It's all right," I assured him. "I'm not here for dinner. I have an appointment with Signore Cordova. My name is Christina van Bell and I'm from *World* magazine in New York."

"An interview? Are you sure?" He seemed rather confounded by this bit of news. "My uncle never sees members of the press."

"Is Signore Cordova your uncle?" I asked.

"All of my employees are members of my family," came a rich baritone voice from behind me. "It keeps the theft of the silverware down to tolerable levels."

I turned and confronted a tall thin man in a navy pin-striped, three-piece suit. There was a gold watch chain hanging across his middle and a diamond pin nestled in his navy-blue silk tie. He had black eyes beneath heavy, straight brows, a prominent nose, and full, sensuous lips. His skin was dark and his black hair showed just a touch of gray at the temples. He's certainly a sexy package, I thought as he smiled down at me.

"It's a pleasure to meet you, Miss van Bell," he said, taking my hand and bringing it to his lips. His eyes traveled over my body, barely visible through the folds of my shawl. I moved my hand so that the front fell open, exposing the long line of my neck and the swell of my breasts, naked beneath the tight-fitting red wool dress. His gaze shifted downward, and I could tell that he liked what he saw.

"The pleasure is mutual," I replied, looking straight at him. "I have heard a great deal about your restaurant, of course, and about you."

"Oh?"

"We have some friends in common," I said, watching him closely. "I ran into Sam Brentwood at the airport when I arrived this morning. We drove into the city together and he asked to be remembered to you." Mr. Cordova laughed heartily.

"I have one of his *Christina*s, as he no doubt told you," he said. "I don't usually grant interviews, but when you called I jumped at the chance to meet the real flesh and blood Christina."

"I have never seen those paintings," I said. "In fact, it was only this morning that I learned of their existence. They were done from some pencil sketches Sam made of me several years ago."

"I thought mine a masterpiece until now," Cordova said. "But it doesn't compare with the original."

"How can you tell?" I asked with pretended in-
nocence. "I'm fully dressed."

"I think we can rectify that situation," Cordova
murmured. "I have a small apartment downstairs inside the cellars. We will have complete privacy. We
can talk, eat, and sample the best of my private collection."

"Perhaps I'll let you sample the best of my private
collection too," I said. I slipped off my shawl, turning slightly. I heard the sharp intake of his breath as
the smooth white flesh of my back and the dimpled
top of my buttocks was revealed for the first time.
From the far side of the room there was a loud crash
as Mr. Cordova's nephew dropped the tray of glasses
he was carrying.

"Vincente, tell the chef to prepare the special dinner I ordered earlier and bring it to me downstairs,"
said Cordova as he opened a large oak-paneled door
and ushered me through. "And see that you clean up
that mess before we open. This way, my dear." As I
preceded him down the narrow winding stairs his leg
brushed my ass as if by accident, sending little shivers
along my spine.

At the foot of the stairs there was a small square
whitewashed room with an immense carved wooden
door. There was a heavy, ornate iron grille in front of
this door, fortified with a wicked-looking electronic
lock.

"The door to my cellar," said Cordova proudly.
"The cellars themselves extend under other buildings
and the Borghese Gardens, and even I would not
know where to blast my way through from the outside, but securing the entrance was a problem, as it is
easily accessible." He pointed to a small box on the
wall with ten numbered push buttons. "This is the
most sophisticated electronic lock available. It is vir-
tually pick-proof." Shielding the box with his body,

Cordova punched in his code number.

It was lucky for David that I had agreed to get his wine bottle, I thought. He never would have gotten through this security system without Cordova's co-operation.

The combination entered, Cordova punched a few more buttons and the heavy lock clicked open. He opened the gate and turned the brass handle on the wooden door. A light snapped on as the door opened, revealing another whitewashed room. A cool gust of air burst from the door.

"Did you say you had an apartment down here?" I asked, shivering slightly.

"Don't worry, the apartment has a separate heating system," he assured me. "All wine cellars are cold. The temperature and humidity in this one are strictly monitored by computer so that conditions are perfect all year round. Wonderful things, computers. The Japanese make terrible wine but they do know their way around the old microchips."

The cellar was truly massive, extending for quite a distance in both directions. Cordova had enough wine to qualify as an exporter, though all of his stock was kept strictly for his private use.

"I'm impressed," I said, wondering how I was ever to find the wine bottle I needed. "How do you keep it all straight?"

"The racks have code numbers," he said, pointing to small typed labels along the horizontal bars of the wine racks, "and the computer has the entire stock catalogued on a single disc. Of course, a lot of this is moderate-priced wine or duplicates of some rarer wines that are for sale to the customers in my restaurant." He led me to a table holding a small computer terminal. It was an expensive model of one of the many popular home computers available. "A waiter can find any bottle listed on the menu by punching the name into the terminal and matching the number that appears on the screen to the number beneath the bottle on the racks."

"I can see how that would save a lot of time," I agreed.

"Time and money," Cordova said, opening another paneled door and ushering me into his apartment. It was a large room with walls of dark reflective glass and a brown ceramic tile floor. The lighting was recessed and the furniture simple and functional. A black lacquered table had been set for two and I noticed a low modular seating arrangement with extra-large throw pillows, covered in natural raw silk. "I love my nephews," Cordova continued as he took my shawl, "but they're not too bright. With this system they just match the numbers of the computer screen to the labels. They get the right bottle and I don't sell a rare wine to some lucky customer for a thousand lire."

Speaking of the devil, at that moment the nephew appeared at the door, weighed down by a large tray.

"There you are, Vincente," Cordova said, waving him into the room. "What took you so long?"

"The tray is very heavy, uncle," the boy gasped, staggering under the weight.

"Then put it down," his uncle snapped, making no effort to help him with his burden. "If you didn't chase whores all night, you'd have more energy."

The nephew placed the tray heavily on the sideboard and leaned against the wall, trying to catch his breath.

"It smells wonderful," I said. "I hadn't counted on a meal."

"But you are a guest in my house," Cordova protested. "It would be discourteous not to offer you refreshment. Besides, that is what your story will be about, the greatness of Ristorante Cordova, and Americans always insist on proof of greatness. You come from, how do you say, the 'give-me' state.''

"That's the 'show-me' state," I said. "But I'm not from Missouri. I think Harry Truman was."

"Harry Truman, of course," he said delightedly. "I remember him from the war. I was just a child, but my father was an American sympathizer. These very cellars were used to house wounded American soldiers, and they taught me all about your great Franklin Roosevelt and Harry Truman." He suddenly rounded on his nephew, who was still leaning against the wall. "What do you know about Harry Truman?" he demanded.

The nephew stood bolt upright. "I don't know who Harry Truman is, uncle," he stammered. "Is he the man who ordered the Lafite-Rothschild last night?"

"You see?" said Cordova triumphantly. "That is why I have to install a computer. This dolt doesn't even know who Harry Truman is." He advanced on his nephew with a threatening air, and the boy began to back away toward the door. "Truman was a great man. He dropped a bomb on the Japanese so that the Americans could spend billions of dollars rebuilding the country so that the Japanese could learn to make computers to help your poor uncle keep his ignorant family from sending him to the poorhouse!" he barked. His nephew stumbled out of the room and Cordova slammed the door behind him.

"There, now we will not be disturbed," he said, walking back to the table.

"None of what you just said made any sense," I said as I took my seat.

"That's true," he conceded, "but I'm the head of the family, and it is necessary to assert my authority at least once a day. How do you like your steak?"

"Rare."

He took off the covers and placed a charcoal-grilled piece of meat on my plate. There was a large green salad with a special house dressing, fresh crusty bread, and a vast selection of hors d'oeuvres.

"This is the best steak I've ever eaten," I said. "It's as soft as butter and perfectly seasoned."

"Ristorante Cordova is famous for its steak," Cordova replied. "The meat is the choicest cut and it is all imported from Tuscany, where Italy's best cattle are raised. I find that simple food is the best complement to a fine wine."

I looked at the wines that Cordova had selected to go with the meal. There was a Romanée-Conti '61, a La Tâche '59, and a Petrus '45. I did a bit of mental arithmetic and realized that the three bottles would sell for close to $3,000 on the open market. But there was no Rumanian wine, and I was afraid that if I asked directly about the wine that I was interested in, Cordova might take a closer look at the bottle and perhaps notice an imperfection on the label. I decided to wait and see what happened. I was very hungry and Cordova was an attractive man. I was sure he could satisfy more than my physical hunger and I was in the mood for some really great sex.

"What do you consider the proper way to drink wine?" I asked as Cordova opened the bottles to let the wine breathe.

"I see you've fallen victim to the usual snobbery that afflicts wine lovers," Cordova laughed, pouring out two glasses of the Bordeaux. "They all have these idiot rituals. They drink from a certain shaped glass. They dip their noses in the glass and sniff. They dip their big toes in. They rinse their mouths with the wine. They use eyedroppers and drip it up their asses. They do everything except just drink the damned stuff. The best way to drink fine wine is in the company of a beautiful woman." He raised his glass in a silent toast and drank, never taking his eyes from mine.

As we ate and drank, we discussed his wine collection and his restaurant and his family and everything else I could think of to ask about. I took careful notes, figuring that Cordova, not knowing that this entire interview was just a ruse to gain access to his wine cellar, would expect to actually see an article about himself in *World* magazine. I would turn the notes over to the feature editor at the magazine, who could write something for publication as soon as I got back to New York.

We had finished our meal and were lingering over the last of the wine. I had asked about Rumanian wine when discussing his collection and Cordova stated that he had several bottles from small vineyards that were considered excellent but that he himself thought inferior to French wine. He did not elaborate or offer to show me any of the bottles, and I did not feel I could press the point without arousing his suspicions. Fortunately, Cordova had shown me the computer terminal. I had a general idea of how those things worked because when we had installed similar devices in the offices of *World* magazine, I had been given lessons on their operation by the overeager salesman. I felt confident that I could use the computer to find the wine, but I would need a few minutes alone. More than a few minutes, if I could swing it. I considered several ways of accomplishing this, but I decided to play it safe and stick to what I knew. Some strenuous exercise, combined with the excessive amount of food and wine we had just consumed, might induce Cordova to take a short nap. Besides, I felt hot and horny and ready for a bit of erotic exercise myself. I looked at Cordova over the rim of my glass. His face was flushed and I could tell by the smoldering expression in his eyes that his thoughts were the same as mine. I put down my glass, stood up, and stretched languorously. I began to undo the zipper on the side of my dress. Though Cordova made no move to help me, I heard the sharp intake of his breath as I slowly and sensuously peeled off the clinging fabric. I am an exhibitionist at heart and enjoy having a man watch me undress. My own excitement is heightened as the promise of my body is revealed in a ritualistic, sensual way. I turned and walked toward the couch, trailing my dress and deliberately affording Cordova an excellent view of the undulating motion of my hips as I moved. I had not worn any underwear. Clad only in stockings, a lace-trimmed garter belt, and gray high-heeled shoes, I bent over to place my dress on the couch. I looked over my shoulder, affecting the same pose as in the painting that Sam had said Cordova had purchased, and smiled invitingly. Cordova had taken off his jacket and tie, unbuttoned his shirt and vest, and loosened the belt on his trousers. His cock rose from the unzipped fly in mute testament to my charms.

I straightened up and walked back across the room, letting my body brush against his shoulder as if by accident.

"Why don't you get more comfortable?" I said wickedly.

I moved in front of him and his hand stroked my rear end as I passed. He was an ass man, no doubt about it. I stopped, letting him fondle my ripe, firm cheeks, then I sat on his lap, entwining my arms around his neck and grinding my naked bottom against the hardness of his cock. His body jerked spasmodically, and I laughed softly, bouncing playfully, then licking his ear in a hot, wet promise of delights to come. I pulled his vest down over his shoulders and flung it wantonly aside. I yanked his shirt free of his trousers. He shrugged out of it and I dropped it on the floor, my breasts rubbing against the mat of thick dark hair on his chest. He was breathing heavily now, his body warm against my naked flesh. His hands trembled as he lifted me off his lap and stood me on my feet. I tugged impatiently at his belt. He laughed at my eagerness, catching my wrists in one hand while the other completed my work in a more dignified manner.

He knelt before me and, cupping my ass cheeks in his hands, he pressed his face against the fragrant triangle between my thighs. He began to plant kisses on my upper thighs and belly on the springy bush of my pubic area. My skin began to tingle pleasurably and little shivers of excitement raced along my spine. Holding onto his shoulders, I stepped out of my shoes and allowed him to remove my stockings and garter belt.

We stood naked for a moment in a puddle of discarded clothing, two bodies taking stock of each other. Cordova's fingers touched my lips and my breasts, then traced a line down the firm, shapely curve of my waist, and I could tell that he was pleased with what he saw. Taking his hand, I led him back to the couch, indicating that I wanted him to lie down. His skin was dark and his body lean yet muscular. His cock too was long and straight, and there was a fuzz of dark hair on his balls. I leaned over his supine form and began to lick at his swollen shaft and the loose, pliant skin of his balls, using my tongue and lips in a way that made him curl his toes and clutch at the cushions in the sheer exuberance of his passion. I breathed in the fragrant smell of his sex, enjoying the feel of his sweet hardness filling my mouth. My pussy was tingling now, eager for a little massaging of its own. I moved my body so that I straddled his waist, crouching down and pushing my aching cunt almost against his face. He took the hint, and as I brought his cock to a full throbbing erection in the hot cavity of my mouth, he separated my ass cheeks and thrust his tongue into my well-lubricated passage. The pressure of his tongue on my joy-button was like a jolt of electricity. Fired by lust, I began to heave and pant. I drew him deep into my throat, my hands moving beneath his hips to tickle the crack between his ass cheeks. As his hips lifted off the sheets, I plunged my finger into his asshole. His buttock muscles contracted and he cried out, his cock trembling in my mouth. His fingers raked my ass cheeks as he fought to keep his tongue against my clit. Near to climax, we abandoned ourselves to pleasure. Suddenly he let go and his passion poured into my eager mouth. I hungrily swallowed as much as I could of his abundant fluid as I spread my knees wider, pressing my clit back against his tongue. My entire body was trembling, then I was coming too in an undulating wave of ecstasy.

"That was great," Cordova sighed as we leaned back against the sweat-soaked cushions to catch our breaths. "You have a body that just won't quit. Tell me, what form of lovemaking do you like best? Straight fucking, oral sex, perhaps some B&D?"

"Yes," I replied, and he laughed and pulled me back against him. I felt the pressure of his leg between my thighs and wriggled suggestively.

"You move like a cat in heat," he growled playfully, his hands fondling my breasts. "Your scent is driving me wild."

"I'd like your cream," I replied. "In my cunt, in my mouth . . ."

"I'd like to shoot it in your ass," he murmured, his hand moving down over my quivering belly. His words, his touch, made my pussy tingle. I pictured his long hard cock skewering my most intimate hole, and my stomach muscles tightened in pleasurable anticipation.

"It's a deal," I whispered back. "Shall I turn over?"

"No, stand up," Cordova said. "Then bend over the back of the sofa. I don't just want to butt-fuck you. I want to make love to your ass."

I did as he asked. Placing my feet shoulders'-width

apart, I bent at the waist and placed my hands lightly on the top of the sofa back. Cordova ran his hands along the flat length of my back, telling me to relax. He fondled my breasts and stroked the flat hardness of my belly until I was almost purring with pleasure. He let his hand rest lightly on the rounded swell of my bottom, and my skin burned beneath his touch. Cordova unscrewed a small opaque jar containing a pure white cream with a faint almond scent. He put a generous dab on each of my cheeks and began to massage the smooth skin of my derriere, letting a well-coated finger slide along the crack dividing my half-moons. I was quivering with excitement and when his finger pushed at my asshole, I groaned and moved back against it. Again and again Cordova's finger teased my slick, loosening hole. I began to breathe more heavily and my grip tightened on the soft padded back of the sofa.

"You like this, don't you?" Cordova murmured. "You like my finger in your ass."

"Oh, yes," I moaned. "Just like that. It feels so good."

"This is just the beginning," Cordova promised. "I'm going to make love to your ass like it's never been made love to before. I'm going to make you beg me to fuck your hot little hole with my cock until you cream."

He knelt on the floor between my spread legs so that his face was on a level with my behind. He began to plant kisses on the smooth, taut skin, his hands playing with the damp hair of my pussy as he worked. Then his hands were on my cheeks, pulling them apart and I felt the rough skin of his tongue as it rasped the entire length of the crevice between them. I gasped and my muscles tightened involuntarily, but he held me firm, urging my legs even wider apart. I relaxed and abandoned myself to the ministrations of his flickering tongue darting at the pink puckered hole of my anus. He probed deeper and deeper until I was groaning madly. My hands clutched the sofa and my spine arched, thrusting my buttocks upward.

"Oh God . . . please!" I gasped. "Give it to me now. I want your cock in my ass!"

He needed no further urging. Placing his swollen cock head at the entrance to my rear passage, he slowly pushed into me. Aching for him, I did not resist. I moaned softly and pushed my ass back against his prick as my tiny anus stretched wider and wider to accommodate his bulk. He ran his hands along the underside of my body, cupping my breasts. I sighed with pleasure as my buttocks nestled against his crotch, my asshole full of his wonderful cock.

He held this position for a few moments, then began a long, slow withdrawal. Every nerve responded to this move, tightening, crying out for release. I was like a violin string being played on an ascending scale. I clenched and unclenched my hands, crying out, whimpering in pleasure. He sank back into me and I moved back to meet him. He became more demanding now, plunging faster and deeper. I was totally relaxed, rendered helpless by the exquisite sensation of his hot hard cock in my tight furrow. I moved with him, bucking wildly, tossing my head like an animal in heat. He held my hips for balance, then rammed into me so powerfully that my entire body shook from the impact of his thrusts. I reached between my legs to touch the inflamed lips of my cunt. My pussy was on fire. I pushed my fingers into the sopping orifice, reaching for the hard knob of my clit. My buttock muscles contracted as I stoked the fires of my own lust, increasing the pressure on Cordova's cock. We gyrated wildly, almost out of control. I cried out with pleasure as I felt myself climax, and a moment later Cordova's cock exploded in my ass. The hot creamy cum filled my hole and overflowed down the back of my thighs as his throbbing tool contracted to normal size. I released my hold on the couch and he put his arms around my waist and helped me straighten up. Cordova threw some of the large cushions on the floor and we sank down onto them, too exhausted even to talk. I wanted desperately to close my eyes, but if I fell asleep now, the success of my mission would be in jeopardy. I took three deep breaths, forcing myself to stay awake as beside me Cordova, overcome with wine, food, and physical exertion, slipped off into a deep, noisy slumber.

I got up carefully and, taking my purse, slipped out of the apartment. I went directly to the computer terminal, hoping that some nosy waiter wouldn't decide to pop downstairs in the next few minutes to get a bottle of wine. A naked woman playing with the computer terminal would be pretty hard to explain. Snapping the machine on, I quickly punched in the name of the wine I sought and pressed the data-entry key. I crossed my fingers and watched the screen anxiously. Everything depended on my using the system properly. I figured that I had ten, perhaps fifteen minutes before Cordova woke up. If there was some other interruption, or if I became too numb from the refrigeration to operate the equipment in my purse, the mission would fail. I certainly could never hope to find the bottle in the maze of Cordova's extensive cellar in such a short time without the aid of the computer.

Luck was with me and the computer quickly read out the code number that corresponded to the bottle. Holding my purse, I padded quickly through the rows of bottles, scanning the numbers on the small labels until I finally found the one I wanted. Reaching into the rack, I took out the bottle and blew off the thin layer of dust that had settled on the label. It was a twin to the one I had delivered to Andrei. With trembling fingers I opened my bag and slipped out the microscope from the bogus lipstick case. I could not repress a triumphant cry as the microdot came into focus exactly where David had said it would be. Using the special stick, I lifted it off the label and carefully placed it inside the watch. With a sigh of relief, I replaced the bottle, hurried back to Cordova's apartment, and lay down next to him, rubbing my frozen feet against the warmth of his legs. The cold stirred him awake.

"You are chilled," he murmured, rubbing my hands between his own. "Come, we will dress and I will order some espresso and dessert. You must be hungry after all that activity."

"I'm always hungry," I agreed, "and coffee sounds great."

It was after ten o'clock when we finally said our good-byes. I promised to send Signore Cordova a copy of the article when it appeared, and to visit him the next time I was in Rome. The evening had been an enjoyable one, and I began to think that being a spy was not such a difficult or dangerous job after all. All that remained was to hand over the microdot to David's partner, and my part in the "microdot affair," as I chose to call it, would be over.

I hailed a taxi and directed the driver to take me to the Colosseum.

"It's closed at this hour," he said.

"It doesn't matter," I replied. "I just want to see it by night."

The request was not an unusual one. By day the Colosseum is an anachronism: a pile of rotting stone surrounded by subway stations, parks, sidewalks, and all the confusion and pollution of a modern city. At night, however, it is floodlit at strategic points, giving it a certain eerie magic. It was also to be my meeting place with Marc Baxter. David had described me to Baxter over the phone and felt that he would have no difficulty in recognizing me. He would wait for me from eight o'clock onward, and my instructions were to make contact with him regardless of the outcome of my mission.

I stood near the Colosseum at the northern end by the entrance to the subway station. The city was dark, but the streets were still crowded with cars and the sidewalks with residents and tourists of all nationalities, so I did not attract any particular attention. I leaned against a wall and waited.

Suddenly there was a tap on my shoulder. I started and turned to see a tall man with a plain face standing next to me.

"Miss van Bell?" he said. "I'm Marc Baxter. I'm sorry if I startled you."

If it was useful for a field agent to have an appearance that allows him to blend into a crowd, Baxter certainly fit the bill. He wasn't ugly, but he wasn't handsome either. He had straight brown hair and regular features and wore a pair of lightly tinted, tortoise-shell glasses that obscured the color of his eyes. His ears were perhaps a bit too big, but maybe not. His nose was not too small or too big. And so it went, no matter where you looked. It was the sort of face that you would never give a second look.

"How did everything go?" he asked.

"Before we start that," I said, suddenly feeling cautious, "tell me the password."

"Do I have to?" he said, looking rather embarrassed. "It's not a very nice word."

"How do I know you're really Marc Baxter?" I said. "I wasn't even given a description of you." He sighed and nodded in agreement.

"Cunnilingus," he mumbled. I laughed and shook his hand.

"You're Baxter, all right," I said.

"Thank God it's an English word," he said. "Connelly used to use Italian curse words. I once nearly got killed saying something that I found out later roughly translated as 'your mother's cunt.' ''

"David certainly has a fine sense of fun," I agreed. "He told me that he likes to pull the Agency's beard a bit."

"It's easy for him," Marc said. "He gives the orders, but I'm the one on the front line." There was a tinge of bitterness in his voice, but I pushed away the thought that he might be really angry. David had spoken of him with genuine fondness and had nothing but high praise for his work. Baxter was probably just tired. He had been waiting for me since eight o'clock and it was now after eleven.

"Well, I had pretty good luck," I said, changing the subject. I slipped the watch off my wrist and handed it to him. "I think you'll find everything in order."

"That's terrific," he beamed. "It would have taken us months to break into that cellar. When Connelly said that he was using a civilian for this job, I was very much against it but he's proved me wrong."

"Always glad to help," I said modestly.

"I wish I could take you for a drink to celebrate but I have to wrap this up. Connelly will be waiting for my call."

"Give him my best," I said. He gave me a sharp look.

"Will you be staying in Rome?"

"No," I replied. "I'm returning to Paris."

"Then perhaps we'll meet again. I'll be working with Connelly until this assignment is finished."

"I don't think so," I said. "This was strictly a one-shot deal. I'm rich and lazy by profession."

"Too bad," he responded. "But this was certainly a fine piece of work. Well, I have to get going. Thank you again, Miss van Bell . . ."

"Christina."

"Christina," he said, smiling.

I watched him walk away, then set off in the opposite direction to find a phone. My job was done, Sam was waiting for my call, and I intended to forget all about secret agents and microdots for the next few hours.

CHAPTER EIGHT

A taxi deposited me at the doorstep of Adaline's Paris home two days later. Upon entering the house, I discovered an agitated Madame Poret waiting for me.

"It is your American friend Mr. Connelly," she complained. "For the past two days he has called three, perhaps four times a day, asking for you. Then this morning after you called to tell me you were coming home, I give him this news and he comes straight over here to wait for you."

"You mean David is here? Now?"

"He is in there," she replied, waving in the general direction of the living room, "reading the newspapers and smelling up the furniture with his filthy cigarettes. I told him that when you came home you would throw him out on his ass but he pretends not to understand me. Go inside and throw him out."

"He is probably just anxious to see me," I said soothingly. "I never said I was coming right back from Rome but I don't think he expected me to be away for so long."

"He is in love with you," said Madame Poret. "That is why he behaves so."

"I'll take him out of the living room," I said. "Then you can empty the ashtrays."

"Do you want dinner?"

"Later perhaps. I want to rest first."

"I don't think you want to do that," said Madame Poret, giving me a knowing look. "Not with that handsome young man, eh?"

"You're right," I laughed. "I did have something else in mind."

"Well, see that he doesn't smoke in bed," said Madame Poret as she went toward the kitchen. "It's very dangerous."

"I'll make sure that he has something to put in his mouth besides cigarettes," I promised.

I found David sitting over a copy of *Le Monde*, a French-English dictionary on the coffee table in front of him. There was an overflowing ashtray near his feet and the room smelled strongly of stale tobacco.

"Having fun?" I said, throwing open a window and letting in a blast of cold fresh air. "Madame Poret tells me you've been a millstone around her neck for days. Why aren't you out there hunting for commies in the public toilets instead of bothering honest Frenchmen in their homes?"

"Christina!" he said, jumping to his feet and catching me in a bear hug that nearly took my breath away. "Thank God you're all right!"

"Why shouldn't I be?"

"You checked out of your hotel two days ago. I expected you to come right home, and when you didn't show up I figured that you'd been kidnapped. I was all set to come after you when your housekeeper told me you'd phoned this morning."

"I think you overreacted," I said. "I was visiting a friend in Rome."

"Oh?"

"Mmmm. Sam Brentwood. You might have heard of him. He's a fairly well-known artist. We met for the first time many years ago, and this seemed like the perfect opportunity to renew our acquaintance."

"How romantic!" he said, glaring at me.

"Jealous?"

"Of course," he admitted, blushing furiously. "Who wouldn't be? But as I didn't know you were shacking up with an old lover, my concern had nothing to do with jealousy."

"I can take care of myself," I said, sitting down next to him and lightly tracing the line of his jaw with my finger.

"This is a risky business, Christina. I would never have forgiven myself if anything had happened to you."

"As nothing did happen, let's just forget the whole thing," I murmured, leaning closer and blowing gently into his ear.

"I don't want to forget it," he grumbled. "I want to talk about it now."

"Are you sure?" I said, licking the outer ridges of his ear and pulling gently on the fleshy part of his earlobe with my teeth.

"Well, maybe not," he sighed, taking me in his arms. His lips closed over mine and I sighed softly and relaxed against him. I put my arms around his neck and snuggled my face against his cheek as he lifted me in his arms and carried me upstairs.

We undressed hurriedly and got beneath the covers in the big pink bed. I had been anything but celibate the last three days, but the feel of David's hands on my body, of his hot lips on mine, were like old friends, familiar yet exciting at the same time. He burrowed beneath the covers and began to kiss and fondle my pubic area, stroking the soft, springy hairs of my pussy and licking the long wet slit of my nether lips. I breathed deeply, my flesh tingling with desire. I took his hand and placed it on my breast beneath the cover, hungry for his touch. His tongue probed the entrance to my slippery canal as his hands massaged my breasts and stroked my hips and thighs. He seemed to be everywhere at once and my cunt juices started to flow, trickling down the inner side of my thighs. I spread my legs and reached beneath the covers to hold my pussy lips apart.

David's tongue plunged the full length of my shivering canal, lapping at my engorged clitoris and then swirling around the tip of my clit until I was thrashing about and screaming in passion. I climaxed in shuddering surrender, but he didn't let me rest. Again and again he stoked my internal fire until I lay panting with exhaustion, the tears rolling helplessly down my cheeks.

"Welcome home," he whispered, emerging from under the covers and stretching out next to me. He held me tightly, his front against my back. His arm encircled the tender fullness of my breasts and his leg thrust between my thighs. He toyed idly with my nipples, his free hand stroking the indentation of my waist and the gentle swell of my hips. I sighed with pleasure as his touch stirred familiar longings, and I moved closer against him in the warm intimacy of the bed. With a swift, sure movement, David guided his prick into my well-lubricated pussy from the rear.

"Oh God!" I moaned softly, relaxing my body to allow him maximum entry space in this awkward position. "That feels so good." My hot pussy juices began to flow as David gently moved his bulging cock in and out of my steamy passage. I lay as still as I could, encouraging him with little moans and gasps of delight. I let him call the shots, relinquishing my body to his pleasure. He understood my lack of response and seemed excited by this total control of my body. He paused every couple of thrusts to let me savor the feeling of his fullness in my cunt, prolonging his own pleasure as long as possible. He was breathing heavily now and I could feel his body trembling behind me. My own body was trembling too, building once again toward climax. My stomach muscles tightened, and unable to control my reactions any longer, I began to move my pussy back against his cock.

"That's right, baby," David whispered as he increased the rhythm of his thrusts. "You want it too. You want it every bit as much as I do."

"Oh, yes," I moaned hotly. "Your cock feels so good. It's so hard inside of me. Fuck me. Fuck me hard!" I squirmed and wriggled against him, my words and my body a lewd invitation.

Fired by my words and my movements, David started pounding his steellike pole into my burning cunt, moving against me in a savage, grinding motion. I tightened my vaginal muscles and he exploded inside me, his climax triggering my own, as his warm, milky cum filled my soaking canal and overflowed down the back of my legs.

Totally spent, we lay for a long time in the pool of our love juices, touching and kissing each other with a gratifying sense of mutual contentment.

At last, driven by hunger from the warm peacefulness of our bed, we decided to eat at an elegant restaurant to celebrate our reunion and the success of my mission.

I sent David back to his hotel to find something more elegant to wear than slacks and a sweater. Then I showered and changed, selecting a simple black dress that showed my diamonds to perfection.

I picked David up in my car, refusing for once to use the government heap. "We'll be much less conspicuous in the Maserati than in that pile of tin," I pointed out, "and we won't get a ticket for having a broken muffler."

David thought this over, then agreed with the wisdom of my remarks. Unlike a great many men, he was not pigheadedly insistent on doing things his own way all the time. I did, however, relinquish the wheel without protest when he offered to drive. I have discovered that men and women hold different opinions as to the proper way to operate a motor vehicle, and I did not want to open up a potential can of worms.

I directed him to a small but very expensive five-star establishment located between Avenue de l'Opéra and Place Vendôme. I chatted briefly with the maître d', dropping a few names known only to the cream of Parisian social circles, and we were escorted to a small table near a window.

David perused the menu carefully, looking for something that would please his miserably American palate.

"All of this damned French bilge," he muttered. "Sauces and crepes and peculiar fish. What's steak tartar? Can I get that with fries, do you suppose?"

"That's raw steak," I said.

"You mean cooked rare," he said.

"No, I mean like off the cow's ass and onto your plate," I said, smiling sweetly. He paled visibly.

"If they heard about that in Texas, they'd probably declare war on France," he moaned. "Texas *would* do that, you know. They're very independent that way."

"You have to expand your horizons," I insisted. "Why not try the blowfish? It's fresh and the head chef here prepares it in a special sauce."

"Listen, little lady," David said, leaning over the table and affecting a heavy Western drawl, "where I come from, people understand the value of good food. We don't puree it, or dunk it in sissy sauces, or eat it raw! We take a big fat old cow and slaughter it, then we dig a pit and stick that dead cow on a spit over a blazing fire and turn it slowly for a few hours. Then we carve it up into big bloody slabs and serve it with a heap of potatoes and a mess of salad and a few cold cans of beer. *That* is your haute cuisine."

"You make it all sound so delicious, I can hardly resist," I said sarcastically. "Especially the part about the bloody slabs. Mmmmm." I stuck my tongue out at him playfully. "Animal! Go live in a tree!"

This argument, the latest in a continuing series, went on for several more minutes, at which time we agreed on a truce in the interests of getting some food into our stomachs before dawn. I ordered Sole Ana-dalouse (sole poached in white wine with peppers and tomatoes) and David had steak tartar, cooked medium rare. I could tell by the waiter's expression as he took our orders that we would have to leave an outrageous tip to avoid being banned from the restaurant in future.

"What happens next in the great microdot hunt?" I asked as we began on our salads. I had impressed upon David that salad was eaten as a separate course, not with the main dish, and that the waiter wouldn't bring his steak until he had finished both his salad and the white wine I had ordered to be served with this course.

"Do you really want to know," David asked, "or are you just trying to stick to a safe topic?"

"A bit of both," I replied truthfully. "I'm glad my part in this caper is over, but I can't help being curious as to how it all turns out."

"Well, while you were . . . ahem . . . vacationing in Rome, we successfully followed up leads on two more bottles. Unfortunately these both proved to be duds."

"That must have been disappointing," I murmured sympathetically.

"It was, but as we continue to eliminate the duds, the chances that the remaining bottles will have a microdot are increased."

"Do you have any other leads?"

"As a matter of fact we do, but there's a bit of a problem with this one."

"Which is?"

"Well, so far most of the bottles have been bought by wine collectors like Cordova, who are likely to put the bottle into their cellars and let it sit for a while. The collector's squirrel instinct works in our favor for it gives us time to get to the bottle."

"I take it that this isn't true in the present case."

"In this case," David sighed, lighting a cigarette, "it appears that the bottle has fallen into the hands of someone who doesn't collect wine and is more than likely to drain the damned thing and throw the bottle into the garbage before we can get to it. We have to move fast or the microdot, if it's really on that bottle's label, will be lost."

"You found the others fast enough," I pointed out. "I thought your agency was giving this job top priority."

"I can tell you don't have a government job," David laughed, but there was a tinge of bitterness in his voice. "Saying that your job has top priority, that you have all the manpower and backup services you could want, doesn't make it true. It's the government's way of making any failure to successfully complete an assignment your fault rather than theirs. My three new agents were just 'temporarily' reassigned to another 'top priority' job," he explained, seeming to put sarcastic quotes around his words. "Both Marc and I are too well known in that area to go there ourselves. In a major city we could get lost in the crowd but not this place."

"Exactly where are we talking about?" I asked.

"India," said David. "Specifically, a little rural town near Poona, on the Arabian Sea, called Pondiswah. Population a few hundred. It's a rural community full of farms and goats and Muslims."

"And a bottle of Rumanian wine," I laughed. "How on earth did it ever end up there?"

"By a pretty crazy series of coincidences," he agreed. "It was originally bought from a dealer by a financier as a present for his mistress, who liked rare wines. Well, the mistress was unfaithful, and in a fit of anger the financier gave the wine to his chaffeur. The chauffeur was a Muslim and didn't drink, so he gave it to his brother-in-law, a poor farmer, who traded it to the servant of the current owner for a pound of English tea."

"That's about three and a half dollars," I said.

"Right. Wine is hard to come by in rural India and the nonnative population will drink just about anything that crosses their path. Because of the climate it's expensive to have a wine cellar, so even good wine will be consumed almost immediately. The present owner is a retired British Army colonel by the name of Edward Brooke Kensington. He joined the British occupation army in India in the late thirties and quickly rose to be governor of a remote southern area near Poona. When India gained her independence after the war, he seemed to get lost in the shuffle. The army kept sending him his pay for a few years, then discovered their mistake and tried to discharge him. He promptly retired, and has been living on his pension ever since. Never went home. He must be in his midsixties by now."

"Perhaps he's planning to give the wine to *his* mistress for Christmas," I suggested. "That would give you about eight weeks unless they quarrel, and you'd probably have your agents back by then."

"Very funny," David growled. "The way my luck is running, he's probably a lush who gets off playing with himself and can't wait to slog the stuff down with his chappatis and buffalo milk. I must get that bottle, Christina, and all kidding aside, you can see the problem I'm faced with, can't you?"

"I suppose so," I agreed.

"Good!" he said heartily. "I knew I could count on you."

"Count on me for what?"

"Why, to go to Pondiswah and recover that bottle, of course."

"Now, hold on, James Bond," I protested. "I've already done you one favor and it was a kick and all, but that was supposed to be a one-time deal, remember? I'm not in the employ of this agency of yours, and I don't have time to go all the way to some backwater town in India to find a damned wine bottle."

David leaned back in his chair and squinted at me through a haze of blue smoke. "I thought you had some patriotic feeling," he said. "Your country needs you, Christina."

"Uncle Sam doesn't need me. You do," I snapped. "You're the one who let them decimate your staff so that you're left with your finger in the dike. I already did my bit for my country, remember? And I already got back to Zelanko for the way he tricked me, so forget about that ploy too. It won't work."

"You're right, Christina," said David seriously. "You're an intelligent woman and I shouldn't try to trick you. How about money? A bribe? A few bucks in the old pocket?"

"I'm hardly in need of money . . ." I began.

"Everybody needs money," he said, pulling out an old wallet and going through the billfold. "Here we are. Twenty bucks, cash. You don't have to declare it on your tax form or anything. The IRS will never know."

"You're a crazy man, do you know that?" I sighed.

"I'll throw in another . . . let's see, fifty cents, seventy-five cents . . ." He rummaged comically through his pockets, the deadpan seriousness of his performance making me laugh.

"Okay, okay, I'll do it," I said softly, feeling for the moment oddly tender and protective toward him. "You obviously need all the help you can get. I'll even do it for free, just for you. You can save the money to pay for dinner."

"That's terrific, Christina . . . I mean *you're* terrific . . . I mean you're more than terrific. I have all the information ready and the transportation arranged. You can use the same equipment to recover the microdot, if there is one."

"When do I leave?"

"Tomorrow morning."

I narrowed my eyes and glared at him suspiciously. "You sound as if you counted pretty heavily on my helping you," I said. "What makes you so insufferably sure of yourself?"

"I know the kind of woman you are," he said, winking. "You wouldn't let me down in a tight spot. That's the code of the brotherhood of spies, and you're one of us now."

"I suppose so," I sighed. "But remember, the last one was for Uncle Sam, this one is for you, and that's the end of it. You don't have any more cards to play from this hand, understand?"

"You're beautiful when you're angry," David teased, leaning across the small table and cupping my chin in his hand. For an instant my cool self-assurance crumbled. I felt as if I had never kissed, never touched, never desired anyone before as I desired this man.

We spent the night making love, and from the passionate force of his lovemaking, I gathered that David was trying to avoid my taking another little vacation after locating this next wine bottle.

David had arranged an early morning flight to Bombay, where a small plane would help me make the connection to Pondiswah. David drove me to the airport, keeping up a steady stream of instructions while I drank a thermos of hot coffee liberally laced with brandy and tried to pay attention to what he was telling me.

Counting on being able to talk me into this assignment, David had called a contact in the British M.I.5, who dug through old army files and came up with the names of officers who had served with Kensington in India. Selecting the name of an officer who was of the same age and likely to have been friends with Kensington, David forged his name to a telegram informing Kensington that his goddaughter Christina was en route to Ceylon via Poona to take part in a geological study. Would Kensington please put her up for the night and look after her as a favor to an old friend? David felt that Kensington would probably agree out of a sense of loyalty to his old comrade and not even think of questioning the veracity of the telegram.

The Air India flight to Bombay took six hours, but as India is five hours ahead of Paris time, I arrived too late to make my connecting flight before the following morning. I booked myself into a deluxe hotel, made some new friends at the bar, then joined them for dinner and a swim and finally for more intimate activities upstairs. I returned to the airport the next morning just in time to make my connecting flight, full of pleasant memories, black coffee, and dexedrine and ready to resume my career as a secret agent.

The plane that took me from Bombay to Pondiswah was a two-engine, propeller-driven DC3 flown by an Indian pilot who obviously thought we were in rehearsal for a World War II John Wayne movie. After he landed me, exhausted and shaking, on a flat strip of land a half-day's journey from the village, I was forced to cover the rest of the distance in the ox cart of a passing farmer. Stretched out on the hay in the back of the cart, my head pillowed on my knapsack and my pith helmet over my face to keep off the sun, I began to see that there was a side to being a spy that I hadn't contemplated. Though I was young enough to easily pass as a graduate student, it had been a long time since I had traveled in anything less than first-class accommodations. I hoped that Colonel Kensington would have a decent bed, indoor plumbing, and something more to eat than bitter tea and rotis.

It was dusk when I arrived in town, and once there I used my limited Hindustani to inquire as to the Colonel's whereabouts. I expected to be directed to his house, or hut, as the case might be, but I was told that he was waiting for me in the town's only restaurant.

It was a far cry from Lutèce, with a packed dirt floor and a beaded curtain over the doorway, but it was wonderfully dark and cool inside. I had dressed for the heat in tight white pants, a tailored white shirt, and low-heeled, knee-high black leather boots, and I stood out among the colorfully dressed, dark-skinned, black-haired natives like a diamond in a coal pile. All activity stopped when I entered.

I recognized the Colonel immediately. He stood well over six feet with the odd erect bearing that is the legacy of years of military training. He had white hair, brushed straight back, keen gray eyes, and the thick mustache favored by British officers of his generation, an emulation of Lord Kitchener. He still wore his military uniform, and his broad chest was decorated with ribbons and medals attesting to a long and honorable career. He turned when I entered, and his eyes lit with pleasure as he came toward me.

"Colonel Kensington? I'm—"

"—Christina van Bell, of course," he said, taking my hand in his and squeezing it painfully. "I got your telegram this morning. I would have fetched you but I did not know where you were starting out from or how you were traveling. We're not on any direct route here."

"I made out just fine," I said, smiling, dismissing almost ten hours of bone-weary travel with a casual wave of my hand.

"That's right. You're Ginger Morton's goddaughter, aren't you? You'd better be up to anything. Rough country for a woman, though. Bet you could do with a hot bath and some proper food."

I didn't need to be asked twice. "My godfather used to hold me on his lap and tell me stories of your adventures," I said as he took my arm and led me outside.

"He did, eh? Well, perhaps later I'll hold you on my lap and tell you some stories of my own," he said. His tone was lightly teasing, but I could tell that he was not averse to the idea of further intimacy. I smiled and held his arm a bit tighter so that we were forced to walk very close together. There is a bit of the little girl in all women. It's what makes older men so appealing.

The Colonel lived in a large, lumpy-looking sandstone house about twenty miles beyond the center of town. It was neither English nor Indian in design, the architect having been unable to reconcile his vision with the building materials at hand, but it was structurally sound and adequately lit, as the Colonel had a small generator which he ran on dung purchased from the local goat herders.

We entered the house and I looked about me curiously while the Colonel called for his servant. "Cuff, where are you, man?" he bellowed in a voice that rang through the house. "We have a guest. Come and see to her bag!"

"Hold your water, you blasted buffalo," came a cracking voice from the next room. "I'm coming!"

Moments later Sergeant Cuff made his appearance. He was at least ten years older than the Colonel, and was considerably smaller than his employer. He was a stiff, spare figure with a fringe of white hair and big hands and feet. He wore a faded military uniform and shuffled long, peering myopically through wire-framed spectacles.

"What's the big emergency?" he wheezed. "I have dinner burning in the oven, can't just walk away from it, you know. Here now, who's this?" he said, stabbing a grimy finger at me.

"I told you we were having a visitor," Kensington said. "Christina van Bell, this is Sergeant Cuff. Miss van Bell is passing through on her way to Ceylon, and we were asked to put her up for the night. She's Ginger Morton's goddaughter. You remember Ginger Morton, don't you?"

"No," said the old man impassively.

"You must remember Ginger," the Colonel said helpfully. "Why, he was the major in our unit. In charge of local transportation or some such rubbish. Big man with flaming red hair . . ."

"Ginger Morton," the old man nodded. "Yes, of course. I remember now."

"Good old Ginger," the Colonel sighed. "And this lovely young woman is his goddaughter."

"Your godfather and I spent many years together out here," Cuff wheezed.

"He's a fine man," I said.

"He was a filthy swine," Cuff spat. "Ran off with the mess fund, as I recall, and left me holding the bag. I did thirty days in the hole. Always hated him after that."

"Nevertheless, Miss van Bell is our guest," Colonel Kensington said hastily. "Take her bags up to the guest rooms and we'll have dinner as soon as she freshens up. She must be famished. I know I am."

"Nag, nag, that's all you do," the old man grumbled, picking up my knapsack and dragging it behind him up the stairs. "Forty-five years of your nagging, it's .enough to drive an honest man bonkers."

I followed him upstairs, hoping that the microdot equipment would not be damaged.

From his appearance and his military background, I had expected the Colonel's home to be furnished like a camp barracks and was surprised to find it a motley collection of mismatched, overstuffed furniture that had probably been left behind by various English officials when they had departed for home. My bedroom had a cherry wood four-poster bed with a faded, handmade patchwork coverlet and a braided wool rug on the floor. There were a number of oil paintings on the wall, including an original by Harry Hall, the famous sporting artist, and I wondered if the Colonel knew the true value of it.

I bathed and changed, choosing a green-and-white striped T-shirt dress and low-heeled sandals. I carefully placed my phony lipstick case and mascara tube in a white cotton purse and went downstairs to dinner.

There was a portrait of King George at one end of the long dining room and of Lord Kitchener at the other. Numerous other photos stood on the sideboard, showing groups of military men standing in rigid poses in front of stately Indian structures.

Sergeant Cuff had prepared a typical English meal —rare roast beef, served at room temperature, boiled potatoes, and some very overdone vegetables. There was a bottle of whiskey on the table and two eight-ounce glass tumblers.

"Would you like a drink with your dinner?" the Colonel asked, placing a thick slab of bloody meat on my plate.

"I'm afraid I'm not used to whiskey," I lied, meaning that I was not used to whiskey with my dinner. "Do you have any wine?"

The Colonel thought for a second, then his face brightened. "I think Cuff got some just the other day," he said. "Some commie brand. Not French. Not red either, for that matter. We're not near a major city and there's no regular supply here. The natives are all Muslims, so they don't drink."

"White wine will be just fine," I assured him, trying not to appear too anxious.

"Cuff, bring that commie wine in here and pour the young lady a drink!" Kensington bellowed, passing me the vegetables.

Cuff shuffled slowly into the room, his face set in a sullen expression. "Don't you have anything better to do than yell at me all day?" he grumbled. "Why don't you get yourself a wife? A nice young girl to give you a heart attack on your wedding night." He was carrying a bottle, and I felt my pulse quicken as he placed it on the table and fumbled beneath his apron for a corkscrew. It was all I could do to remain calm when I saw that it was indeed the bottle of wine that I sought.

"Would you like me to pour?" said the Colonel helpfully.

"You'd only show yourself up," Cuff said. "Probably pour the stuff into the bloody tumbler. You'd drink bloody sterno if I didn't stop you." He produced two wine glasses from his apron pocket and carefully wiped them clean. "I'll pour it. Mind if I have a drop myself or would that be too much to ask his Lordship?"

"Not at all, help yourself," said Kensington grandly. "You bought the stuff."

"Traded your best tea for it," said Cuff gleefully, handing me a glass and filling his own.

"Here's to our lovely guest," the Colonel said, raising his tumbler.

"Up yours," Cuff toasted him, tossing back the wine in a gulp. "Pardon me, Miss van Bell, but I have to assemble the trifle." He wandered off to the kitchen.

"Rather cheeky for a servant, isn't he?" I asked.

The Colonel laughed and nodded. "After forty-five years with me, I'm afraid old Cuff has a touch of cabin fever," he agreed. "He misses the excitement of army life. He used to bully all the young recruits and now there's only me to fight with. But what the hell, eh? Adds a bit of spice to the day."

He refilled my glass, and as we ate and talked, I kept trying to figure out a way to get alone with the bottle before we finished our meal and Cuff cleared the table. Colonel Kensington did not seem inclined to excuse himself for a side trip to the bathroom and even if he did, there was still Sergeant Cuff to worry about. I considered finishing the wine and asking to keep the bottle as a souvenir but dismissed it as too obvious a ploy.

I studied the Colonel over the rim of my glass. He was handsome in his uniform, and though the difference in our ages was considerable, I found myself attracted to him. I am not usually reticent where my sexual desires are concerned, but here, as with the wine bottle, I felt it was important not to be too obvious.

We had both consumed a great deal of alcohol. We had discussed the incompetence of the Indian government, the deplorable condition of the Indian roads, the superiority of the English educational system, and how much better things were when the Colonel was my age.

"The trouble with the modern generation," said the Colonel sagely, "is that they're too tense and anxious all the time. They consult astrologers and headshrinkers, invest in group therapy and biofeedback and marriage counseling and est. All utter rubbish!"

"Why is that?"

"It's too verbal. People should talk less and touch more. The art of relaxation lies with the hands, not the head. I have a little gadget that, if used properly, will do more than all the pill pushers and head doctors put together."

"Sounds great," I said. "Why don't you show me."

"It's rather an intimate technique," the Colonel stammered, getting very red. "You may not like being placed in my hands in quite this manner."

"Oh, but I would," I said softly. "It sounds very . . . educational."

His face lit up as he took in the meaning of my words. "Well, very well then. I suppose we can give it a go if you're really keen on the idea. Why don't we go upstairs where we can have a bit more privacy."

He led the way out of the dining room, and I casually picked up my empty wine glass and the bottle and followed him upstairs. The Colonel's bedroom was a bit more spartan than the rest of the house, with simple wood furniture and a large four-poster bed with a plain white cover. The room was warm, and a large ancient wooden ceiling fan circulated slowly, creating a hot breeze. The Colonel went over to a tall armoire and opened the doors. I put my bottle and glass down unobtrusively on the nearest dresser and went to look over his shoulder. Kneeling down, he opened a small drawer in the lower right-hand corner and removed a carved mahogany box, which he handed to me. Inside was an elaborate battery-operated vibrator with an assortment of removable tips. Keeping to my pose as a naive graduate student, I pretended to be surprised.

"I've never seen one of these," I said. "What is it?"

"It's . . . ahem . . . an electric massage," said the Colonel. "Lie down on the bed, my dear, and I'll demonstrate it for you."

I did not need to be asked twice. Slipping off my shoes, I lay down on the bed. The Colonel picked up an attachment with many small rubber teeth and, sitting down next to me, began to move the vibrator gently over my neck and shoulders. I closed my eyes and sank back against the pillows, letting the low hum of the vibrator and the light touch of the rubber needles lull me into a state of total repose. My body began to grow warm. I was not wearing a bra and as the Colonel moved the vibrator over my breasts, I felt a stirring in my loins as my nipples swelled and stiffened. I gave a faint moan and instinctively opened my legs, arching my hips slightly upward. I was breathing more heavily now and my skin burned beneath the thin material of my dress.

"Would you like to feel this against your bare skin?" the Colonel murmured, centering the vibrator on my mons in a way that made me gasp.

"Yes, please," I moaned, turning over onto my stomach so that he could reach the zipper on my dress. I heard a soft whoosh, then the material parted and a current of warm air blew across my bare back. He moved the dress over my shoulders and peeled it down over my arms, slipping them from the sleeves so that I was naked from the waist up. He placed the vibrator against my flaming skin and my hands clutched at the covers as the rubber needles slid up and down the hard, bumpy curve of my spine from the base of my neck to the top of my buttocks. Now he very slowly finished undressing me, rolling my dress down over my hips and legs and flinging it aside. He deftly removed my panties, and I heard the sharp intake of his breath as his eyes devoured my naked form, spread out for his enjoyment. He continued to move the vibrator over my back for a few moments longer. Then with a click he switched the vibrator tip to one with a phallic shape. He gently parted my ass cheeks with his fingers and began to tease the small pink hole of my anus. I gave a loud cry, my hips involuntarily bucking up and down.

"Get up on your knees," he whispered, and I did as I was bid, crouching in the center of the bed. I spread my knees, thrusting my behind up into the air.

He moved in back of me and, switching the vibrator to a higher speed, pushed it against the swollen lips of my pussy. My entire body tensed, then relaxed as the vibrator slid deeper and deeper into my aching hole. The Colonel knew just how to manipulate the tip to keep me on the brink of orgasm without allowing me the ultimate release. I could hear his heavy breathing as my body responded to his unspoken commands. I knew that he was excited and this turned me on even more.

Finally, by an almost imperceptible increase of pressure on my clit, he brought me to an explosive series of orgasms. I felt as if a string of firecrackers had gone off as the vibrator continued to move in my spasming hole until I collapsed face down on the bed, too exhausted to move.

When I rolled over and opened my eyes, the Colonel had taken off his jacket and unbuttoned his shirt. His face was flushed and a thin film of sweat matted the white hairs on his chest. The material of his pants was stretched taut by what appeared to be a massive hard-on, and my body tingled at the thought of taking it into my mouth.

I quickly sat up on the bed and, reaching out, gently massaged his swollen organ through the material of his trousers. The Colonel's body responded immediately to my touch. He did not protest or pull away, so I reached for his zipper and slowly released the turgid pole of his manhood till it stood almost straight out in front of him. I slid to the floor so it was inches from my face, a drop of moisture glistening at the tip. Holding it almost reverently, I took his quivering shaft hungrily into my mouth. I have sucked a great many cocks, yet I never tire of performing this particular sexual act. No two cocks are exactly alike, just as no two men are the same, and this simple ritual is new and exciting for me each and every time. The Colonel was not a young man, yet his cock was surprisingly soft and smooth and of a particularly delicate shade of pink. As I slid my lips over the applelike head and down the silky shaft, the Colonel's hands caught at the golden tresses of my hair to steady my head as he silently urged me to swallow as much of him as I could. I felt my body softening as I worked, melting toward him. I closed my eyes, letting the smell of his maleness and the feel of his cock in my mouth dominate my senses. I could easily have brought him to orgasm, but I took my time, prolonging both his pleasure and my own as long as possible. The Colonel's eyes were closed, his muscles tensing and relaxing as I licked and sucked furiously at his swollen shaft. My hands tugged at the belt of his pants and they dropped around his ankles. I pulled his shorts over his hips, cupping his throbbing balls in my hands, then raking my fingernails along his ass cheeks. With a hoarse cry his control broke and gushes of hot, creamy cum spurted deep into my throat. I fought the gag reflex and swallowed every bit of his precious gift, relishing the salt-sweet taste of it.

He was still trembling as he pulled off his shirt and stepped out of the puddle of clothes on the floor. I had climbed back on the bed, and he sank down beside me, his body now totally relaxed. His penis lay soft and limp against my leg, but I was not ready to retire it just yet. I was hot and horny, and with the real thing in my hand, I would be damned if I was going to masturbate myself to orgasm.

I began to softly stroke his limp organ, coaxing it awake. His eyes were half-closed but as his breathing quickened, I could tell that he was not indifferent to my expert ministrations. I continued to work my magic until, like a snake awakening from a long rest, his prick began a slow but certain resurrection.

I sat up and straddled his prostrate form, spreading my legs as wide as I could. Holding his cock in my hand, I guided it to my well-lubricated pussy, rubbing the tip along the outer edge before inserting it inside. His eyes were open now, watching me. He arched his hips as I slid down his swollen shaft until I felt the slap of his balls against my ass. In this reversed missionary position, it was I who controlled the rhythm and tempo of our lovemaking. The Colonel gripped my buttocks as I raised and lowered myself on his slick, engorged pole, leaning forward so that my breasts were in tantalizing reach of his mouth. He took the hint, catching greedily at the distended nipples with his lips and teeth as his hands roamed over my hips. I could feel my orgasm beginning to build and I speeded up the tempo of my movements, sweeping the Colonel along with me in a sweating, groaning confluence of passion. I threw back my head and gave a loud cry as I forced his climax from him. My own orgasm exploded seconds later as his hot cum coated the throbbing walls of my cunt.

I tightened the muscles of my vagina to hold him inside of me as long as possible, then I collapsed down next to him, letting the hot air from the fan dry the sweat on my body and the gentle hum of the motor lull the Colonel into a deep, peaceful sleep. Mata Hari must have also done a lot of work on her back, I thought as I eased myself off the bed and padded over to the dresser where I had left the wine bottle. I took out my equipment and surveyed the label through my magnifying lens, giving a small cry of triumph as the microdot came into view. Within seconds it was safely secreted inside my watch, and I tipped the last of the wine into the glass and toasted myself.

"Christina van Bell, superspy," I said softly, then smiled as I thought of how pleased David would be with my success.

CHAPTER NINE

The powerful engines of the 707 hummed as the pilot dipped the jet slightly to starboard, dropping below the cloud bank and bringing the panorama of night-time Paris into view. Far below, the city was a multi-colored fairyland, and an unaccustomed wave of homesickness washed over me. David would be waiting for me, and I found myself eagerly looking forward to seeing him again. Madame Poret would have said I was in love, and I toyed with the idea as I fastened my seat belt but could come to no satisfactory conclusion. There was a romance, a mystique about the adventure I had been involved in these past few weeks and David was part of it. I could not separate him out, imagine him, say, in the living room of my New York penthouse. It was a bit like being in a movie and falling in love with the leading man. My hand strayed to the watch I still wore on my left wrist. The microdot was nestled safely in its secret compartment beneath the crystal and I smiled, happy that the adventure was drawing to a successful close.

The gentleman in the next seat noticed my smile. He was a middle-aged Englishman, wearing a conservative blue suit and carrying a small attaché case.

"You seem to be pleased about something," he commented.

"Just glad to be back in Paris," I replied.

"It's a very romantic city from all I've heard," he said wistfully. "I wish I had time to stay and visit, but I have to catch a connecting flight to London. I have a board meeting tomorrow morning. Someday I'm going to stop in all the places I've been forced to rush through on my way to the top of the corporate ladder."

"I know how you feel," I said. "I was in India for just two days. Finished my business and had to rush right home. I didn't even see the Taj Mahal."

"What sort of business are you in?" he asked.

I looked around carefully, then wiggled my finger to motion him closer. He looked surprised but played along, putting his ear next to my lips.

"Can you keep a secret?" I whispered mysteriously.

"Cross my heart," he said, making the appropriate sign.

"I'm a spy," I said.

"Well, you certainly could have fooled me," he said. "It must be very difficult work."

"Difficult on the lower back," I said, giving him a sly wink. "But it's all in the service of my country."

"The Americans are very lucky to have you, Miss . . . er . . ."

"I travel under the name of Countess Von Plume," I said. "My real name is known only to three people. And my mother, of course, but she's sworn to secrecy."

"You can count on my discretion," he said, smiling. "I understand how it is."

We both laughed and I could see that he considered me nothing more than an enchanting liar. I wondered what he would think if he knew that I was telling him the truth. I bet his mustache would curl.

The plane bumped gently as it hit the runway, and less than half an hour later I was walking through customs and out into the crowded terminal. I had commandeered a redcap to haul my knapsack and he trailed behind me as I searched the floor for David. For a moment I thought he had not come—he had never actually said he was going to—but then I spotted him standing near a bank of telephones, and I called his name and waved. He smiled and walked quickly toward me, catching me in a bear hug and whirling me around.

"Hello, darling," he said loudly, kissing me passionately. "Pretend you were on a geological expedition," he whispered in my ear. Then, loudly, "Did you have a good time?"

"As good a time as possible in a place like that," I said conversationally as he tipped the redcap and retrieved my knapsack. "It isn't the sort of place I would recommend for much beyond a rest cure for the terminally nervous. It's like a Midwestern town with curry. They roll up the flying carpet at nine o'clock."

"Did you get the rock samples you went for?" he said, taking my arm.

"Oh, yes, all taken care of," I replied coolly. "Do you want to see them?"

"Later, dear, let's get you home first," he said lightly as we exited the building.

"What was all that about?" I asked when we had settled ourselves into the car and David had started the engine.

"Airports are to espionage agents what the Bellmore Cafeteria is to New York cabbies," David explained as we raced toward Paris. "We meet each other here to have coffee and exchange gossip about newcomers, but it's not a safe place to conduct business. So you were a success, huh? I knew you would be.''

I carefully slipped off my wristwatch and dropped it into the inside pocket of his sports jacket. "As I recall," I said, "this places you heavily in my debt. I think you can start paying me back tonight. I want to have a nice late dinner on the Champs-Élysées, then a riotous evening in the sack." I leaned over and nibbled at his ear, blowing softly into it, then licking around the outer rim. David gripped the steering wheel, fighting to maintain control.

"You're on," he gasped. "But I have to take care of a little business first."

"Are you sure?" I whispered, reaching down to cup his genitals through the soft wool of his pants. He groaned audibly and the car swerved slightly.

"Chrissakes, not when I'm driving," he moaned. "They'll be scraping us both off the pavement if you keep that up."

"Can't the business wait?"

"I have to get this microdot back to the States," he said firmly. "Marc is waiting for me, and there's no sense in keeping him on pins and needles while I'm off having a good time with you."

"Why can't I go with you?" I asked. "It won't blow your cover. I've already met Mr. Baxter, remember?"

"How could I forget?" David laughed. "He asks about you every time we talk."

"That's sweet," I said absently, trying to remember what he looked like.

"He's obsessed," David continued. "But so am I and I'm not going to risk losing you by letting you two meet again."

"You don't have to worry," I said. "We only met for a few moments that one time and he seemed rather a cold fish. Not my type at all."

"I suspect he's just shy," David said, "though he's not exactly a Good Time Charlie. He's the kind of hard-working, serious stiff that the Agency likes. Probably be head of the department someday. But Marc's forgettable personality notwithstanding, I can't take you with me. I expect to be followed, and it's easier for me to shake a tail when I'm alone."

"Marc's not the only hard-working, serious stiff in your agency," I grumbled. "You pay more attention to the job than to me."

"Not to beat a subject to death," said David seriously, "this is important. If I don't tend to business, you could wake up one morning speaking Russian. Get my drift, comrade?"

"Da," I grunted, as we pulled up in front of David's hotel.

"That's the spirit," he grinned, giving me an affectionate hug. "I'll only be a short while and then we can celebrate. Is there anything you need?"

I shook my head. "I have an extra dress in my knapsack," I said, "and I remember where you stashed your scotch."

"Good," said David, helping me from the car and slinging my knapsack over his shoulder. He locked the car and we started toward the hotel.

"I thought you had an errand to perform," I said.

"The man in the blue sweater leaning against the doorway in that building across the street is watching the hotel," David explained. "He's been on my tail all week, and I've been deliberately open about my movements so that he's become careless and overconfident. We'll go up to the room together and I'll duck down the back stairs and out the side entrance. I'll take the Métro. I've been careful to always use my car when I go out, so he'll be watching that."

David made a point of talking to the desk clerk on duty, yawning broadly and stroking my buttocks in a lewd, possessive way. The clerk gave us an understanding wink as he handed David his key and promised to hold all calls till morning. We walked to the lift and David pressed the button for his floor.

"Forgive me for fondling you that way," he apologized as the lift door clanged shut behind us, "but I wanted to make sure that the desk clerk remembered us. If our friend asks, he'll be told that I went upstairs with a beautiful woman and an obvious hard-on, and I don't think he'll check further. He's been working alone, which makes this even easier. He's such a dumb clod, I feel almost guilty giving him the slip."

"*Do* you have a hard-on?" I asked innocently, looking pointedly at the bulge in his pants.

"You know I do," growled David, reddening. "I have a perpetual hard-on when I'm around you, and it's cruel of you to keep teasing me."

"I know," I said, ruffling his hair affectionately, "but I like to see you blush. It's a trait I find particularly endearing."

We exited the lift and David quickly unlocked the door of his room, opening it for me and handing me the key. "Just take a shower and relax," he told me, catching me to him in a hard embrace. "I'll be back soon." His lips brushed mine, but I deepened the kiss, pressing myself against him and fondling his genitals as my tongue snaked around his. He was flushed and breathless when I let him go.

"I just wanted to be sure you'd come back," I said lightly, whisking into the room just in time to avoid the slap aimed at my rear end. I closed the door, then opened it again and peered around the edge to watch him walk down the corridor until he disappeared around the bend.

First things first, I thought, turning the lock and hauling my knapsack into the room. I had had a long and tiring journey and had not eaten a proper meal since leaving India. I cannot stand airplane food and usually spend my flight drinking. I wondered if this shabby hotel had some semblance of room service. Unlike many countries where food quality is commensurate with price, there is no such thing as bad French food. Despite David's assurance that he would be gone only a short time, I worried that he might be delayed only to find my starved, emaciated body lying in a pitiful heap on the rug when he returned. I looked around for a list of telephone numbers and finally discovered one Scotch-taped to the wall near the mirror. Though the hotel had only a limited kitchen, I was assured that for the paltry sum of twenty francs, the chef would arrange a plate of cold meats and cheese and send it up with a bottle of a house wine that was the very same as that served at the Ritz at a much higher price.

While I was waiting for room service to deliver my meal, I poured myself a glass of scotch and soaked off the grime and fatigue of the past forty-eight hours in a perfumed bath. David had apparently anticipated having to leave me in his hotel room and had laid in a supply of toiletries purchased at a small exclusive shop on the Left Bank. I was struck again by this thoughtful and extremely generous gesture from a man whose yearly income was probably less than my laundry bill.

I dried myself off and slipped into a pair of white satin bikini briefs and a matching camisole top edged in baby-blue satin ribbon. I have a year-round tan, the result of frequent trips to the world's sun capitals, and I could not help admiring the contrast of the white satin against the gold-hued color of my skin. I was brushing out my hair before the bathroom mirror when I heard a knock at the front door. David's blue terry bathrobe was hanging behind the bathroom door and, thinking it was room service with my dinner, I hastily wrapped it around myself before answering the door.

A short brutish man in sagging brown pants and a blue sweater stood in the doorway. I started to slam the door but he forced his way in, blocking my escape. Holding my arm in a grip that made me wince, he closed the door and deftly turned the lock. I aimed a vicious kick at his shins, but I was not wearing shoes and succeeded only in stubbing my toe.

"Let go of my arm!" I said angrily, struggling in his grip. "Who the hell do you think you are?"

"I think you know that, Miss van Bell," the man said. He spoke English with an Eastern European accent, an accent that was becoming all too familiar. He had straight, heavy eyebrows, a rather bulbous nose, and a short thick neck and jowls that reminded me of a bulldog.

"How do you know my name?" I demanded.

"You ask a great many questions," the man said, smiling without warmth. "That is quite a coincidence. I too have many questions to ask. Perhaps we will take turns, yes?" He let me go but stood squarely in line with the door, blocking my escape. I backed away, rubbing my arm.

"I'm not going to answer any questions!" I snapped. "If you don't leave this instant, I'm going to call the police!"

"Please, comrade agent, let's not play games. You may be able to wind that moon-struck dolt you're working with around your finger, but I am not a fool."

"I don't know what you're talking about," I insisted. "I don't know who you are and I've never seen you before in my life."

"You passed right by me less than an hour ago," he replied impassively. "I was in doorway across from the hotel. I have been sure to trip over your American's feet all week while I wait for you to return, and I see him point me out. I think to have our little talk when you return from Rome but he never lets you out of his sight. So, I lay out bait and he bites, yes? He is so busy giving me the slip—how you say, outsmarting me?—that he leaves you alone and I make my chance. I admire your caution, comrade agent, but we have little time. My name is Stanislas Vronsky. You've heard of me?"

A shiver of fear raced along my spine, but I fought to keep my expression neutral. Obviously Mr. Vronsky was under the impression that I was a communist agent. If he knew the truth, he would not be pleased and I doubted that I would leave the hotel room alive. I had to be careful not to let on that I not only wasn't a communist agent, but that I hadn't the slightest idea of what he was talking about.

"I wasn't told about you, Mr. Vronsky," I said boldly. "My orders were pretty explicit but they didn't include you."

Vronsky frowned and his eyes narrowed dangerously. "You were seen with Nicholas Zelanko in New York and received instructions from him. Is that correct?" I shrugged slightly, neither confirming nor denying this statement. "Zelanko was arrested by American police after you arrive in France. I know he has recruited American agent to continue with work if he is suspect. You have done fine job. I know you have recovered two microdots, first in Rome and now India. But what has become of them?"

Now I understood. Vronsky was under the impression that I was a double agent and a backup for Zelanko. He assumed that I was collecting the microdots for his side under the guise of working for the Americans.

"I have my orders," I said as coolly as I could, "and I have been transporting the microdots as arranged. But the details are classified, and I cannot reveal them. If you were meant to know what was going on, I'm sure you would have been told."

This statement seemed to touch a nerve. Vronsky scowled and spat out an expletive in his own language, advancing toward me menacingly. I began to back away, but the room was small and in a moment I felt the edge of the bed pressing against my legs. I could go no farther and I tensed, waiting for his next move.

Suddenly he grabbed me and threw me roughly on the bed. He slapped me hard across the face.

"I do not like this situation, comrade agent," he hissed. "I get the distinct feeling I am being shut out of operation and I do not care for implications of freeze. First I am denied knowledge of identity of American double agent. Then I am denied control over microdot assignment. I am director of operation in this part of Europe. Everything passes through my hands, you understand? But I do not see microdot. Why is this, comrade agent? Who is trying to squeeze me out?"

My cheek was burning from the force of his slap. I blinked back the tears and tried to sit up, but he grabbed my shoulder and hit me again.

"I don't make the rules, Mr. Vronsky," I said pleadingly as he raised his hand for the third time. "I just follow them. Honestly. If you have some sort of dispute with your boss . . ."

I flinched away as his hand descended again and the blow caught me on the side of the head. There was a ringing in my ears and the room turned black.

When I opened my eyes, my robe and underwear had been removed and my hands and feet secured spreadeagled to the bedposts with strips of cloth. Fear made my mouth feel dry and my stomach muscles tighten. I was completely helpless. Vronsky could commit any atrocity he wished. I was completely at his mercy and he was a desperate and dangerous man. He leaned over me now, dark eyes blazing with anger, his mouth a cruel gash against the dull red color of his face.

"You will listen to me," he said in a low, even voice. "I do not care about orders. I am director of sector and you will obey me. Now you will tell me where are the two microdots you have recovered?"

I felt a rising sense of panic. I could not tell him the truth nor could I think of a lie that would sound convincing. I was damned either way. I could only stall for time and pray that David would return soon.

"I can't tell you," I said. My voice sounded high. I licked my dry lips, trying not to look as scared as I felt.

"You refuse?"

"I have my orders," I said weakly.

"You're a fool," he said in measured tones. He was breathing heavily, his face mottled with angry red blotches. Stepping close to the bed, he began very slowly to take off his clothes, his eyes never leaving my face as he undressed. "You understand," he continued, "that I will never allow my enemies in department to freeze me out. This is a very important assignment. Many honors will be handed out when it is successfully completed and I intend to have a full share of those honors. I will do whatever is necessary to achieve this. Whatever is necessary . . ."

My heart was beating painfully. I struggled against my bonds, outraged, frightened and, strangely enough, excited. I had experienced some mild B&D but I had always been a willing participant. My partners knew my limits and acted accordingly. But now, bound and helpless, I was at the mercy of a total stranger. There were no rules, no limits. Vronsky could do anything he wanted to me, but, despite my very real fear, I found the idea a powerful aphrodisiac.

He was totally naked now, his short square body covered with a pelt of dark hair. His penis, too, was short and thick, swollen with his lust.

He bent over me and bit the soft flesh of my cheek, hard. I cried out, turning my head and jerking at my bonds, but he only laughed sadistically, biting my ear and my shoulder, leaving dark purple bruises on my flesh. He bit his way down to my breasts and, gathering them in his hands, bit on the nipples. I was screaming now, begging him to stop, and he slapped me viciously across the face, knocking the breath out of me. He slapped me again and again, the force of his blows making me half unconscious. I no longer knew where I was. My body felt suspended in space. Kneeling over my outstretched form, he grabbed my hair and, yanking my head up, he forced his swollen member into my mouth. It was so big that I almost choked. Still holding my hair, he jerked my head back and forth so that my tongue and lips slid along his cock.

"Suck me!" he commanded suddenly, smacking me again. "Make me come. I want to come in your mouth!"

He let go of my hair and held his cock as I obediently began licking and sucking its steellike length. My body, raw with pain, began to respond to the pleasurable feeling of a hard cock in my mouth. I relaxed my throat muscles as Vronsky fed the entire length of his manhood into me, watching me, his face contorted with pleasure. The combination of acute pain and incredible pleasure, of fear and excitement had me so turned on that I was on the brink of orgasm. Seconds later he came, his orgasm exploding in my mouth. I hungrily swallowed his hot cream and he followed this by a stream of urine which overflowed my mouth, bathing my face and breasts. This took me over the edge and with a gasp I let myself go, climaxing with an intensity that I had never experienced before.

For a few moments he stood looking down at me, an expression of triumph in his eyes. "You see how

you will be treated if you disobey me?'' he said at
last. I nodded, too exhausted by my ordeal to speak.
''The punishment will be hard but I can reward as
well as punish,'' he continued. ''Your position is a
difficult one. I understand that. You have contradict-
ing orders. To obey one is to betray the other.'' His
fingers probed my pussy, and he smiled as he felt the
wetness there. ''You like what I did to you just
now,'' he said softly. ''You were frightened but you
were excited too. From now on it is I whom you will
obey. You will trust me and I will protect you.'' His
eyes gleamed, and, glancing down, I saw that his
shaft had swelled and stiffened.

''You are not talking of microdots,'' I whispered.
It was obvious he wasn't finished with me yet.

''You are clever, comrade agent,'' he murmured
almost to himself, ''and very beautiful. Many Russian women are beautiful but not like you. Your skin
is soft and smooth . . . like cream.'' His hands
stroked my breasts, pinching the nipples so I flinched. ''You will trust me,'' he said again. ''You will offer yourself to my discipline as a sign that you will
obey me.''

He cut my bonds and I sat up on the bed, rubbing
my chafed wrists and calculating the distance to the
door. I would never make it. Vronsky was too fast
and too strong. In the end I would be forced to submit and I knew that the punishment would then be
even more severe. Vronsky took the long thin belt
from his pants and my heart began to beat wildly as
he ordered me to kneel on the bed. He fastened my
hands behind my back with my torn panties, then
positioned me with my head down and my butt stick-
ing straight up. He ran his hand over the rounded
curve of my behind and I shivered in anticipation of
the first blow.

There was a whistling sound as the strap descended
and I felt a searing pain across my defenseless be-

hind. The second blow landed a few inches below the first, and I gave a stifled sob as my body arched and my buttocks rose even higher. Vronsky continued to whip me until my ass cheeks were raw and flaming hot. I could feel the sting of each blow even as the next one landed, but despite the intense pain and the humiliation of the position I had been forced to assume, I found myself getting turned on, my pussy juices flowing freely. A moment later, Vronsky stopped whipping me and I felt his hands separating my ass cheeks and the tip of his prick nudge the puckered hole of my anus. I spread my legs, relaxing as he pushed into me. He held me tightly as he moved his cock in and out of my rear end, at the same time pushing his fingers into my sopping cunt. I gasped and cried out. Hampered by my position from taking an active role, I could only submit as his frenzied movements fired my lust. The thickness of his cock stretched my tender asshole to its limits. He used quick, hard thrusts, pulling his cock out almost to its tip, then ramming it back in, keeping his fingers pressed against my clit so that my body experienced the pain and the pleasure simultaneously. All of a sudden he withdrew his fingers from my pussy and slapped me hard across the rump, triggering a violent climax that had me screaming with release. A second climax followed seconds after the first as his orgasm burst forth, his pumping organ shooting jets of hot cream into the aching well of my rectum.

It was all over. Vronsky cut my bonds and I collapsed onto the wrinkled, soaking sheets. The violence of his emotions exhausted, Vronsky quietly began to put on his clothes. He did not stroke or cuddle me the way a lover might. He was all business, cold and efficient. He had degraded and punished me, and his face was set in stern lines as he stood looking down at me.

"You have learned lesson, comrade agent," he

said harshly. "In future we will understand each other. I will worry about your friends in high places and you will not be harmed. But you will do as I tell you and deliver recovered microdots directly to me."

I nodded weakly. It was a moot point. There would be no more microdots. If I got out of this alive, I planned to give that smart-ass David a piece of my mind, then take the next plane back to New York.

Vronsky grunted and withdrew a long brown envelope from the pocket of his trousers. "You see," he said, waving the envelope in front of me, "I have begun to gather strings into my own hands. It is now I who have information about wine bottle. You are good agent, Comrade van Bell. You have fooled the Americans and, thanks to you, it is we who have microdots. Now I, Stanislas Vronsky, will take control of assignment. This envelope contains information you will need for recovery of next wine bottle. Young woman who has it is alone, not married. She has few friends, but I am sure you are capable of making her acquaintance. You are resourceful and will not fail to carry out assignment as instructed. I will remain in Paris. You will bring microdot, if there is one, back here."

I was careful not to let the surprise I felt show on my face. Vronsky was handing me a valuable piece of information. David would be thrilled right down to his toes, though he scarcely deserved to have me give him the envelope after his carelessness in letting Vronsky get to me.

"How will I find you?" I asked, sitting up and gingerly feeling my bruised face.

"You will hear from me. I will know where to find you. But do not betray me, comrade agent, or next time you may not get off so lightly." He handed me the envelope, then turned and quickly left the room.

CHAPTER TEN

By the time David returned thirty minutes later, I had worked myself into a state of nervous agitation. I had spent the time pacing the room, peering out the window and checking and rechecking the bolt on the front door to be sure it was securely fastened. When David entered the room, I lashed out at him, pounding my fists ineffectively against his chest.

"Take it easy," he said, trying to catch my hands. "What's the matter?"

"You've made me a living target, you prick!" I yelled, squirming away and backing toward the window. "I was just minding my own business and you dragged me into this mess and now I'm going to end up on the bottom of the Seine with concrete shoes! You told me there was nothing to this, just a harmless little caper, and now look what's happened! I hope you suffer terminal guilt after I'm dredged out of that river!"

"You're hysterical," he said, walking slowly toward me. "Now, stop hitting me and calm down. You're not making any sense."

"Why the hell shouldn't I be hysterical?" I demanded. "I'm going to be erased by some ugly commie in a Perry Como sweater. He's a sadist to boot! He'll probably torture me before he drops me out of the rowboat!" My body touched the window ledge and David swiftly caught my arm. He hugged me close, and with a stifled sob I burst into tears.

David carried me to the bed and sat holding me in his arms, rocking me gently until I had cried myself out. Then, while I told him what had happened, he bathed my body, putting cold compresses on my bruised face and swearing under his breath as he examined the long red weals on the tender flesh of my buttocks. I was not seriously hurt, but I enjoy being fussed over and catered to and played my situation to the hilt.

Room service finally arrived with the cold buffet and wine I had ordered earlier, and David plumped up my pillows and served me in bed, pulling up a chair and sitting down next to me.

"Are you sure you're okay, Christina?" he asked anxiously. "Do you want to see a doctor?"

"I'm all right," I assured him. "I'm sorry I carried on like that."

"You were more frightened than hurt," David agreed, "but you have every right to be angry. The commies have men equally as smart and capable as ours, and by being such a pompous ass I walked right into a trap. I'll never forgive myself for letting you pay the price of my carelessness."

"That's all right, Cap'n Connelly," I said, giving him an offhand salute, and he laughed and smiled across at me. I poured another glass of wine, then sat staring into my glass, not knowing how to broach the subject that was on my mind without hurting him. The silence stretched between us until at last David leaned forward and took my chin in his hand.

"It's not all right, is it?" he said gently. "What's wrong, Christina?"

I pulled away, not wanting to look at him. "The

game is getting serious," I said, "and I'm not so sure I want to play anymore. I didn't mind running your errands when it was all just harmless fun, but now the commies seem to think I'm one of their agents and things could get pretty hot if they find out the truth. So, if you don't mind I think I'll just take a powder, as they say in the trade, and go back to New York where I can hide under the covers."

"I wish you could, Christina," said David ruefully, "but it's not that easy. The commies know you picked up those two microdots. If you didn't give them to their side, then you had to give them to ours. There are no other sides in this game, and those microdots are not terribly valuable as collector's items. Once this fact is established, your life isn't going to be worth very much."

"That's a comforting thought," I said, pushing away my tray and pulling the covers over my head.

"Stop being childish, Christina. You're perfectly safe. I won't let anything happen to you."

"You're too late," I said from beneath the covers. "Something already has."

"Anything *else*," he corrected. "Give me a break, Christina. I didn't know that Zelanko had a backup, so how could I know that those idiots would mistake him for you? However, now that I understand the situation, I can take steps to cover all contingencies."

"Good! Cover them from New York. I'm leaving on the next available plane."

"You don't understand. Vronsky will be watching you from now on, and if you make any untoward moves, he's going to want to know why. Your only chance is to stick with me. As long as the commies think you're still working for them, you're safe, and we want them to continue thinking that for as long as possible."

"In other words, I'm stuck here keeping up this charade? Is that what you're saying?"

"That's it exactly," he agreed. "Look, Christina, I know you're worried, and I understand, but I've been in this business a long time. Believe me, this is the safest course of action. If you just stick with me and do as I tell you, we can deal with anything that comes up."

"I don't like it," I muttered sullenly, "but I suppose I have no choice."

"I knew you'd listen to reason," said David heartily. "Now, come out from under the covers like a good girl and let's discuss business."

"Let's discuss dinner," I said.

"You just ate."

"Dinner, or I'm not coming out."

"Dinner it is, then," David laughed. "Put on some clothes, Mata Hari, and we'll go to Le Petit Escargot and give Maurice a treat. He asks about you everytime I go in."

An hour later we were seated in the small upstairs dining room eating Beouf sans Oeuf and Veal Prince Orloff. The food and the change of scene had restored my sense of perspective and I began to see that David was right. It would be safer to play along and help recover the microdots. If our side won, commie headquarters would probably send Vronsky to some remote gulag in Siberia where he couldn't get to me, and if the commies won, I would still probably be given a medal by our side. I smiled at David over the rim of my wine glass.

"Dinner was delicious," I said. "Now I'm ready to discuss business. What's our next move?"

David cleared his throat and took the brown envelope from the inside pocket of his sports jacket. "I think this is our next logical move," he said, waving the packet. "Our own people have turned up nothing in the last week, so, as Vronsky has just handed us the location of another wine bottle, we might as well follow it up and see if we can retrieve it." He opened the envelope with his butter knife and scanned the contents. "Brussels, eh?" he grunted, lighting a fresh cigarette with the end of the one in his mouth. "The owner is a woman, almost a recluse according to this file. This should be quite a challenge."

"Vronsky said the same thing," I said, "but I don't think so. Women are much more social than men as a rule. They're more trusting and easier to get to know. Should be a piece of cake."

"Well, we'll find out soon enough," said David. "Thanks to you, Vronsky has saved us a great deal of work. I have to make a few phone calls but we can probably leave tomorrow."

"Does this mean you're coming with me?"

"Absolutely. Somebody has to protect you, and since the commies have blown my cover, I might as well go along and do the job instead of assigning it to another agent."

"I see," I said. "It's the most efficient way. That's the only reason?"

"Is that what you think? It's a justification, not a reason. I would prefer to have my superior's permission to accompany you, but I'd go in any case . . ." He stopped for a moment, frowning.

"What's the matter?" I asked.

"There's one other problem we haven't considered," David said. "If there's a backup agent for Zelanko, and it isn't you, then who is it?"

"Vronsky spoke English," I said. "He assumed I was an American."

"That's a good point," David nodded. "And even if the person isn't an American, it would at least be someone who wanted to pose as one and knew the language. I'll advise Washington of the situation and have them put someone on it. Hopefully, we'll discover his identity before he can blow your cover."

"Perhaps he's dead and that's why he hasn't shown up so far," I suggested.

"It's a possibility," David said. "But we'd better not take any chances till we know for sure. I'll take you home. You'll be safe there while I make final arrangements. That dragon of a housekeeper would scare off the dead."

"Shall I have her stand guard outside the bedroom door?" I teased.

"For a while," David laughed. "You can retire her when I return."

David was especially creative and tender that night. We lit a fire, drank champagne, and made love in the big pink bed. My anxiety over the events of the day had heightened my sexual appetite, and we came together with a fierceness and hunger that transcended our earlier experiences.

Our flight to Brussels was uneventful. David had arranged for a rental car to be waiting for us at the airport, and shortly after clearing customs we were motoring from the Brussels Airport into the city itself.

Brussels is an international business center and one of the art and antique capitals of the world. David and I had agreed that we would pose as representatives of a successful American art gallery, in Brussels to shop for the upcoming Christmas season. At my insistence, we had booked a suite at the new Brussels Hilton on Boulevard de Waterloo, not far from the Palais du Roi. I had argued successfully that in case we were found out I did not want my bruised and bleeding body to be found in a second-rate hotel.

We arrived shortly before lunch and were greeted at the desk by the manager, a small round gentleman with a pin-striped suit and an effusive manner. He shook hands with David and kissed me three times on the cheek. The Belgians do this to be one up on the French, who traditionally only kiss the cheek twice in greeting. We had traveled under our own names, David having decided that arranging for false passports would be time-consuming and unnecessary, and I was surprised when the manager remembered me.

"I could not forget you, Miss van Bell," he said, beaming at me. "I was an assistant at the Regency when you stayed there."

"But that was three or four years ago at least," I protested. "You must have served millions of people since then . . ."

"Ah, but none of them caused quite the sensation your party did that particular night," the manager sighed. "The local fire department still talks about it."

"I remember now," I laughed. "That was quite an evening, wasn't it? So now you are manager of this fine new hotel. It's beautifully decorated. Givenchy, isn't it?"

"That is correct, mademoiselle." The manager nodded. "You have a good eye. When I saw your name on the arrivals schedule, I immediately aranged for one of the VIP suites on the sixteenth floor to be reserved for you. You will, of course, be our guest for lunch."

"You're too generous," I protested, but the manager held up his hand.

"It is you who are generous, mademoiselle. There were many in your position who would not have even paid the cost of the damages that night. You not only did so, but recommended the hotel to all of your friends. The Countess Von Pleitz still occupies the entire third floor."

"Dear Carlotta, she must be nearly seventy. Does she still have those horrendous dyed pink poodles?" I asked.

"*Oui*, mademoiselle, and three chauffeurs." He winked at me broadly and summoned a bellhop to handle our luggage and escort us to our rooms.

In the lift David glared at me, shaking his head in disbelief. "So much for our cover identities," he said. "We were supposed to be unassuming business people, remember?"

"The Hilton wasn't even built the last time I was here," I protested. "How could I know that the manager would recognize me?"

"Perhaps if you'd behaved less outrageously he wouldn't have remembered you," said David self-righteously. "What exactly did happen in the Regency that night? Why was the fire department called in?"

"Water under the bridge," I said. "It's not really worth discussing."

"Sounds to me as if they've discussed nothing else around here for the past three years. I'm not making a judgment, you understand. I'm just curious."

"You're making a judgment," I snapped. "I can tell by the tone of your voice. It wasn't really all that sensational. It's just that the Belgians are a bit provincial."

"I see . . ."

"Well, you know the Belgians love fairs, and there was a troup of acrobats from Munich in town. I always wanted to join the circus, so I decided to take a few lessons and things got a little out of hand. They had to hose down the tumblers and there was a little disturbance, I suppose, but it's not worth talking about."

"Maybe we should just take out an ad in the newspaper, announcing that we've arrived in town and do the job up right," David grumbled as we walked down the lushly carpeted corridor to the door of our suite.

"Think of how disappointed you'd have been if you had bothered to get those false passports," I pointed out, but he ignored me.

Our rooms were spacious and beautifully appointed with a breathtaking view of the city. The Belgians have always been traditionalists, and the comfortable chairs and sofas in the sitting room were covered with a bright floral chintz that was complemented by a muted velvet rug. There was a beautiful Georgian fireplace with a basket of fresh flowers on the mantel and a gleaming silver coffee pot on a small white porcelain stove near the bar. Coffee is the favorite drink of the Belgians and most of the residents are addicted to it before they start school. It is served in the French manner with plenty of hot milk and chocolates, if it's after dinner. Another favorite national beverage is beer, some of the finest of which is brewed in Belgium, and I found a small refrigerator/bar amply stocked with their finest lager as well as other types of spirits.

While I poured myself a cup of coffee and admired the view, David carefully inspected the walls, doors, lamps, telephones, and other obscure corners of the rooms for bugging devices, all the while keeping up a patter of innocent chitchat.

"Would you look at that view," he said, kneeling on the floor and lifting up a corner of the rug. "Nothing but the best, eh? Did you say this painting was an original?"

"It's a Frederic Remington," I said, trying not to laugh, since David was squinting into a lamp base. "Would you like some coffee or beer?"

"Coffee, please, black," he replied, putting down the lamp and going to the bathroom to wash his hands. "Looks pretty clean," he said when he came out. "We should be able to talk freely here. Be careful what you say outside the room, though, especially in crowded places." He sat down next to me on the couch, lit a cigarette, and sipped his coffee appreciatively.

"Don't get too comfortable," I said. "We've been invited to lunch by the manager, and I haven't eaten since breakfast."

"You had a second breakfast on the plane, remember? And we stopped for a snack on our way in from the airport," David reminded me. "I don't know where you put it. You eat six meals a day and your figure is perfect."

"I exercise a lot," I said. "Horizontal exercise. Let's eat now, and after lunch I'll show you how to burn off a few calories."

David readily agreed to this, and we took the lift to the top floor where a table had been reserved for us in the famous El Plein Ciel restaurant. The entire room was glass-enclosed, giving patrons a spectacular view of the city from every angle, and the lush decor was dominated by a huge Val St. Lambert chandelier.

We were quickly seated at a choice table and spent several minutes scanning the menu.

"You've hit paydirt this time," I said sarcastically. "Brussels has a national love affair with the french fried potato."

"A very civilized place," he said, nodding approvingly. "From what I can see the Belgians like good, plain home cooking. That's probably what makes them so friendly. Their stomachs aren't filled with that fancy French muck. Here it is, Bifteck et Frites, steak and fries. What are you having?"

"I think I'll have one of the other national favorites," I said casually. "Anguilles au Vert."

"My French is a little weak there," said David cautiously. "What is that, exactly?"

"Cold baby eels, prepared with mint, sage, sorel, and a few other herbs," I said, smiling sweetly. "No fancy sauces, just plain home cooking." David paled visibly but made no comment. "The best thing about them," I continued blandly, "is that you can suck them into your mouth like thick strands of spagetti and, if you're extra lucky, you might get one that's still wiggling . . ."

"Stop right there," he choked, holding up a protesting hand. "Just stop right there, or I swear you can have lunch with Vronsky instead."

"Like you said, a civilized people," I reminded him. He scowled at me and hid behind the menu.

After lunch we returned to our rooms where I spent a pleasant two hours pretending David's cock was a baby eel that had slipped off my plate. We then showered and changed and took a stroll across the Place Royale and through the Parc de Bruxelles, admiring the beautiful landscaping and ponds that make this park one of the most popular in the city. David wanted to discuss our next step, but I was tired of being indoors and suggested that we find a quiet place in the park where we could conduct our business undisturbed.

We stopped to rest in front of one of the park's notable landmarks, a replica of Frampton's famous statue of Peter Pan, the original of which is in Kensington Gardens in London.

David drew the envelope Vronsky had given me out of his coat pocket, and shuffled through the papers inside. He handed me the photos of our quarry, whose name was Lynette Broullard. The photos were in black and white and showed a tall, angular woman with a long nose, high cheekbones and round rimless glasses. She was dressed in a plain skirt and blazer with dark ribbed stockings and sensible shoes. Her long thick hair was coiled in a bun at the nape of her neck.

"She seems rather an ugly duckling," I said, "but perhaps these photographs don't do her justice. They give no hint of her coloring, after all, and those clothes she's wearing would make the most glamorous model look like a shopping-bag lady."

"Skin fair, hair auburn, eyes gray . . ." David read, lighting a cigarette and squinting through the smoke at the notes in front of him. "She is unmarried, has no family, no real friends, and no contacts in society that you can use to gain an introduction."

"How about interests?"

"Miss Broullard's passion is art and she seems to have a fairly single-minded devotion to it. She is a graduate of the Sorbonne, and holds a doctorate in Art History. She writes a critical column for an obscure art journal and is something of an artist herself. She taught at the university level until two years ago, when she decided to quit and devote all of her time to painting. She almost never goes out . . . except on Sunday."

"Oh?"

"She gives art lectures at the museum on Sunday," David said. "There's a list here of her various gallery shows and clippings of some promising reviews, but few painters can live solely on the sale of their work."

"It looks like the museum is my best shot then," I said. "And tomorrow is Sunday. That's a lucky break, isn't it?"

"I don't know," David replied, frowning. "If we had a bit more time, you could have taken a few books out of the library and boned up on art history. It would have given you something in common, something to talk about."

"Oh, I'm fairly knowledgeable about art," I said airily, "and if that doesn't work we can talk about men . . . or women as the case may be. I bet Miss Broullard is one of those women who look better with their clothes off than fully dressed."

David gave me a hard look but said nothing. He was a man of the world and undoubtedly knew what I was referring to, but his starchy upbringing made the open admission of the possibility of sex between women a social taboo. He dragged on his cigarette and looked at the park. Dusk was falling and the street lamps were snapping on throughout the city.

"You'll know best how to handle it," he said finally. "Still, in light of the recent developments in this case, I think I'll cover your movements just to keep an eye out for Vronsky or his friends. You won't see me, but I'll be in the neighborhood so you'll be perfectly safe. Now, if you've had enough fresh air I suggest we find someplace for dinner. You've only had four meals today, and I wouldn't want you to faint from hunger."

"Did you know that the Belgians are famous for their chocolate," I said, as we walked out of the park. "We could buy a five-pound box after dinner and spend a quiet evening in our room making love and pigging out."

"That's an offer only a fool would refuse," said David, smiling.

Part of the sacrifice involved in my service to my country was getting out of bed before eleven the following day. My body was in a state of shock, but I had no choice. I had to get showered and dressed and over to the museum in time to link up with Lynette's lecture, which started promptly at noon.

Fortunately, the Musée Royal d'Art Ancien was located on Rue de la Régence, just a few minutes walk from our hotel, so despite my lingering under the spray of the shower, my inability to choose between three different outfits, and several vain attempts to get David back into bed with me, I still managed to get to the museum on time.

The Royal Museum of Ancient Art is devoted to several schools of Flemish painting, but Lynette was lecturing in the Baroque section, where the museum was hosting a special exhibit devoted to the work of Peter Paul Rubens. A small but attentive group was gathered before one of the paintings, listening to Lynette as she lectured in French. Some appeared to be students, perhaps from her former classes at the university, and others were obviously tourists.

"This painting dates from late in Rubens' career,

shortly after he had married his second wife," Lynette was explaining as I quietly joined the group. "It is, in fact, a portrait of his wife, Helene Fourment, painted shortly after their marriage."

A short bald man, wearing a shirt with a map of Florida on the back and holding an unlit cigar clamped between his teeth, nudged his fat wife in the ribs. "Wha'd she say, Sarah?" he demanded of the woman, who apparantly understood French.

"That's a paintin' of his wife," she translated.

"You're kiddin'," the man exclaimed. "She's naked as a jaybird, fer cryin' out loud! What kind of man paints his wife starkers like that so's the whole world can see?"

"Hush! I think it's lovely," Sarah hissed. "The man loved her and wanted to immortalize her beauty. You wouldn't understand, Sam. It's called romance."

"Dirty pitchers ain't romance," the man grumbled.

"Rubens had had a fairly unsatisfying first marriage to a pious woman named Isaḅella Brandt," Lynette continued. "When he was fifty-three he married Helene, who was then sixteen years old. He was hopelessly in love with her, especially with her physical beauty, which he idealized as the perfect female form."

I studied the portrait of Rubens' wife. She was typical of the women he painted, with chubby arms cupping lush, full breasts. Her legs and thighs were full and heavy and she was naked save for a fur coat that was slipping from her body, barely concealing her buttocks. She had golden hair, cherry lips, and wide blue eyes, and her expression was startled, as if someone had just walked in on her unannounced.

"You see, Sam?" Sarah said smugly. "A great artist like that, and he considered her the height of feminine perfection. And she's two hundred pounds if she's an ounce. So maybe you ought to stop complaining when I put on a few extra pounds, huh?''

"You don't put on a few extra pounds," Sam snorted. "You put on a few extra people. Besides, she's sixteen years old. You ain't no sixteen, Sarah.''

"You stink, Sam, you know that?" the woman snapped.

"So? Sue me! Go live with Rubens! Maybe he'll paint you in the buff too, and you can hang it in the den." He laughed at the thought and his wife shot him a dirty look.

I decided that I would have to attract Lynette's attention and raised my hand to ask a question. She saw me and nodded.

"Didn't this marriage have a profound effect on Rubens' painting style?" I asked.

"Yes indeed. I'm glad you mentioned that, mademoiselle," she said. "As you know, Rubens was born in Antwerp, where his father was a magistrate of that city, and he was quite a solid citizen. He had already gained a considerable reputation for a solemn, majestic style of painting, quite typical of the Flemish school, but after his marriage to Helene, love—or perhaps passion—transformed him considerably and this is shown in his work."

"I can see the change quite clearly," I said. "He's abandoned many of the subtler earth tones and adopted a wider palette of bright colors. His brushwork is freer and his use of lighting less slavishly realistic."

"That's correct," Lynette said enthusiastically. "You have a good eye, mademoiselle . . .''

"Van Bell," I said. "Christina van Bell."

"It's as if in his later years Rubens' painting took on some of the fanciful, buoyant qualities typical of young childen. He always loved full-figured women and after marrying his young bride, he was happy for perhaps the first time in his life, and as later portraits show she became even more abundantly endowed as she grew older.''

"It must have been hard on his wife," mumbled Sam. "An old man like Rubens must have been pretty worn out by then. Those paintings are very nice, but to a young girl they'd be a poor substitute for a good night in the sack."

"You're wrong there," I said. "Helene bore Rubens five childen. And the last, Constance Albertine, was born in 1641, a full nine months after Rubens died. I think that's testimony enough to his prowess."

"Or to what killed him," Sam chuckled, but I could see that I had made my point. The group laughed appreciatively and the lecture ended on a high note.

"Remember the painting, Sam," Sarah said as they walked to the door. "We'll buy a postcard of it and send it home to Mrs. Fourage next door."

"You can't send a picture like that through the United States mail," Sam said, obviously shocked at the thought. "They may allow that sort of thing over here but not back home. Mrs. Fourage's got young children and she wouldn't thank you for sending her such a postcard, believe me . . ."

The room cleared and Lynette and I were left alone.

"Thank you for your help," she said shyly. "I never know what to do when I come up against people like that. They're prudish . . . and a bit vulgar, but they're curious too. You handled it just right. They'll remember that painting everytime they talk about their trip."

"I've always liked Rubens," I said. "He venerated women, real women, with breasts and hips and stomachs. Women today are expected to look almost androgynous, tiny breasts, no hips. I don't mean that women should let themselves go, but some men want

more than a bag of bones in bed. Some women too,"
I added, looking directly at her.

She did not blush or look away. "I too love the
female form," she said softly. "I have made a study
of it over this past year, sketching many different
women to prepare for a theme show next spring."

"I'd love to see some of your drawings," I said.

"And I would like you to see them," she replied.
"You seem to have a solid knowledge of art, and I
would value your opinion. Why not be my guest for
lunch? We can have some wine perhaps, and I will
show you my work."

I readily accepted her invitation, and after getting
our coats, we left the museum together. As we
walked down the steps outside the building, I
couldn't resists looking around for some sign of
David, but he had either hidden himself very effec-
tively or had gone back to bed as soon as I left.

Brussels is a small city full of pedestrian malls and
restricted traffic zones, and Lynette explained apologetically that she usually left her car parked near her
home and traveled to the museum on the tram.

I never take public transportation and found the
short trip in the crowded little bus a novel experience.
Lynette and I sat very close together and the fresh-
scrubbed scent of her skin mingled with the body
odors of the other passengers and the pungent smells
of garlic, tobacco, and ripe cheese.

Lynette lived in a small house in the Quartier Léo-
pold, not far from the Museum of Natural History.
In Brussels houses are taxed according to how much
of the sidewalk the front occupies, so the thrifty
Belgians build their homes narrow and deep. Lynette's home was similar, a mere eight feet wide, but
three times that length front to back. The decorative
ironwork that adorned the building was character-
istic of the style found throughout the city.

Lynette lived on the top floor of the four-story

building. "I'm lucky to have a skylight," she explained as she opened the door and ushered me inside. "I get the northern light and it is very helpful for my painting."

Lynette's apartment had several small rooms, arranged railroad-style to accommodate the strange shape of the house. The furniture was small scale, not expensive, but tastefully arranged. The rooms were all painted white, and red dominated the color scheme along with touches of green from her plants. The scheme was repeated throughout the apartment, and the colors reminded me of Christmas. The center room, which contained a large skylight, doubled as studio and dining area, and it was obvious from the small rectangular table and two chairs that Lynette seldom entertained more than one person at a time. I heard a musical whistling from the far corner and turned to look. Framed by two stepladders overflowing with plants was a bird cage with a pair of green-and-red birds inside.

"You have lovebirds!" I cried, going over to look at them.

"Max and Pauline," Lynette said, waving in the general direction of the birds as she disappeared into the kitchen.

"Hello, birds," I said, but they were busy nibbling at each other's necks and paid no attention. "They seem very happy together," I said, taking a platter of fruit and cheese from Lynette's hands and placing it on the table.

"They are," Lynette concurred, setting out plates, napkins, and cutlery, "but then, they have a nice clean place to live, plenty of food, fresh water, safety from predators or any adverse effects of the environment, and each other. They're like an old married couple."

"That may be enough for birds," I said decidedly. "It might even be enough for some people, but not for me. I couldn't stand being cooped up in the same place day after day."

"I wouldn't mind that," Lynette said thoughtfully. "I seldom go out except to the museum. I'm a very private person and I like to have my own space."

"Don't you ever get lonely?"

"Sometimes," she said softly, turning away. She rummaged in a cupboard and brought out a bottle of wine and two glasses. "We will celebrate a bit, I think," she said. "This bottle was given to me as a gift by my employer at the museum. He is a great connoisseur."

I held my breath as she placed the bottle on the table, then breathed out in a long sigh of relief. Vronsky's information had been correct. It was indeed the bottle I sought.

Lynette poured out two glasses and as we ate and drank, we talked of art with the ease of two people who had known each other a long time. After lunch, Lynette showed me her paintings. They were mostly nudes, done in a stark realistic style. The artist had chosen working women and housewives rather than professional models, strong women whose bodies were used to rough labor and childbearing. They were painful portraits, expressing hunger and loneliness, but they had a spellbinding quality that came from more than just technical proficiency.

I cannot say why it is that sometimes my attraction to a person is immediate and at other times, as with Lynette, it comes as a gradual thing. She had taken off her blazer and slipped a loose-fitting white smock over her tailored skirt and blouse. The more feminine attire softened her features and the wine brought color to her clear fair skin. She was not used to drinking and it made her animated and a bit giddy, but when she suddenly stopped talking and kissed me full in the lips, I found myself returning her kiss with equal passion and desire.

Lynette's bedroom was tucked away behind the kitchen at the very back of the apartment. Lynette lit a gas fire in the grate, and we undressed slowly in its radiant warmth. Divested of the shabby, tasteless clothes, Lynette's body gleamed in the firelight like a marble statue, her full, heavy breasts and rounded hips a sensuous promise. She unpinned her hair and the massive copper tresses cascaded over her shoulders and breasts, and when she smiled her whole face seemed to light up, striking a deep erotic chord inside of me.

We moved to the bed and our bodies took it from there. We fell into each other's arms, kissing and sucking each other's breasts and fondling each other's buttocks and the hot mounds of each other's sex. Blonde and auburn pubic hair meshed together, and I gasped as she pressed herself against me, her hot, searching lips opening to mine, our tongues probing, exploring each other's mouths. I was flushed and exhilarated by the feel of Lynette's body moving against my own. My aching pussy overflowed with warm cream. As if sensing my need, her hand moved down to the juncture between my legs, her fingers slipping between my pussy lips to probe the dark wetness within. The walls of my cunt clung to her fingers as I arched, then relaxed. She pushed deeper and I felt myself opening to her. Wanting to give as well as receive, I mirrored her actions, my fingers searching through the springy hairs for the puckered lips of her vagina. I felt her warm juices flow over my fingers as they probed her honeyed depths, pushing against the swollen knob of her clit. We moved together now in the timeless rhythm of two people making love. I no longer knew where my body stopped and Lynette's began as our mouths pressed together and our driving fingers worked on each other's sex. Our mutual orgasm made the room spin, pushing me almost to the edge of consciousness. When it was over, we lay gasping in each other's arms, our damp, trembling bodies bathed in an afterglow of deep mutual satisfaction.

"That was perfect," Lynette sighed. "But it was too quick. I don't mean rushed, but over too soon. I never wanted it to end."

"I know what you mean," I said. "We were being totally emotional, and our feeling just ran away with us. Let's start again, shall we?"

All of Lynette's longing for physical contact showed in her face. Her body quivered as I gently traced the outline of her hips with my fingertip and she closed her eyes and sighed deeply. We kissed long and slowly this time, letting our tongues explore the hidden treasures of each other mouths, inhaling the sweat-filmed scent of each other's perfume.

I eased Lynette back against the pillows and kissed her eyelids and her cheeks and the soft hollow in her neck. I could feel her pulse fluttering wildly against my lips as her whispered sighs of pleasure echoed in the stillness of the room. I moved downward to her breasts. I licked around each pale pink areola, then took each nipple into my mouth, teasing it awake. Lynette stirred beneath me, her hands moving lightly over my back. I moved over the soft roundness of her belly to the thick, lush forest of her pubic hair. The sight of Lynette writhing helplessly beneath my touch, her face suffused with passion, had me thoroughly aroused. When my fingers brushed her thighs, she spread her legs and parted her pussy lips with her own hands so that I could see the tiny erect knob of her clit.

I let my tongue slid along the inner edge of each thigh, then blew gently into the exposed hole of her cunt. She cried out and dug her heels into the bed, her hips arching upward. I consider myself an expert in the art of cunnilingus and have tongued a great many pussies in my time, but Lynette's hot, juicy cunt was a special treat. My tongue licked eagerly around her clitoris in slow, swirling laps, then I began to rub back and forth over the tip. Lynette's love juices were flowing freely, and, gripping my hair, she literally ground her pussy against my darting tongue.

My own excitement was at fever pitch as I brought Lynette to an explosive series of orgasms. Hardly pausing for breath, I quickly shifted my position so that I was crouched over her body, my rear inches from her face. Taking the hint, she parted my thighs and pushed her tongue between the swollen lips of my cunt. As she swabbed my steaming slit, I again plunged into her syrupy depths, inhaling her pungent female odor and sucking wildly at the sweet nectar within.

Our bodies moved against each other, melted and fused with the frenzied fire of our mutual lust. We drove each other to the brink of orgasm, then came together in a dizzying spiral of emotion.

We drifted off to sleep, awakening hours later in each other's arms. We made love again and again, holding nothing back, the smells and tastes of our lovemaking pungent on our lips and fingers. Lynette took the lead with a new aggressiveness, licking every inch of my body, from the creamy curves of my breasts and belly to the inner recesses of my most intimate holes. She made love to my toes and my armpits and my asshole, and I responded with an unbridled passion of my own, scouring her sweet love-nest until she was trembling and crying out with the force of her orgasm.

It was late when, lying naked in her arms with my head nestled between her breasts, I suddenly remembered my mission. Murmuring excuses about the bathroom, I gently disengaged myself from her embrace and, picking up my handbag, padded to the bathroom, which was on the other side of the studio. I picked up the empty wine bottle on the way and barricaded myself in the tiny room. Under the harsh white light of the bathroom bulb, I quickly withdrew the magnifying glass from its container and examined the label. The microdot was there, in that special spot, and I deftly removed it, placing it carefully in my wristwatch compartment. Then, after flushing the toilet and running the water loudly in the sink, I stepped back into the room, quietly placing the bottle on the table before rejoining Lynette in bed.

CHAPTER ELEVEN

The lobby of the hotel was deserted when I returned late Sunday night. The businessmen who populate the city during the week had all gone home and the hordes that were expected for the following day had not yet arrived. A bored-looking clerk sat at the desk, leafing disinterestedly through a magazine. He ignored me as I walked quickly to the lift and sped up to my suite.

I found David sitting in the living room, nursing a drink and dropping cigarette ashes into a clean ashtray. There was a greasy bag of french fries on the table, and his overcoat was draped over a nearby chair. It felt cold when I touched it.

"Did you just get back?" I asked as he came over and hugged me.

"Yes, I did, Sherlock. Sit down and relax. Would you like a drink?"

"Brandy," I nodded, taking off my coat and kicking off my shoes. "What were you doing? Buying out all the french fries in Brussels? I certainly didn't see you."

"I was keeping an eye on you," he said. "I

watched you make your connection with Mademoiselle Broullard at the museum, then I followed you
back to her house. I waited until you left and tailed
your taxi back here. I used the freight entrance and
arrived just a few minutes before you did, as you so
cleverly deduced. Did everything go as planned?''

"Yes, it did," I said, slipping off my wristwatch
and handing it to him. "Vronsky handed us a real
present. I've done your dirty work once again, David
Connelly. Why don't you take me to dinner?''

David looked at his watch and frowned. "It's getting late. I have to meet my contact and get this microdot back to the States first. It won't take long.''

"Liar! It will take two hours, at least. And what
am I supposed to do while you're running around the
streets? I can't just sit here and vegetate.''

"I'm afraid you'll have to," David said, reaching
for his coat. "I can't take you with me. I have to be
careful and not attract attention, and I can't let you
run around unattended. Vronsky or one of his co-
horts may be waiting for an opportunity to chat with
you again and I'm sure you don't want another encounter with him.''

"If he offered me dinner I might consider defec-
ting," I said. "Hunger does things to me.''

"Have a french fry.''

"I'd rather starve!''

"No, you wouldn't," David laughed. "Somebody
else maybe, but not you.''

"You're right," I conceded. "What else have you
got?''

"Chocolates," said David, emptying his pockets.
"Peanuts. Here we are, a Belgian waffle.''

"You're a regular bodega," I sighed.

"Look, Christina," he said more softly, putting
his arms around me and stroking my hair, "I know
how difficult all this is for you. I've reported the

latest developments to headquarters and in light of your personal danger, they have assigned extra personnel to the task of rounding up the microdots. We have a team in Germany right now, and it looks as if they might have found something there. Just hang on a few more days. It will be finished soon, I promise you."

"I just feel so confined," I complained. "I usually come and go as I please, and I'm not used to being tied down like this."

"Read a book or watch TV," David suggested. "But whatever you do, stay in the room. Keep the door locked and chained and don't open it for anyone. Not room service or the maid or anyone. Do you understand?"

I nodded glumly. David kissed me absently on the lips and slipped out of the door, waiting outside until he heard me turn the lock and hook the chain into place.

I rummaged in my bag for my gold cigarette case, lit a joint, and inhaled deeply. I poured myself another drink and prowled the room like a nervous tiger, flipping listlessly through magazines, turning the television and radio on and off, and picking at the leftover food on the table. I looked resentfully at the clock and saw that instead of hours passing, as I had thought, David had been gone less than thirty minutes. The brandy and hash made me high and I had a raging case of the munchies.

"I'm going stir crazy," I said out loud. "I'm going plain nuts, and I don't see why the hell I should put up with it." I turned to the mirror and spoke plaintively to my image. "After all, I'm over twenty-one. I should be able to do what I want." My image nodded agreement, so I put on my shoes, picked up my coat, and headed for the door.

I was confident that I could slip out of the hotel

without being followed by Vronsky's men even if they were actually watching for me. After all, David did it, and I could certainly do anything David could.

I took the elevator to the third floor, then went down the back stairs and left the hotel through the garage, which had a side door on a quiet street. I carefully scanned the street and saw no one. Having assured myself that I had no unwelcome companions, I walked quickly to Rue de la Loi, near the St. Michel Cathedral, where I hailed a taxi.

The driver was a thin young man with a rakish cap perched on his head at a jaunty angle. I slipped into the rear seat, and he turned around to smile at me.

"You're a tourist, aren't you?" he asked, speaking French in a friendly manner.

"What makes you say that?" I asked in the same language.

"Only tourists are on the streets of Brussels on a Sunday night," he said with a shrug. "Good Belgians spend their weekend nights in their homes with their shutters closed and their televisions blaring. It makes it difficult for an enterprising taxi driver like me to make a decent living."

"Well, you can take me for a drive," I said. "I've been cooped up long enough and I need a change of scene."

"Any particular destination in mind?"

"No," I said. "I would like to stop for some chocolates, then perhaps a tour of the city." I reached into my bag and pulled out ten thousand francs, which I handed to him. "Just drive this off," I instructed, settling back in my seat. "When it's gone, I'll decide what to do next."

"It will be a pleasure," he smiled, stuffing the bills into the inside pocket of his jacket. He slipped the car into gear and we drove off. I bought a large bag of assorted chocolates filled with various liqueurs, then

we drove at a leisurely pace through the center of
the city, eventually reaching the Grand' Place. The
marketplace is the city's showplace, floodlit at night
with changing colored lights. The driver slowed down
to allow me to admire the Hôtel de Ville, with its impressive Lion Stairway and copper statue of Saint
Michael forever crushing the figure of the Devil
beneath his metallic feet. Over the main gate were the
Claus Sluter statues of Peace, Prudence, Justice,
Strength, Temperance, and Law, and just beyond the
gate two splendidly lit fountains sent their silver
spray into the moonlit sky.

"You certainly have a lot of statues in this city," I
said to the driver.

"A lot of artists have lived here," he laughed.
"Exiles mostly. They got thrown out of Paris and
came over here to work. The city is littered with their
creations, like bronze bird droppings."

"I thought only New Yorkers were that cynical," I
said.

"You get blasé about the stuff when you've lived
here all your life," he replied. "It becomes part of
the scenery. When was the last time you stopped and
admired the Empire State Building or Rockefeller
Center?"

"I don't remember," I admitted ruefully. "You're
absolutely right."

"I'm not totally indifferent," he said, driving on.
"I still enjoy visiting the city's oldest inhabitant."

"And who is that?" I asked politely, my attention
focused on the bag of chocolates in my lap.

"You mean you don't know?" he asked in amaze-
ment. "It's the first thing a tourist rushes to see in all
its grotesque splendor. Come, we'll visit the old fellow now. He's right in the neighborhood."

On Rue de l'Etuve the driver stopped the car in
front of a small bronze statue of a young boy. The

statue was dressed in a red velvet suit, elaborately embroidered in gold thread. His bronze penis protruded from the open fly and a steady stream of water poured into the fountain.

"Manneken Pis," I said, reading the inscription. "It's a statue of a kid urinating. Why on earth did they ever erect such a thing? It's hardly in the same league with the statues in the Grand' Place."

"He is regarded as a symbol of the changing fortunes of Brussels," the cab driver replied. "No one really knows why the original stone statue was erected, or when, though there are a great many legends to choose from. This bronze model was done in the seventeenth century by Duquesnoy. Once, during the war of 1695, the statue was kidnapped by the French. Louis the XV was so taken with it that he had some special suits of clothes designed for him. Since then, it has become a custom to dress Manneken Pis in various outfits to commemorate different special events. Foreign dignitaries often bring a new outfit for the statue to wear when they come on state visits. After World War II, for example, the Allies presented him with various uniforms from their armies, and when Great Britain entered the Common Market in 1973 they presented him with a John Bull outfit. So you see, Manneken Pis has a long and dignified history in this city."

"I suppose so," I said, "but it still seems a bit bizarre. I mean, the fortunes of Brussels could be symbolized by anything. A general, a king, a national hero . . ."

"New York has a red apple, doesn't it?" the driver laughed. "That's equally as bizarre, if you ask me. The Belgians love children and they aren't prudes about natural functions the way you Americans are. Brussels has public urinals for men right out in the streets, just a stone wall and a gutter." He leaned over the back of the seat and said in a more confidential tone, "I understand that for some, urination can be a form of sexual intimacy."

"I've heard that," I said noncomittally. "Is it a popular form of sexual diversion here?"

"It's not everybody's cup of tea, you understand, but in a city whose prurient interest runs to urination there are many who enjoy it. There's even a private club, La Douche d'Or that caters to this particular form of intimacy. I will take you there if you like. They welcome newcomers."

"The Golden Shower," I murmured. "Why not? I've seen enough statues for one evening."

We drove east to a small street near Avenue Louise in a mostly residential district, which was quite deserted at that hour. The narrow houses were dark and shuttered as good Belgians snored their way toward the next workday, but one particular house was still lit. The only thing to distinguish it from its neighbors was an ornate gilded wood door.

I tipped the driver handsomely and got out of the cab. "Have a good time," he said as he gunned his engine. "Ask for Pieter. Tell him Marcel sent you."

I was greeted at the door by a tall, broad-shouldered blond with magnetic blue eyes and a dazzling smile. He was wearing a beige turtleneck sweater tucked into dark brown corduroy pants that showed off his splendid proportions to perfection. I gave him my warmest smile and he smiled back.

"I'm looking for Pieter," I said.

"I am Pieter, mademoiselle," he replied. "You are most welcome."

"Marcel sent me," I said, feeling like I was trying to get into a speakeasy. "He told me to ask for you."

"Marcel is a good friend," Pieter acknowledged. "May I buy you a drink?" I nodded and he took my coat. His fingertips brushed my arm as he removed the coat, and I felt a tingling sensation through the thin material of my blouse.

The first floor had been gutted, and the long narrow room that contained the bar reminded me of the many small private clubs in the Greenwich Village of my teens. The walls were painted a metallic bronze, the moldings edged in a darker shade of umber and the chocolate-brown tile floor buffed to a mirror shine. The sepia photos that covered the walls were suggestive rather than blatantly erotic, the women partially clothed in Victorian lingerie.

Pieter and I spent the next half hour exchanging small talk and consuming great quantities of excellent Belgian beer. There's a saying about beer—that it can't be bought, just rented for a short period —and my bladder was soon full to bursting.

"Excuse me," I said politely. "I have to powder my nose."

"If you want a mirror," he said, a gleam of amusement in his eyes, "there's one over the bar."

"You know perfectly well that's not what I want," I mumbled, blushing. "Where's the bathroom?"

"I'll show you," he said, "if you'll let me watch."

An electric gaze passed between us, and I caught my breath as his hand gently touched my pubic area. I found the thought of this handsome, virile man watching me perform this very personal function strangely exciting. He took my hand and led me upstairs into one of the largest public bathrooms I had ever seen. There was a row of gleaming porcelain and brass toilets and urinals set against a dark blue and white tiled floor. There were four shower stalls and at the far end of the room I glimpsed a huge sunken tub with whirlpool attachments at each end. Men and women in various stages of undress were using the facilities freely, and my breathing quickened as I took in the tempting display of buttocks and pussies and cocks. No one seemed the least bit embarrassed.

The toilets were separated from each other by side walls, though there were no front doors on the booths. I looked at Pieter. His face was flushed and his eyes glowed with excitement. I was still high, and as I entered one of the stalls I stumbled slightly. He caught my arm to steady me.

"Let me help you," he whispered, getting down on one knee in front of me. I held onto his shoulders as he slowly ran his hands along my legs and up under my skirt. He pressed his face against the soft swell of my abdomen, his hands squeezing the firm roundness of my buttocks. Then he very slowly removed my panties, letting his fingers brush the line between my ass cheeks as he pushed the silken material over my hips. A tremor ran through my body at his touch and my buttock muscles tightened convulsively. I held my breath as I stepped out of my panties and slowly raised my skirt, bunching it around my waist. Urging my legs apart, Pieter slipped between them, lying on his back so that my cunt was directly over his face and his legs stretched out in front of me. He loosened his belt and unzipped his fly. His cock thrust upward, full and erect, and I took it in my hands as I crouched over his face. I was still holding my urine, but when he reached up and slipped his fingers into my pussy, I could do so no longer. The first tentative golden drops splattered over his fingers and he gave a soft sigh of pleasure.

"Come on, baby, you can do it," he urged. I felt his penis throbbing in my hands and heard the harsh sound of his breathing. Catching his excitement, I squatted down and, letting go at last, urinated full force over his face, my hands manipulating his prick until a stream of cum jetted into the air.

I felt his fingers parting my soft pink nether lips, his tongue licking the lingering drops of urine from

my inflamed orifice, then slipping inside, deeper and
deeper into my steaming slit. My hips began to move
and I almost ground my pussy against his face as his
flickering tongue brought me to a shattering climax.

I got up and unbuttoned my skirt, letting it drop to
the floor and kicking it aside. I stepped out of my
shoes and eased my stockings and garters over my
legs. Pieter watched me undress, his pupils dilated.
His breathing quickened, and looking down, I could
see his cock beginning to swell with new life.

I knelt beside him and kissed his urine-coated lips,
breathing in the pungent, acrid smells of our lovemaking. Then, with trembling fingers I pulled at his
clothes, wanting the sight of his naked body, the feel
of his warm flesh against my own.

I crouched over him again, easing my aching pussy
onto his rigid pole. I closed my eyes as I sank down,
feeling the pleasurable slap of his balls against my
ass. When I opened them again a pair of short, trunk-
like legs and an immense penis were inches from my
face. It was thick and full, begging for relief. The
man said nothing, and deliberately looking no higher
than his waist, I opened my mouth and took his
swollen manhood hungrily inside. I began to move,
tightening and releasing my vaginal muscles and
sucking furiously on the pulsing organ in my mouth.
Pieter's hands played with my breasts, and I gripped
the buttocks of the faceless man in front of me, our
three bodies movies like a giant sex machine. My
head was spinning as my body raced toward orgasm.
I relished the feeling of two cocks inside me at once
and I could tell by the groans of my partners that
they were as excited as I was. A hot burst of semen
spurted into my mouth, and as I struggled to swallow
the creamy fluid, Pieter's orgasm exploded in my
pussy, triggering my own mind-blowing climax. I
gave a low moan as the man in front of me released a

searing stream of urine full blast into my mouth. I found the pungent fragrance stimulating and the taste pleasantly acrid. I held his balls, drinking the burning liquid, climaxing again and again as Pieter's golden shower bathed my love canal, mingling with my own juices and trickling down my thighs.

I made a gradual recovery and slowly opened my eyes. Pieter was holding me in his arms, and a short, stocky dark-haired man was crouched beside him, brushing the damp hair from my face.

"This is Heindrik," Pieter introduced us. Heindrik gave me a warm smile and I smiled back. I could not believe the intensity of my fulfillment. Having engaged in this most basic form of intimacy, all feelings of strangeness had been stripped away. I felt a special bond with the two men beside me, as if we had known each other for years instead of hours.

By common consent we adjourned to the bath, where we joined others who had been engaged in similar forms of mutual pleasure. I slipped into the water between a curvacious blonde beauty with pendulous breasts and a slight Oriental woman with long black hair that floated around her like a net. A communal joint was being passed around and I inhaled deeply.

There were perhaps a dozen men and women in the bath at any one time, and, still somewhat dazed by my recent experience, I leaned back against the side of the tub and watched the changing kaleidoscope of shapes, sizes, and skin tones. There is an infinite variety to the naked body and I never tire of looking and touching and tasting. When the blonde offered me her ample breasts, I did not refuse. I licked the large pink areolas, sucking the splendid nipples to hard points of pleasure as, beneath the surface of the water, she fingered me to orgasm. I lost track of the time and count of the number of cocks and breasts and pussies I made contact with. I was like a rich kid in a candy store. I wanted it all but I kept returning to Heindrik and Pieter as to longtime favorites.

When at last wrinkled skin and imminent starvation put an end to our watery games, the three of us decided to continue our activities in a drier, more intimate setting. Gathering our clothes, we headed for Pieter's apartment, which was on the third floor of the building. As Pieter cooked a giant omelette in the small kitchen and Heindrik kindled a fire in the bedroom fireplace, I stretched out happily in the king-sized bed, contemplating the joyful possibilities of the night ahead. The thought of David's concern at my absence crossed my mind, but I pushed it resolutely away. It was his own fault for leaving me alone. In the morning I would think up some story to tell him, and David would probably be so glad to have me back, safe and sound, that he wouldn't even bother to question its veracity.

CHAPTER TWELVE

A few hours of healthy exercise between the sheets had a salutary effect upon both my physical and mental state. Sandwiched between the warm, firm bodies of Heindrik and Pieter, I drowsed happily, the tensions of the past few days totally banished.

Beside me Heindrik stirred slightly and let out a contented sigh. "What time is it?" he murmured into my neck. The touch of his lips sent little shivers along my spine.

"Dunno," said Pieter on my other side. He opened one eye and squinted at the window. "Morning, though. It's light out. Anyone for breakfast?"

"Can we have it in bed?" I asked.

"Don't see why not," Pieter replied. "One of us will have to get up to make it, though. The cook only works nights."

"I'll keep Christina happy while you do that," Heindrik said, turning slightly and putting his arms around me.

Pieter glared at him but sat up and stuck one leg

out from beneath the covers as if testing the temperature of the room.

Suddenly there was an unexpected noise in the hall outside the apartment, then the click of a lock and the sound of the door swinging open. Still holding the pick that he had used to jimmy the lock, David walked into the bedroom. He was dressed in a tan trenchcoat with the collar turned up against the early morning chill. A cigarette dangled from his mouth, and there was an angry glint in his eye.

"So here you are," he said in English, glaring down at me.

"Your husband?" Heindrik asked in French, a note of surprise in his voice.

"No, I'm not married," I assured him. "This is Mr. Connelly. He and I are working together. He has no business being here, and I'm sure that once he realizes his mistake, he will go out the same way he came in."

"It's you who have made the mistake," said David evenly. "I expected to find you in the hotel when I returned."

"I got tired of waiting for you," I said, shrugging my shoulders indifferently, but deliberately avoiding his gaze. "I decided to take a walk."

"Don't play games with me, Christina. You're halfway across town and you've been gone for hours. This isn't taking a walk. You deliberately disobeyed my orders."

"If you'll give us a minute to dress," said Pieter politely in French, "we'll all have breakfast." He had not understood the conversation and had obviously interpreted it as a lover's quarrel. "I'm sure you'll see things differently once you've eaten and we've had a chance to talk."

David seemed to notice the two men for the first

time. "Stay out of this," he said shortly, switching to French. Then to me, "Get dressed and let's get out of here."

"I'm not so sure I'm ready to get dressed," I said petulantly. "I've promised to have breakfast with Pieter and Heindrik here, and I'd hate to disappoint them. Besides, I'm not so sure I like your attitude."

David threw his cigarette butt into an ashtray and walked quickly across the room. He reached down and, seizing my wrist in a powerful grip, hauled me forcibly to my feet, scattering sheets and blankets everywhere. Their offer of truce ignored and their privacy violated, Pieter and Heindrik scrambled quickly to their feet.

"See here," Pieter said angrily. "I don't care for your manners at all. You'll have to treat the lady a damn sight nicer, at least while she's with me."

"She is not with you," said David in his minimal French, maintaining his grip on my wrist. "She is coming back to our hotel with me."

"Let me go, you baboon!" I howled, kicking ineffectually at him with my bare feet.

"I don't think she wishes to go with you," Heindrik pointed out.

"I don't think it is your business," David replied. "Now, I do not like to hit a man with his cock out in the morning air, but my good manners have a limit."

Pieter and Heindrik realized their disadvantage but stood their ground, making no move to search for their clothes. "With you that's not very far," growled Heindrik, his eyes blazing. "Unhand the lady at once, while you can still do it under your own power."

David made no reply, but he didn't release me. Heindrik took a menacing step toward him, fists clenched, and Pieter quickly moved in from the other side. A shiver of fear rushed through me.

"Now, wait a minute, fellows," I said in a small voice. "I don't think we have to prove anything here. This can be settled amicably . . ."

Without warning, Heindrik's fist rushed through the air. Dropping my wrist, David quickly blocked the blow to his face, following it with a left that landed squarely on the side of Heindrik's jaw. Heindrik staggered back, trying to maintain his balance. Pieter, a bit more timid than his friend, circled the room, trying to attack David from the rear, but David quickly maneuvered his back against a wall, keeping both his adversaries in view. I could see that talk would be useless at this point and sought shelter in a far corner of the room.

Both Pieter and Heindrik were considerably younger than David, with powerful bodies and quick reflexes. However, David's years on a football field, in the Green Berets, and in his current occupation had sharpened his fighting skills and it quickly became apparent that it was he, not they, who had the advantage.

Catching up a small wooden chair, Pieter charged at David, who ducked just in time to save his head, taking the force of the blow with his shoulder before the chair splintered against the wall. He recovered immediately, slamming his fist into Pieter's solar plexus as he turned, leaving Pieter doubled over and puking his dinner onto the floor.

Heindrik hurled himself on David's back, struggling to get a firm full nelson, but David managed to throw him over his shoulder, and he landed with a painful crash against the bureau.

Pieter had staggered to his feet, but he swung wide and David's fist crashed into his ribs, knocking him into a pained, panting heap on the floor.

Heindrik stirred like an angry bear, but seeing David standing over him, fists ready, he subsided back against the broken bureau with a low groan.

Breathing heavily, David straightened his clothes and searched his pockets for a cigarette. "Got to quit smoking," he muttered. "It cuts my wind. It never used to take me this long to handle two goons." He looked at me with an angry frown. "If you're through causing trouble, young lady, get your clothes and let's get out of here."

Shaken by this uncharacteristic display of aggression, I dressed in silence and allowed David to lead me out of the building and into a waiting car. David drove toward the hotel, chain-smoking silently and ignoring me. He did not speed or disregard red lights and his hands on the wheel were totally relaxed, but I could tell by the tense line of his jaw that he was angry.

I was a bit frightened by this new side of David Connelly, but I was intrigued at the same time. He had always seemed so good-natured and mild-mannered. In all the weeks we had been together he had treated me with a courtly deference to my desires, both in bed and out, that had led me to believe that I could do or say anything I liked. The situation had been to my liking. I'm the first to admit that I'm a bit spoiled and self-centered and that I like to have my own way. Though I know that every man has his limits and that David had a legitimate reason for being angry, I resented being treated like an errant child and was in no mood to apologize for my behavior or to forgive him for his. I folded my arms across my chest and turned away from him, staring stonily out of the window.

When we arrived at the hotel, I preceded him into our suite, went straight into my bedroom, and slammed the door behind me. I kicked off my shoes and stamped angrily into the bathroom to wash.

When I reentered the bedroom fifteen minutes later

in a knee-length, white velour robe, with my hair clinging damply around my face, David was sitting in a chair by the window, casually smoking a cigarette.

"Go drop ashes in your own room," I snapped.

"We have to discuss what happened," he said gently.

"You discuss it. I have nothing to say to you."

"You behaved very foolishly," he said.

"And you behaved like a macho moron! Connelly the Barbarian, kicking down the door to a private apartment and working over two innocent young men before dragging his woman back to the cave. Yes sir, it was a performance to be proud of. I'm sorry they didn't have you arrested. I would have really enjoyed that."

"I didn't start that fight," David reminded me, "and it was two against one, though I can't say much for your choice of bodyguards. If it had been Vronsky who had found you instead of me, your friends would have been dead instead of bruised, and it would have been as much your fault as if you had pulled the trigger yourself."

His point hit home. "I'm sick to death of commies and microdots and anything else connected with this caper," I yelled defensively. "Besides, nobody saw me go."

"No one had to. You left a clear trail, whether you know it or not. Vronsky's been in this business since before either of us was born, he's run rings around me, and if I found you you can be sure he could have as well. Admit it. You put yourself in danger and your friends as well and caused me no end of trouble tracking you down. You were just lucky that nothing worse happened to you."

If it's one thing I hate more than a wise-assed bastard, it's a wise-assed bastard who's right. David's calm control and logical reasoning only made me more determined to put him on the defensive, to have him apologize to me instead of me to him. I decided to switch the argument to more emotionally charged ground and attack rather than continue to defend myself against his irrefutable arguments.

"I don't think you were worried about my safety at all," I said. "I think you were just jealous."

"What the hell are you talking about?" he demanded, blushing furiously.

"See? It's true," I continued triumphantly. "You're all red in the face and defensive. You knew I had been fucking those two hunks the moment you walked into the room. It got the hairs on the back of your neck standing on edge and you couldn't control yourself. You were raving jealous, admit it!"

"You're nuts," he snapped. "Ranting, raving nuts. What do I have to be jealous about?"

"Two terrific looking studs doing what they do best," I taunted him. "I bet it's gnawing at your insides. Were they better than me? Do I rate? Do I even match up? Go on, ask me. Maybe I'll tell you."

"I don't have to compare myself with anyone," he said angrily.

"You don't have to, but you will. You're dying to know if they were bigger or better or kinkier, but your constipated Midwestern upbringing won't even let you get the words out of your mouth, will it? You can't even admit you're curious because you have twenty generations of provincial morality sitting on your head and you're probably afraid you're turning homo. Maybe you should have jumped into the sack with us. You might have had an enlightening experience and improved your chances for getting a date next Saturday night!"

"That's enough, Christina," David said, walking toward me. "I don't know how you talk to those pansy doormats you usually hang around with, but

I've had just about all I can stand from you today. Now, listen to me. As long as I'm saddled with the job of keeping your skin intact, you'll do what I say. Is that perfectly clear?"

"What if I refuse?"

"I'll take you over my knee and give you the spanking you deserve."

"You wouldn't dare," I gasped.

"Just watch me," he growled, seizing my wrist in a powerful grip and pulling me toward him. I struggled against him, kicking ineffectually at his shins with my bare feet. I called him every name I could think of, but he didn't respond. He continued to hold my wrist, and when I had exhausted myself struggling and screaming, he dragged me over to the bed. Sitting down, he pulled me across his lap. I gave a little sob of protest, then lay perfectly still.

When it came to women, David was not the tough-guy type. I knew that I had only to apologize, or even beg for mercy, and he would stop immediately, but having fought him and taunted him every inch of the way, I had no intention of letting him back down now. The brutal scene in Pieter's apartment had excited as well as frightened me and I was turned on by the thought of unleashing this savage side of David's personality within the bounds of our sexual relationship. I was wearing only a thin pair of panties beneath my short velour robe, and as I anticipated his next move, my body grew warm and my pussy juices started to flow.

David arranged me across his lap so that my behind would get the full impact of his blows. He was breathing heavily, and as I lay helpless and vulnerable over his thighs, I could tell that the thought of spanking me had turned him on as much as it had me, but he hesitated, his hand resting lightly on my velour-covered ass.

"Are you going to spank me with my panties on, or shall I take them down for you?" I asked wickedly, goading him.

"This is not a joking matter," said David sternly. "I'm going to spank you first with your panties on and then with them off." He lifted my robe above my waist, and I heard the sharp intake of his breath as he took in the rounded curve of my cheeks, half exposed by the high cut of my bikini briefs. I closed my eyes, tensing slightly. He brought his hand down hard, but not too hard, and a shiver raced through me. The next slap was harder, and the third harder still, causing me to cry out involuntarily. I squirmed on his lap, feeling his growing hard-on as he whacked away at my panty-covered cheeks. I was crying in earnest now, but I was lubricating freely, my juices soaking my panties and dampening David's thigh as he continued to spank me. Suddenly he stopped, and I felt his fingers on the waistband of my bikini briefs.

"Oh no, please! Not on my bare ass," I cried out, but he ignored my plea for mercy, which was, of course, exactly what I wanted him to do. Very slowly he peeled my soaking panties over my reddened ass, letting them constrict my thighs. His hand came down on my quivering bottom, and I gasped at the feel of his palm on my naked flesh. David spanked me a few more times in this position, then took my panties off entirely. Though my bottom was burning and I cringed as each blow fell, I relished my humiliating punishment. I was completely turned on. I spread my legs, allowing David a glimpse of my pale pink pussy lips peeping through the thick golden bush of my pubic hair as I arched my ass to meet each blow.

With a final rain of blows, David brought me to a shuddering climax. I lay exhausted and gasping across his lap while his fingers stroked my flaming cheeks, tracing the line between them and teasing my anus and the swollen lips of my pussy. I spread my legs farther, and his fingers slipped inside my aching cunt, triggering another climax. My entire body was drenched and trembling with desire. I wanted David in a way I had never wanted him before, and when he finally let me stand up, I slipped to the floor. Kneeling between David's legs, I fished his swollen manhood out of his pants.

I took it hungrily, letting my tongue and lips slide over the smooth, silken skin, feeling him tremble in my mouth as my fingers played with the downy skin of his balls. I tilted my head and relaxed my throat muscles, struggling to take him as deep into my mouth as I could. He closed his eyes, groaning with passion as his hips began to move, plunging his cock in and out of my mouth. We were both completely out of control, and as I sucked furiously at David's thrusting cock, I reached down and fingered my throbbing clit. Suddenly, with a final groan David exploded in my mouth, his creamy gift pouring down my throat. I fought the gag reflex to swallow as much of it as I could, bringing myself to climax at the same time.

Our spanking session had not only relieved the tension between us, but removed any lingering inhibitions to our lovemaking. We stripped off our clothes, both totally aroused. David pulled me into his arms and kissed me hungrily. I pressed myself hard against him, opening my mouth to the explorations of his tongue and grinding my pelvis against the lengthening hardness of his cock.

"I want you, Christina," he whispered savagely in my ear, kissing my eyes and my cheeks while his hands fondled my hair. "I've never wanted anyone like I want you right now."

"I want you too," I whispered back. "My body is

hot for you, my mouth, my pussy. I want your cock in every hole at once."

Lifting me in his arms, David carried me to the bed. He was not gentle. We were both too stimulated for tenderness. His hands and lips explored my body with an almost brutal passion, but I met his challenge with a fierce intensity I had not known I possessed. We were locked together like two cats in heat, clawing and biting wildly. I gave a sharp gasp as, without preliminaries David separated my thighs and thrust his steellike pole to the hilt inside of me. I relaxed my muscles and my pussy widened, the soft, moist tissue clinging around his slippery hardness as if to imprison him inside of me.

I wrapped my legs around his waist, arching my hips to allow him maximum penetration as David's cock pounded into me with hungry, savage thrusts. It was the most dynamic fuck I could remember. I lost sense of everything around me except the feel of his cock reaming my love canal, pushing so deeply that I felt the tip at the entrance to my womb.

I sobbed out loud and screamed his name over and over, raking my fingernails along his back as we moved together in an ascending rhythm of passion. I felt a sudden rush, then the floodgates opened and I was overwhelmed with the force of my orgasm. David gave a final grunt as my hot juices washed over his cock, then exploded in his own pulsating climax.

CHAPTER THIRTEEN

I awoke the next morning to find a short note from David taped to the bathroom mirror, informing me that he had gone to attend to some business and would return shortly. I found his dirty breakfast dishes and a full ashtray on the table in the sitting room, indicating that he had been up early and had already eaten.

I ordered an elaborate breakfast from room service and by the time I had showered and dressed, the room had been cleaned and the table relaid. There was a pitcher of Bloody Marys, a large green salad, a platter of assorted smoked fish and cheese, and a basket of bread and rolls, freshly baked that morning. I was on my third helping of fish and my fourth drink when the door opened and David walked in. He did not say good morning but took off his coat and joined me at the table. He seemed ill at ease and there were dark circles under his eyes. I suspected that he was embarrassed by what had occurred the previous evening. His conservative upbringing and chivalrous attitude toward women made such overt displays of raw passion almost nonexistent. As I had instigated the behavior in the first place, I felt a twinge of guilt, but I waited, sipping my drink.

David poured himself a cup of coffee and lit a cigarette.

"I want to apologize for last night," he said at last. "I've never hit a woman before."

"You don't need to apologize," I said lightly. "I goaded you into it. I wanted you to spank me. Besides, I thought you enjoyed it."

"I did," he admitted truthfully. "That's what bothers me. The darker side of my nature is not one I'm proud of."

"You needn't be ashamed of it," I said. "You can't be Mr. Nice Guy all the time."

"You're right, Christina, and though I'm sorry I lost my temper, your actions last night very much prompted my behavior. But concerning what's happening right now, I've just picked up some information from headquarters, and I have to leave Brussels this afternoon. If you choose to come with me, you must understand that I will not tolerate a repeat of last night's hedonistic, egotistic, self-destructive performance."

"What if I choose to back out?"

"I'll arrange for your return to New York, where you will be placed in protective custody until this assignment is concluded."

"What do you mean by protective custody?"

"In your case, a man will be assigned to insure the safety of your apartment, and any phone calls, visitors, or requests by you to leave the apartment will have to be cleared through him."

"That's not protective custody. That's house arrest!"

"A question of semantics," David conceded, "but last night proved to me that such measures would be necessary to insure both your safety and my peace of mind."

I was trapped. I realized that I would have to give David the promise he demanded and continue to co-operate on his terms or I would be held a virtual prisoner in my own home until the affair was wrapped up. On the other hand, I couldn't bear to admit to David that he had been right all along. I decided on a face-saving compromise.

"I've been in on this affair from the start," I said casually, stirring my coffee, "and I don't want to run with my tail between my legs just because the action's starting to get a little rough. I'd rather stick with you and see this through to the end." I looked him in the eye. "Just to make sure that *you* get through it okay."

David smiled and nodded, accepting my statement without challenge. An unspoken truce was declared and any lingering tension between us forgotten. He withdrew some papers from his inside jacket pocket and placed them on the table in front of him.

"Our men have been working overtime these last few days," he said, lighting another cigarette and smiling at me through a haze of blue smoke. "Several more wine bottles were located and the fifth micro-dot was recovered by a team working in Berlin. There are only three bottles unaccounted for from the original shipment and only one more microdot out-standing, so you can see that we're in sight of our goal. Now, Marc Baxter has sent a report indicating that he's located another bottle, and the odds are pretty heavy that this one has the last microdot. I'd hate to blow the job when we're this close, so we'll have to move fast. Can you get your stuff packed quickly?"

"Of course," I said. "But where are we going? Who has the bottle?"

"Marc only said that he's in London and that he has a line on the location. He didn't say exactly where it was, and it's possible that he hasn't pin-pointed the precise spot as yet. He should have further information for us when we get there. Now, hurry and pack. I've made reservations for both of us on the four o'clock flight to London. It can't hurt to think positively," he added, noticing my hangdog look. He came around the table and took me in his arms, kissing me in a way that made my temperature soar.

There is a popular myth that I am incapable of packing my bags for a quick getaway, but I laid such rumors to rest that afternoon, successfully assembling my possessions and preparing myself for the trip to the airport in a record three hours and twenty minutes. David pointed out that he was ready in twenty minutes, but I discounted this because, as I triumphantly pointed out, he had neglected to shave before we left.

By late afternoon we were seated comfortably in the first-class section of a plane bound for London. I had insisted on paying the difference between these and the economy seats the Agency allowed, though David, knowing my dislike of being crowded, had made the offer first.

"If you're worried about your expense account," I said, sipping my drink as the plane plowed through the clouds, "we can stay at my townhouse in London and save the cost of the hotel."

David frowned and shook his head. "I'm afraid not," he replied. "We still have those thugs on your tail, itching to get their hands on the recovered microdot they assume you're carrying from Brussels. I haven't the time to secure an entire townhouse, and in any event it would cost more than a first-class hotel bill. The Agency maintains a suite in a small hotel in Central London which we use as a safe house when security is required. The rooms are protected against bugging devices and there are extra security mechanisms to prevent a break-in. We can work out of there. If you like, you can have someone bring you some fresh clothes. I assume you have a household staff?'' I nodded. "No harm in letting them know where you are. The commies have known about the hotel room for years, though they've never breached its security. They have a similar suite in the Kensington area so it's more of a gentleman's agreement than anything else. Neither side wants to be forced to relocate.''

"I hope it's decent," I said. "Not some hovel in Soho or some equally attractive neighborhood."

"It's not the Savoy," he admitted, "but it's a pretty nice neighborhood and the rooms are comfortable. We built it before the budget cuts."

A few hours later we had cleared customs at Heathrow, and David bypassed the taxi stand to pick up an Agency car waiting in the airport parking lot. It was one of the new Minimetros from British Leyland, and I cursed our government's stinginess as I wedged myself into the small front seat.

Night was falling in London, and street lamps were snapping on as we glided into the center of the city. People were crowding into the underground as they rushed home from their jobs, and hoards of cars crammed the streets. In contrast to the drivers of most countries on the Continent, British drivers are orderly and polite, yielding to pedestrians and drivers all over the place and consequently slowing rush hour traffic to a mere crawl. David, accustomed to a faster pace on the road, was showing signs of frustrated temper after the first hour.

"Look at that idiot!" he growled, consciously resisting the urge to slam his fist down on the horn.

"He refuses to pass the crosswalk. We could sit here all night!"

We finally made our way through the traffic to Piccadilly Circus, where David slipped the car out of the traffic circle, onto Piccadilly proper. We drove along the darkened streets past Green Park, with the familiar view of Buckingham Palace on the far end. David turned right, driving past the Mayfair Theater and pulling up in front of a small, elegant luxury hotel located on a side street near Berkeley Square.

"This isn't half bad," I commented as we walked into the hotel lobby, followed by a bellhop wheeling a hand truck with our luggage. "It's a bit garish and not in the *best* part of town, of course, but I guess it'll do."

"I'm glad it meets your highness' requirements," David muttered as we stopped at the desk. The clerk was a gaunt man with a large nose and a thick mustache. He had overheard my comments and eyed us with disfavor.

"My name is Mr. Brown," David said. The man's eyebrows raised slightly.

"Not *the* Mr. Brown," he gasped. "Heavens, what a red-letter day for our humble establishment. And this must be Mrs. Brown."

David didn't rise to the bait. "I want the Red Suite," he said quietly, placing emphasis on the name. The clerk apparently recognized the code name, for he handed over the key without further comment.

"They don't know who rents the suite," David explained as we went up in the lift, "but they have standing orders to cooperate with us and no nonsense."

David took the bags at the door of the room, which was located on the third floor, and dismissed the bellhop before opening the door. He explained that the room was cleaned and maintained by Agency employees, and that the regular hotel staff never entered the secure suite.

The door opened on a large sitting room, comfortably furnished in the leather-and-wood style men find so appealing. The leather was all dark red and there was a soft gray carpet on the floor, overlaid with an expensive Oriental rug. I was suitably impressed and mixed myself a drink at the bar while David stowed our suitcases in one of the bedrooms.

"I don't see any antibugging devices," I said as he reentered the room.

"This isn't a James Bond movie," David laughed, "but rest assured that the rooms are as secure as American technology and ingenuity can make them. We can talk freely here."

"Good! Let's talk freely about dinner. I haven't eaten since this afternoon, and I'm famished. I could even eat English cooking."

"The English really know what to do with a roast beef," David sighed, evidently missing the implications of my remark, "and they make the best french fries outside of America. But I'm afraid dinner will have to wait a bit. I have to check with our London office and see if Baxter has sent through any further information on that wine bottle."

"Don't tell me I'm going to be stuck in here again while you traipse all over the city," I protested. "Damn it, David, I'm hungry!"

"We may have to retrieve that bottle on a moment's notice," David replied. "We can't toss out all our hard work just for some greasy fries."

"I wasn't going to have greasy fries," I reminded him. "You were going to have them."

"Have another drink," said David placatingly. "I swear on my father's name, I'll be back as soon as possible and I'll take you anywhere you like."

"Bring an undertaker," I grumbled. "They'll have to embalm me or I'll leak on the rug."

"That's the spirit," said David, deliberately missing my point. "You just sit tight. And remember our agreement. No repeats of what happened in Belgium. Keep the door locked and don't bother to try to get room service because there are no deliveries allowed to this suite."

He gave me a quick hug and left, locking the door behind him. I briefly considered trying to slip out and find a candy machine, but I didn't know what kind of security devices were at work in the room. For all I knew, opening the door could bring the Palace Guards from Buckingham swarming through a hidden tunnel behind the bookcase. Dejected, I sat on the sofa and pouted.

The second hand on the clock was making its fifth sweep around when I heard a key turn in the lock. Thinking David had changed his mind, I jumped up and started for the door, but I halted when I saw that the visitor was Marc Baxter. He was dressed in plain brown slacks and a tan overcoat, and he peered at me owlishly through his glasses as he silently closed the door behind him.

"I hope I didn't startle you," he said apologetically. "It's against procedure to answer knocks in this room. If you have business in here, it's assumed that you have a way of getting in."

"No," I said. "I just thought you were David. How are you, Marc?"

"Well, thank you," he said, looking quickly around the room. "I've been very busy the past few days, as you probably know. I take it David isn't here?"

"No. I think he went out to find you, as a matter of fact," I said. Marc frowned and shook his head.

"Crossed communication wires," he muttered.

"It's an occupational hazard. Unfortunately, time is of the essence here, and I have a problem that requires his immediate attention."

"Does it relate to the microdots?" I asked.

"It does," he sighed, sitting on the couch. "I've located not one, but two wine bottles side by side in a small liquor store in Knightsbridge. They're just sitting there, waiting to be bought, but they have a rather hefty price tag and I don't have enough cash. I was hoping David would requisition the funds from our London office, as I don't have the authority to do so myself."

"That doesn't sound like such a terrible problem," I said, seeing a way to do my patriotic duty, bring the caper to an end, and get out of that damned hotel room all in one move. "I have a bank account in London. I'd be glad to get the cash and buy the wines."

"It's evening," Baxter noted. "The banks are closed."

"The bank is never closed to Christina van Bell," I assured him. "My banker will still be in his office at this hour, and I'm sure I can get him to accommodate me."

"If you could, that would be wonderful," Marc said, almost managing a smile. "I had thought it would be necessary to break into the store after closing and steal those damned bottles, but this would be a far more satisfactory solution."

It was just seven o'clock. Marc obtained an outside line by giving a code word to the operator, and I quickly dialed the private number of my banker, Geoffrey Landsdale. When he heard my voice, the tired dullness I had detected in his greeting quickly disappeared.

"I didn't know you were in town," he said.

"I only just arrived," I told him. "I have a problem I hope you can solve. I know you usually work late, and I figured you'd still be at your office."

"I like my work," he said, "and I've no reason to rush home. No bachelor does. What can I do for you?"

"A small business matter has come up," I said, "and I need five hundred pounds in cash quickly. Could I impose upon you to stretch business hours just a bit and cash a check for me?"

"It's no imposition," he assured me. "It will be a pleasure. Come down immediately and ring the bell on the side door."

I thanked him and hung up. "It's all set," I told Marc. "We can go to the bank, pick up the money, and buy the wine."

"This is very decent of you," Marc said.

"It seems more sensible than trying to break into the store after dark," I shrugged, "and I'm more anxious than you to get this affair wrapped up."

Marc and I went down in the lift and he led me to his car, which was parked near the hotel. Following my directions, he drove us up Oxford Street, into High Holborn, then Cheapside, and finally to Threadneedle Street, where the Bank of England and the Stock Exchange are located. My bank was an ancient building on Old Broad Street that catered exclusively to a small number of wealthy clients. During the drive, Baxter concentrated on the traffic. He made no effort to engage me in conversation, and I admit that I didn't encourage him to talk. Though I knew that David held the blank-faced agent in high regard, I found him difficult to warm up to.

While Baxter waited in the car, I walked quickly to the side door of the bank and rang the night bell. A uniformed guard let me in, and I was ushered immediately to Geoffrey's impressive, wood-paneled office.

The room was like a small museum, for Geoffrey was knowledgeable in many areas of art and antiques and had the money to indulge his whims. Even the floor was covered in a Tbriz medallion-and-cartouche carpet which dated from the early 1500s and was valued at several hundred thousand dollars.

Geoffrey stood as I entered, and his smile of welcome banished the tired lines on his face. He was an elegant figure in his three-piece, banker's blue pinstriped suit. It seemed to have just been pressed though he had been wearing it since early morning.

"It's lovely to see you again, my dear," he said, bowing briefly over my hand, "even if it's only for a short business visit."

"I wish I could make it a real visit," I said, "but I have to complete this deal quickly or it will fall through."

"I have your money right here," he said, producing a small brown envelope stuffed with pounds, "and a blank check, since I had a feeling that you wouldn't have your checkbook with you."

He was right as usual. I filled in the check and accepted the envelope. "This is very kind of you," I said as he escorted me to the outside door. "I wish we had more time to talk."

"It was no trouble," he assured me. "Why don't you have dinner with me soon? I have acquired a set of Victorian gold figurine salts that I'm dying to show off."

"I'm sure they're lovely," I said. "As soon as my business is over, I'll give you a call. I remember your cook."

"You almost lured him away at my last dinner party," Geoffrey laughed. "I'll look forward to your call." He kissed my hand and I slipped out the door and hurried to the car.

"Do we still have time?" I asked as Baxter turned

the car west toward Knightsbridge.

"Plenty of time," he assured me. "I think we got the drop on Vronsky after all."

I sat back and watched the buildings flash by as Baxter drove quickly through the nearly dark streets. I felt my pulse quicken as I thought of handing David the final microdot. I had done it alone too, or almost alone. Marc had been following my game plan, and David would be forced to acknowledge that there was more to Christina van Bell than a beautiful face and figure and a great set of moves between the sheets.

The little wine shop was on Trevor Square, overlooking a small park. It was still lit when we arrived, and Marc quickly parked the car in a handy spot a few feet from the door.

"You can wait in the car," he said. "This should only take a moment. I'm not sure if this spot is legal, but if the cops come, just drive around the block. I'll leave the keys in the ignition." Without waiting for a reply, he opened the door, stepped out, and walked quickly toward the wine shop.

I sat in the dark car for several minutes, daydreaming about my plans now that the end of the affair was within reach. I would catch up on my social engagements, possibly throwing a party within the month to let Europe know that I was still alive. I would serve only hard liquor. I had had quite enough of wine in the past few weeks. Then I wanted to . . .

"Good evening, Miss van Bell," said a voice to my right. I felt an eerie chill run down my spine as I looked up and saw Vronsky's smiling Slavic face peering at me through the window. Marc had left the door on the driver's side unlocked and Vronsky yanked it open, forcing his way into the car. I started to scream, but he clamped his hand over my mouth, forcing my head back against the seat. I struggled wildly, but he was a powerful man and I was no match for him. He pulled a heavily chloroformed rag from his pocket and held it over my nose and mouth. The harsh fumes made my head spin and after a final feeble effort to resist, the darkness closed over me.

When I opened my eyes I was lying on a strange bed, on a mattress that smelled strongly of damp and mold. I moaned and struggled to sit up, but my limbs felt like lead weights and I fell back exhausted. My movements had attracted the notice of my captor, however, for I heard heavy footsteps approaching the bed and Vronsky's face came into my line of sight.

"Ah, you are back among living at last," he said. "I was afraid for moment that I give you too much chloroform. You feel well, yes?"

"I feel like shit," I muttered, closing my eyes in the insane hope that this was all a bad dream. I opened them again, but Vronsky was still there, bathed in the harsh yellow light of the single bulb that dangled on a wire from a hole in the ceiling. The room was not large. The walls were covered in a faded pink-flowered paper that showed evidence of water seepage from the outside walls of the building. Besides the bed there were several wooden chairs, painted bright green, and an ancient chest of drawers that was missing a leg and leaning crazily to one side. I heard the sound of a foghorn and realized that I must be somewhere near the docks. There were hundreds of old tenements and warehouses in the area, and my heart sank as I realized how difficult it would be for Marc or David to find me.

"Your involvement in this affair has been most unfortunate," Vronsky said, "but even old veteran like myself can make mistake."

"What are you talking about?" I demanded.

"I know you are not backup agent for Zelanko."

"Oh?" I hoped my fear didn't show in my face.

"Yes," he continued, sitting down on one of the green chairs and taking a pack of Russian cigarettes from the inside pocket of his jacket. "My concern about my position in Moscow made me careless." The blue smoke drifted lazily to the ceiling, and he flicked the ashes carelessly on the floor. "I jumped to conclusions for which I had no proof."

The acrid smell of the cigarette burned my eyes and throat. I struggled to a sitting position and managed to look Vronsky in the eyes. He returned my gaze with a bland, unconcerned expression that clearly showed he felt he had the upper hand.

"If you know I'm not a double agent," I said, watching him carefully, "then you must also know that the Americans are in possession of all the microdots that I've been collecting." Vronsky's expression remained unchanged. I wondered uneasily what he knew that I didn't but decided that my only course of action would be to put on a bold front and try to bluff my way into a position of strength. "You were foolish to nab me outside of that wine shop," I said. "I wasn't on my way to Harrods. While you were busy chloroforming me, another agent from our side was buying two of the last three bottles of that wine. By now that microdot is safely in American hands. Your country's plans to deploy that terrible chemical weapon are useless because now that they have the formula, our scientists will easily find a defense against it."

Vronsky's smile was that of the cat who had swallowed the proverbial canary. He didn't seem in the least bit intimidated, and I began to think that I wasn't being bold or forceful enough. "Not only that," I rushed on, "but the minute our agent sees that the car and I are both gone, his men will be on your tail like bloodhounds. I know they'll find me. They've done it before because you guys leave invisible trails or something else they can spot, and when they arrive you'll go to spy jail or wherever, and rot. So maybe you ought to let me go now and perhaps you can escape back to the tundra or wherever it is you normally escape to before they break down the door, okay?''

Vronsky laughed out loud, a deep hearty laugh. I am usually a fairly convincing liar, but I had obviously failed this time.

"You are very amusing, Miss van Bell," he said, taking a handkerchief from his pocket and copiously wiping his eyes, "and very naive. How I could mistake you for backup agent is mystery even to me. But you are so beautiful, it is hard to think rationally when I look at you. As for your American friend with the glasses, I'm afraid you put far too much faith in him, my dear."

"We'll see," I said threateningly. "Baxter is an experienced agent with the full confidence of his superiors . . ." My glowing litany of Baxter's traits was cut short as I heard the sound of a key in the lock. The door to the room swung open and Baxter himself walked into the room. He carried a brown paper bag and kicked the door shut behind him. He nodded at Vronsky, who looked as if he had been expecting him. Vronsky's overconfident attitude suddenly became clear, and I saw my hope of rescue sinking like a leaky boatload of bricks.

"Comrade Baxter, come in," Vronsky said, waving him over. "Miss van Bell was just telling me about your loyalty to America."

"Was she?" Baxter said, looking at me impassively through his glasses. "I hate to disappoint you, but then, things are not always the way they seem, are they, Comrade Vronsky?"

"I see that you two know each other," I said bitterly.

"That is correct," Vronsky nodded. "You see, Miss van Bell, Comrade Baxter turned out to be double agent. He is good, yes? Even I was fooled. He was in employ of Americans for so long even I believe he works for your side, but my agency checked the records and they confirm his status."

"Then you've been working for the commies all this time," I said, searching Baxter's bland face for some clue to his reasons.

"I'm afraid so," he nodded. "Oh, I'll admit that I was loyal to the Agency once upon a time, but things do change over the years. I was praised as a loyal agent and a good worker, but when the promotions were handed out they always seemed to forget that I was there. You know, I've been with the Agency longer than Connelly, but they passed me over and promoted him instead. So when I was approached by Mr. Vronsky's people and offered a chance to better myself professionally, I accepted. I was treated very nicely too. They knew I'd eventually be the right man in the right place, and when this microdot affair started, I managed to get assigned to it. Every time you and David passed one of those microdots to me, you thought it was being passed back to Washington. Even Vronsky thought that, but you were all wrong. I've been keeping them safe and sound in a bank vault. The last of the microdots is here, on one of these wine bottles, so now I can reveal my true role in this matter and ship the entire formula back to Moscow. It doesn't matter if David and the Agency know, because I'll be living in Russia from now on."

"You were supposed to be sending those microdots back to Washington," I insisted. "Didn't they notice that they weren't arriving?"

"I sent phonies," said Baxter proudly. "I know enough chemistry to fake a basic formula, and without all six of the microdots, Washington didn't expect the formula to make sense anyway. I didn't risk sending the real ones to Moscow because the Agency spies on their own employees as well as everyone else. We're no better than the commies, you know. Freedom and individual rights and justice are just words used by the oppressors to fool those they oppress." His face twisted in a sneer. "Power is what counts, Miss van Bell, even more than money, and it's power I will have after today."

"I hope you have a wonderful life," I said sarcastically.

"Oh, I will," he assured me. "In the Soviet Union I'll be a privileged person. I'll have an apartment in Moscow, a car and a summer house in the country. I'll have access to all the specialty shops and a servant to shop and cook and keep house for me. It won't be quite what *you're* used to, perhaps, but I'm sure you'll adjust to it in time."

"Me?"

"You're coming with us."

"Are you out of your mind?"

"Not at all," he said earnestly. "Surely you didn't think we'd leave you here and risk having you blow our cover before we were safely out of the country?"

"No more talk," said Vronsky, glancing anxiously at his watch. "We have plane to catch."

My mind raced as I tried to think of a way out. I wasn't sure how much time had passed but it must have been several hours. David would have returned to the hotel room by now, and as Marc and I had left the hotel by the front door, the desk clerk would no doubt be able to furnish him with our descriptions. The game was not over yet. It was a long shot, but David had found me in Brussels with even less to go on. I had to remain calm and play for time. Once we were on a plane for Moscow all would be lost.

"What do you plan to do with me once we get to Moscow?" I asked.

"That will depend on you," said Marc, not looking at me directly. He seemed a bit disconcerted.

"In what way?"

Marc flushed and shot Vronsky a look of mute appeal. Vronsky cleared his throat and lit another cigarette. Both men were clearly embarrassed and under any other circumstances the situation would have been humorous. I wondered why they didn't just kill me and be done with it. Neither Vronsky nor Baxter was a squeamish man, and even I could see that this isolated room was the ideal place to do it. Why this elaborate plan to take me to Moscow?

I looked from one to the other, and an idea suddenly occurred to me, an idea so ludicrous that I felt certain of its truth.

"You're planning to kidnap me," I said accusingly. "Once inside the Soviet Union, you could probably arrange a set of false papers and my American identity would be lost. Escape under those circumstances would be impossible."

"You've a clever woman," Marc nodded. "The choice is yours, of course, but now that you understand the situation I'm sure you'll agree that it is infinitely preferable to a quick death."

"Perhaps," I said carefully, "but what do you expect in return?"

"You will be . . . ahem . . . appropriately grateful . . ."

"If you're expecting me to keep house for you," I said, "I'm afraid that I don't know one end of a vacuum cleaner from another and that my culinary skills are strictly limited to mixing drinks and passing around a tray of hors d'oeuvres."

"You have other skills," said Vronsky, eyeing me meaningfully. "You will not have to cook."

"So that's it," I said softly. "You want someone to warm up those cold Russian nights."

"There are no electric blankets in Russia," said Marc as if this were an explanation.

"And you want me to light your fires," I said, looking at them provocatively. Though nothing had changed, I felt a subtle shift in the balance of power. I was on familiar ground here, and if I played my cards right, I might just gain the time I needed.

I was still sitting on the bed, and I shifted my position so that I leaned back against the wall. I slipped off my shoes and put my feet on the edge of the bed, letting my skirt fall back to reveal a healthy expanse of creamy white thigh. I was wearing only panty hose, and the golden bush of my pubic hair was clearly visible through the sheer gauze. I slowly unbuttoned my blouse to reveal the twin treasures of my lush round breasts, the nipples already stiffened with excitement. I heard the sharp intake of Marc's breath as I deliberately exposed my body, and I could tell by the look of the faces of the two men that I had their complete attention.

A moment later I felt Marc's hands on my breasts. He pushed me roughly down on the bed, bending over me to take first one breast and then the other into his mouth. I tried to relax beneath the sudden fierceness of his assault. There was a tearing sound as he ripped my silk blouse from my body, leaving me totally exposed from the waist up. He pulled impatiently at the waistband of my skirt, and I hastily loosened the buttons, helping him take it off.

"I'm here, baby," I murmured gently. "Slow down. I'm not going anywhere."

A shudder ran through his body. I was wearing

only my panty hose and his hands were burning hot against the coolness of my flesh.

"Stroke me," I whispered. "Make me hot for you."

He obeyed my instructions, using his hands and lips to cover my body in warm, moist waves. I writhed beneath his touch, urging him on, pressing myself against him and feeling for the buckle of his belt. I loosened his trousers and, plunging my hand inside his fly, withdrew his throbbing penis, holding it firmly in my hand.

"It's so hard," I whispered, pressing it against the hardness of my belly. "Let me feel it against my bare skin." Marc's trembling hands touched the waistband of my panty hose, and I guided them over my hips as he removed this final layer of clothing, leaving me totally, enticingly exposed. "You too," I urged. "Let me see you. You've a beautiful body," I murmured as I fumbled with the buttons on his shirt.

Marc shifted position, jerking at his clothes with the frenzied need of a young boy with his first woman. I glanced sideways at Vronsky and saw that he had opened his own pants and was masturbating freely. His rapid breathing and rapt expression told me that he was getting turned on by the sights and sounds of our lovemaking. I spread my legs farther and pulled my pussy lips apart with my fingers to let him glimpse the slippery pink wetness within.

Marc's body covered mine again, his cock moving over my abdomen. I reached between his legs to cup his balls, then let my nails rake lightly along the underside of his shaft. I closed my eyes and moved with him, moaning audibly. His fingers slipped between the swollen lips of my cunt, fumbling for the hard knob of my clit. I felt a rush of hot moisture and I arched my hips, begging him to enter. When he hesitated, I placed the tip of his cock at the entrance to my primed cunt. I held my breath as he plunged into me without restraint, moving inside me with growing confidence and passion. I had played the wanton seductress and had succeeded in fooling myself as well as Marc. Now I closed my eyes and let him take control. My body wanted him, his hands touching my flesh and his cock deep inside me.

I wrapped my legs around his, thrusting my hips upward to allow him maximum penetration. His cock drilled my aching hole, and as his orgasm burst forth I tightened and relaxed my vaginal muscles, causing him to cry out with the force of his passion. My nails raked his back and I kept my legs spread, pressing my clit against his pulsating tool until there was so much juice flowing out of me that I could feel it trickling along the crack in my ass. I hovered on the brink of orgasm, not willing to let myself go.

"Eat me," I whispered to Marc. "Lick me out."

He slid down my sweat-filmed body, and, grabbing my half-moons in his strong hands, he started licking me almost at my asshole.

I opened my legs wider as his thrusting tongue penetrated my cunt, pushing its way along my love canal to the hard knob of my clit. My hot juices bathed his face, and withdrawing for a moment, he dipped his fingers into my steamy slit. He brought them to my mouth, letting me taste myself as I drenched each finger with my saliva, then he probed my anus, causing me to cry out as I held the top of his head and practically ground my pulsing cunt against his face.

I was totally open now, grinding and moaning and sweating with passion. My writhing body crashed against the bed, the sheets sliding against my skin.

Soon I was dangling over the edge, my ribs stretched taut and my long hair sweeping the floor as Marc feasted on my greedy flesh. From this upside-down position, I saw two naked feet approach the bed. It was Vronsky, who got down on his knees and, supporting my head in his lap, leaned over and brought my breasts to his mouth. I closed my eyes and enjoyed the sensation of my cunt, my ass, and my tits all being catered to at once. The fire in my body raced along my limbs, centering in my cunt and igniting a volcanic series of orgasms that had me crying and screaming with passion.

I was completely on the floor by now and Vronsky turned me on my stomach, lifting my hips so that I was positioned on my hands and knees. He thrust into me doggy style, emitting a low growl as he centered on his own pleasure.

Marc dropped to the floor in front of me and, getting on his knees, held his hard-on against my lips. I obediently opened my mouth, letting my tongue glide along the steellike shaft. Both men were totally involved with their own pleasure, and the three of us moved together like a giant sex-machine. My tongue wrapped around Marc's cock as my vaginal muscles tightened and released Vronsky's penis. I was totally filled with cock and my entire body vibrated in ecstasy. As Vronsky shot his load into my cunt, Marc let go in my mouth and my own orgasm burst forth amid the inundation of warm milky cum.

I collapsed on the floor with Vronsky on top of me. Both of us were panting and spent. Marc lay on his back, eyes closed.

"Get up," Vronsky wheezed, struggling to a sitting position and shaking me by the arm. "We have a plane to catch."

"We'll make the next one," I sighed, deliberately not moving.

"There is no next one." Vronsky put his arms around my waist and hauled me to my feet, but I leaned against him like a dead weight and he was forced to deposit me on the bed. "Let's go!" He shook me hard, then slapped me across the face.

"Let her be, Vronsky," snapped Marc.

"You're a fool," said Vronsky angrily. "She does this on purpose to make us miss plane."

"Get dressed," Baxter ordered, pulling on his pants. "I'll handle her."

Vronsky started to pick up his clothes, but before he could get far I heard footsteps pounding down the hallway, then a thundering crash against the door. With a splintering sound the wood gave way and David burst into the room, brandishing a pistol. Several blue-uniformed policemen crowded in after him.

"Don't even think about moving," David said, cocking his gun and aiming the barrel directly at Vronsky's head. "Just keep very still and don't tempt me."

As both men were half-naked, unarmed, and out-numbered, they wisely followed his advice. They were securely handcuffed and led away, leaving David and me in the room alone. There was no need for words. All we wanted to tell each other was written on our faces, and, throwing myself into David's arms, I pressed my lips to his.

EPILOGUE

David let out a long, low whistle of appreciation as I walked into the living room of my London townhouse. I was wearing a black silk velvet evening dress with a spectacular skin-fitting line, the tight bodice and deep décolletage set off by big puffy sleeves. A knee-to-floor black satin flounce intermittently exposed black satin sandals ornamented with diamonds, and diamonds sparkled against my ears and nestled in my hair.

"Like it?" I asked as he took my floor-length sealskin coat from my maid. "I thought the occasion called for basic black and diamonds. It sets off my blonde hair, don't you think?"

"It sets off more than that," David sighed as he helped me into my coat.

I expected the usual government heap and was shocked when David led me to a black Jaguar XJ-12 four-door saloon with tan leather upholstery.

"I like your car, David," I said as I slipped gracefully into the front seat. "Is it stolen?"

"The Agency has considerable resources," David replied. "You just have to know the right people."

"Did they supply that dinner jacket as well? You look very handsome, David."

"I happen to own this fine outfit," he said in a miffed tone. "I often get invited to formal affairs. A sharp pair of eyes and ears at an embassy function is always useful. In fact, I first met Comrade Vronsky at a formal dinner in Paris many years ago."

I shuddered at the mention of the agent's name. "What will happen to him?" I asked.

"That depends on his own government," David replied, "but I would guess that after a brief period of official disfavor and perhaps a demotion, he'll be reassigned to another front. He is one of their best men."

"I find it hard to believe you let him go," I said. "After all the terrible things he's done."

"There was no point in keeping him," David shrugged. "He'd never tell us anything useful and it would just escalate tension between the two sides. Besides, we know how he operates, and in this business a known enemy, no matter how dangerous, is always easier to deal with than a new man."

"Yet his accomplice is facing a federal grand jury on charges of treason. It doesn't seem fair."

"It is fair," said David bitterly. "Vronsky was merely doing his job, but Marc Baxter is a traitor, pure and simple. We were just lucky to have found out in time. His safe-deposit box was opened yesterday, and the microdots are all safely on their way to Washington, thanks in large measure to your help, Christina."

"It was nothing," I said, waving my hand grandly. "I'm happy to accept the modest accolades of my government. A Congressional Medal of Honor, perhaps, or a night in the sack with the Congress . . ."

"Dinner and a night in the sack with me will have to do," David said. "The Agency can't advertise their successes, so our work goes largely unrecognized by the general public."

"That's why I'm glad to be out of the business," I sighed. "No presidential handshakes, no cheering ticker-tape parades, just the satisfaction of a job well done. That doesn't appeal to me at all."

"You're impossible," David laughed. "I hope you like the restaurant we're going to tonight. I had a lot of trouble finding a place where we could both eat the food."

"I'll enjoy it if you're there," I said. "After all, this is our last night together."

He nodded. "I'm being ordered back to Washington, but it won't be forever. You could come with me . . ."

"I'd love to," I said. "But I have to get back to work too. This little interlude has been fun, but I have a magazine to manage."

"I know that," he said quietly. "But it's hard to lose you."

"We'll meet again," I promised. "You get around a lot, and I'm frequently in one major world city or another. Just ask any desk clerk if I'm in town."

"I'll do that," he chuckled, stopping the car in front of a large fast-food hamburger stand. A neon-lit hamburger and overflowing bag of french fries winked garishly in the darkness, and the place was crammed with greasy-looking teenagers, each attached to his own set of earphones.

"What do you think?" he said with a straight face. "Dinner for two?"

"I'll slaughter you," I growled. "You have exactly fifteen minutes to drive to the most expensive restaurant in town or I'll eat you instead."

"I may take you up on that offer," he said, pulling me against him and pressing his lips to mine.